P9-CCC-132
2024

The
Tan-Faced Children

Also by Frank Calkins:

ROCKY MOUNTAIN WARDEN
JACKSON HOLE

The
Tan-Faced Children

FRANK CALKINS

DOUBLEDAY & COMPANY, INC.

GARDEN CITY, NEW YORK

1978

For A.C. who knows that trout feed on blueberries.

This is a work of fiction. All the characters are imaginary. Although some of the places mentioned are real, others are not, and nothing described herein, beyond a few instances of historical fact, ever happened anywhere.

Library of Congress Cataloging in Publication Data
Calkins, Frank. 1932–
    The tan-faced children.

    I. Title.
PZ4.C15545Tan [PS3553.A4175]   813'.5'4

ISBN: 0-385-14410-5
Library of Congress Catalog Card Number: 78-18556
Copyright © 1978 by Frank Calkins
All Rights Reserved
Printed in the United States of America
First Edition

COME, my tan-faced children,
Follow me well in order, get your weapons ready;
Have you your pistols? have you your sharp-edged axes?
Pioneers! O Pioneers!

—Walt Whitman, *Pioneers! O Pioneers!*

Chapter One

The house is still standing. You can see it from the new highway. But no one lives there, and the front door has been padlocked for twenty-five years. The old lilac by the back steps has gone wild, and bricks have been falling from the top of the kitchen chimney.

But when the Bakers owned the big, two-story log house it was the valley's show place. A lot of famous people have sat on its front porch, and Clay Baker shot elk and coyotes from there many times. That was long ago, before he got sick.

In his last summer, 1934, Clay Baker used to sit in the screened-in part of the porch and watch his hired man irrigate and slap mosquitoes. Probably no place in Wyoming raises more mosquitoes than Jackson's Hole.

Incidentally, the valley's right name is Jackson's Hole, with an apostrophe "s." It was named for the trapper, David E. Jackson in the 1820s. It was named "Jackson Hole" to be more pleasing to the tourists a long time after that.

Clay Baker was proud of having pioneered in this valley. He had led an active life and hated having to sit on the porch. But he was still recovering from the operation he'd had the previous fall. Mr. Baker wasn't a tall man, but he'd been broad and strong. A lot of the valley's old-timers would not have recognized him in 1934. By then he was just a skinny old man sitting on his porch in a red-striped bathrobe. He didn't look like a millionaire, but those who knew him said he was one.

Mr. Baker enjoyed reminiscing about early days in the valley. And, because he didn't have many visitors, his audience was usually his hired man.

"I came into Jackson's Hole in the fall of 1884. I was twenty-two years old, broke, and lookin' like what the little boy shot at. I came with Johnny Kelly and his wife, Mary. She was a full-blooded Shoshone Injun. Mary couldn't read nor write, but she was a fine woman all the same.

"Mary was the best hand I ever saw with horses. I used to have an old Injun saddle of hers out in the barn till the mice ruined it and we threw it out."

After Mr. Baker got sick, Mrs. Baker took over their businesses and she didn't have much time to sit on the porch with him. She was a big, energetic woman. She had worked hard in her life and it showed. But she dressed well, and it was almost a local scandal that she paid fifty dollars for hats. She also read a lot.

Clay Baker had never been much of a reader. He told their hired man, "I could write a lot better book than the ones Mrs. Baker is always buyin'.

"I brought the first dairy cattle into this valley. Did you know that?"

"No, sir."

"Well I did. I brought ten bred Holstein heifers from Market Lake as soon as the Pass opened in the spring of ninety-one. Bought 'em for twenty-five dollars a head and sold 'em for fifty. In them days no farmer had fifty dollars cash so I also got ten per cent interest and half their heifer calves. I took some of those Holsteins back a half-dozen times. They were gold mines. I made almost five hundred dollars off a couple of 'em."

"Yes, sir," said the hired man. Like most residents of the valley he was painfully aware of Clay Baker's interest rates.

Baker continued, "Nobody remembers me for bringing in those cows. All they remember is that Herb Winters brought in the first automobile. They thought gettin' that first machine was wonderful; even if Herb did have to pull it two thirds of the way over the Pass with a team of horses. What most of 'em don't know was that I lent Herb the money to buy the damned thing.

"Herb had big plans. He was gonna have a taxi-ambulance service an' take sick folks out to the doctors. Course even the Model T's couldn't buck our snow and cold weather, an' they had to be backed up the steepest grades. So Herb's ambulance business ended up like most of his schemes, broke.

"In the early days we didn't have a doctor here. Folks either got well or they didn't. Cancer was about the worst. I've seen many a good man and woman waste away with it. We gave 'em opium to kill their pain, if we had the opium. The pain gets so bad you don't even want to move enough to breathe. I know. But mine's cured. My doctors said they just kept cuttin' till they reached healthy tissue."

When Clay Baker told about his own operation he usually ended by taking a sip from a coffee cup that contained as much Bourbon as it did coffee. Once he said, "Course what these doctors tell you is just bull. They'll keep cuttin' till they hit a man's pocket book."

If Mr. Baker talked about cancer too much his hired man would try to change the subject by asking him why he chose to settle in this valley. Even in 1934 it was far from the markets and miles from the nearest railroad.

Baker replied, "I've always said it was because I saw so much oppurtunity here. Make 'em feel bad because they missed out. But that's not quite right. I came because there wasn't much choice.

"My folks were poor. My old dad was a Liverpool Englishman. He worked in a woolen mill there from the time he was eight. After he got to this country he worked in the mills here. One day a land agent sold him a farm in Wisconsin sight unseen. But when he got there it wasn't a farm. It was just raw land with a swamp in the middle of it.

"The best thing he found there was my mother. She was a farm girl and knew how to work; came from a German family. Mother always had an accent. But, bless her old heart, she was the one that kept us together. She taught me not to give in to anything."

Clay had had to help with farm work so often during his school years that he did not complete the sixth grade until he was fourteen. When he graduated his parents were extremely proud. Clay was their eldest son and the first one in the family to have a grade-school education.

It was his father's conviction that Clay should complete his education by getting a job in a bank. Clay was smart and quick with figures, and it was easy for his father to convince him to become a banker.

But, like so many of his father's plans, this one was ill-considered. No banker they approached wanted to hire a big, ruddy-faced farm boy who was barely fifteen years old. In the end, Clay's father found a labor contractor and sent his son off to work as a field hand. For four years Clay followed the harvests. His sandy hair bleached in the summer suns. His shoulders broadened from endlessly swinging a pitchfork, shovel, or ax. The smart alecks who had teased him as a boy learned to pass him by or seek his friendship. Still, he never abandoned his goal of becoming a banker. And he applied for jobs in dozens of banks.

Once he said, "I got turned down so much I was scared I'd run out of banks. I studied all I could. I learned about loans and land values and interest. While the other fellas were raisin' hell and puttin' a prop under it, I had my nose in some finance book.

"I wouldn't give up, and I finally landed a job in a little state bank in Colorado. But I wasn't a banker. I swept up, polished the woodwork, and ran errands. I kept wood in the stoves during the winter and shoveled snow. Because I was husky I stood in the lobby and discouraged the grifters that'll hang around in a bank if you let 'em.

"The banker was a fine old fellow by the name of Meggs. He used to have me stand outside his office door and listen when he did business. Afterward, when the customer had gone, Meggs called me in an' we'd ask each other questions until I understood what had gone on.

"It was through Meggs that I got recommended to J. M. Warburton's bank up in Eagle Rock, Idaho. Idaho was still a territory then, not even a state. The boosters were puttin' beautiful names on sagebrush flats up there and tellin' folks to come out and 'grow up with the country.' I knew better'n to believe all that. But, it was a brand new country. And, lookin' back, I'd have to say it was an adventure."

A train trip West in those days, however, was more ordeal than adventure. Clay left the Union Pacific at its Ogden, Utah, depot and took the Utah Northern Railway for Eagle Rock, Idaho Territory.

It was early on a chill winter evening when the small train lugged into the Eagle Rock station. Getting directions from the agent, Clay hurried to the hotel. On the way he tried to see all he could of this rough, young Idaho town where the wind blew cold down muddy streets.

That evening Clay played pinochle in the hotel bar with three salesmen. It was a friendly game and as they played the salesmen all spoke of the wildness of the surrounding country and its people. One man said, "It's not too many years since there was Indian trouble here. This trip I rode up on the train with a U.S. marshal. He said all the road agents and stock thieves in the West were goin' into hideouts around the new National Park."

Clay took that with a grain of salt. And when he went to bed that night his thoughts were more on his banking career than on road agents. Nevertheless, he was disappointed the next morning when he entered the lobby of J. M. Warburton's bank. The room was shabby. The plaster walls were smoke- and water-stained and badly in need of a fresh coat of calcimine.

Adjacent to the two tellers' cages was a closed door marked, "PRIVATE   J. M. Warburton, Pres."

Only one of the two tellers' windows was open. Behind its bars a young man was coldly appraising Clay. Clay said, "Morning. My name's Baker. I have a letter to Mr. Warburton from P. J. Meggs of the Valverda State Bank in Colorado."

The teller, whose name plate identified him as, "V. Charles," took the envelope and said, "You can wait here. I'll take your letter in to the boss."

Clay left the window and took a place along one wall. There were no chairs or benches. In a moment V. Charles returned, "OK. He says for you to wait. He'll see you when he can."

For two hours Clay waited in the lobby. Finally he asked the teller, "Do you think Mr. Warburton has forgotten me?"

"No." The teller grinned. "He never forgets anything. He's a busy man, and you didn't have an appointment."

Clay stood against the wall for another hour watching more customers come and go. Suddenly a freckled, red-haired man appeared at the private door. "You Baker?" he snapped. "I'll see you in five minutes," and then he closed the door.

Clay watched the clock on the wall and when exactly five

minutes had passed he went to the door, knocked, and walked in. Seated behind a roll-top desk in the gloomy office was J. M. Warburton. Clay waited in the middle of the room until the banker looked up. J. M. Warburton was about forty-five. Under his red hair and freckles he was pale. He had a paunch, too. But Clay was not misled by that. Warburton's blue eyes penetrated him like a pair of sharp icicles.

There was no smile or handshake. Without a word of welcome Warburton asked, "Why do you want to go into banking here? It's a lot rougher than doing business in a horse-and-buggy district like Valverda."

Clay said, "I came here to make money. I've seen new districts open up before, and I've seen a lot of money made. I grew up poor and I saw what it did to my folks, especially to my mother. That's not going to happen to me. People claim you can grow up with this country. That's not right. You have to make the country grow up with you."

Warburton interrupted, "That's a nice little speech. If I were you, though, I'd shorten it to just the part about making money." The banker turned in his chair to study the young man before him. After a long, silent moment he began giving Clay a rigorous examination in the banking business.

Although Warburton gave little sign of it, Clay's answers apparently satisfied him. Eventually he said, "That'll do. In this business it's more important to know the right questions than the right answers. I want a young fella to go out to Riggs. Asahel Cannon, my chief teller, is moving there this spring to run a new bank for me. Come back in the morning, and I'll let you know." Warburton turned in his chair and began to write in a ledger.

For a moment Clay didn't move. He couldn't believe this indifferent dismissal. Then Clay bristled, "Mr. Warburton, thanks for seeing me. I left a good job to come here. It was a gamble. In the morning I'll let you know whether or not I want to work here." Clay turned and started for the door.

Warburton glared at Clay. "Whoa, Baker! You're a gutty whelp. When I offer you a job in the morning I think you'd better take it."

Chapter Two

Clay stood outside the bank squinting in the harsh sunlight.
Eagle Rock was not an impressive town. Its streets were muddy
and stank from the accumulated droppings of horses and oxen.
The business buildings were typically frame with false fronts although a few of the smaller ones were simple log cabins with
sawn-lumber facades.

Hanging from the porch that covered the boardwalk in front
of the Emerson and Feltch Mercantile Company were buffalo
coats, wash tubs, and several pairs of gum-rubber overshoes.
Farther on, toward the end of the business district, Clay found
Overmire's Rooming House.

He entered and, after inspecting the accommodations, paid
$7.00 for a week's room and board. Mr. Overmire was a bris-
tling little man who said, "No refunds, no women, no drinkin'
or smokin' in the rooms. Do your chewin' outside or on the
porch. Breakfast is from 5:30 to 7:30. Cook'll pack your lunch
for seventy-five cents a week extra, six days a week. Supper is
7:00 sharp on weekdays and 3:00 on Sundays. Better be on
time."

Clay left his bag in the room he had agreed to share with another boarder. Then he walked back to the center of town and
bought a pair of overshoes from Mr. Feltch at the Emerson
and Feltch Mercantile Company. Afterward Mr. Feltch took
him to lunch at the hotel.

Marvin Feltch was an ex-cowboy in his late fifties. He was
tall and spare with a face deeply lined from years outdoors.
Good humor sparkled in the man's blue eyes.

Feltch explained that he gave up cowboying when a horse
fell on him, "Busted my leg in three places. I was in a wagon
two days gettin' to Fort Laramie where a Army surgeon set it.

He really wanted to whack it off—him bein' a Civil War doc. But I promised to kill 'im if he did, so he set it and put on a cast. I've had a stiff leg ever since, have to wear a leather brace, too. But at least I ain't no peg-legger."

As they waited to be served Feltch said, "This 'hardy pioneer' stuff is a lot of horse apples. Most of the Honyockers comin' West these days don't know their butts from fried mush. I can't help feelin' sorry for 'em. Some of 'em has bought railroad farms sight unseen. I remember one pore Eyetalian that landed here with all kinds of grape vine starts and balled fruit trees. He'd hauled 'em all the way from It'ly. He wanted to start a vineyard. Well, what there was of his stuff that didn't burn up or winterkill got ate by the antelope and jack rabbits. I finally bought him out and put him on the train. He got hisself a vineyard down in Californy. Sends me a kega good wine ever' Christmas.

"This was really wild country back before the War," Feltch said. "Me an' Dan Emerson first come in here to hunt and trap beaver. We had some trade goods, too; mirrors, bolts of cloth, and ten-cent butcher knives that we traded to the Injuns. That year wasn't what you'd call a howlin' success. We ended up livin' on the Injuns, but it did get me started in the trade."

Feltch's partner, Daniel Emerson, had been killed by a grizzly bear many years before. Feltch stopped eating. "I always kept Dan's name on the business, but most folks around here now don't know who the hell he was."

Their meal over, Feltch took out a briar pipe and filled it with tobacco from a beaded pouch. Clay looked at the pouch with an interest that Feltch recognized. "Pretty ain't it? My wife makes 'em."

"You could have fooled me," said Clay, examining the pouch. "It sure looks Injun."

Feltch laughed, "It should; my wife is a full-blood Crow. I'm related to half the Injuns in the Territory and all of 'em in Montana." Feltch's lined face grew thoughtful, "The new people comin' in don't understand that. But that's the way life goes. I know my comin' in here made it hard for some other folks."

Clay hoped to talk more with Feltch, but now he was eager

to continue his inspection of the town. As he walked he saw Indians and a few soldiers lounging around the stores and saloons. Firewood for some of the businesses had been dumped in the street and was apparently left there all winter to be used as needed. He saw bearded farmers and their moon-faced wives in the mercantile stores. At least half of them jabbered to each other in Swedish or Norwegian.

He also saw a pair of rough-looking squawmen riding into town on shaggy horses. They were followed by two stolid Indian women on their ponies. One of the squaws rode a pinto that was also drawing a travois on which were piled antelope and deer skins.

Standing in front of a saloon and eyeing them was a clean-shaven man wearing a dog-skin coat and fur cap. Clay decided he was a gambler.

Some mounted cowboys passed wearing woolen caps, angora chaps, and heavy coats made from red-and-black-striped Hudson's Bay blankets. A half-breed woodhawk clad in buckskin pants and an old, blue Army tunic walked along beside the yoked oxen that were drawing a wagon filled with cord wood, "Hey! Wood! Wood! Hey! Wood!" Run together it sounded like an Indian chant.

At the end of the street Clay found a collection of shacks in the cottonwoods by the river. Wisps of smoke came from some of their stove pipes. A passing farmer saw him looking, "That's the Hog Ranch, son. Good place to keep out of. That crew has floated more than one wise Johnny down the river. Right here's the deadline." The man indicated a red-painted post planted at the corner of the building they stood beside. Whatever was allowed down in the shacks was forbidden up town, beyond the red post.

Muttering, "Thanks," to the farmer Clay hurried back to Overmires.

At supper that evening Overmire introduced Clay to the six other diners. "Your roomie is Pat Jennings," said Overmire. "He's a brakeman on the Utah Northern. He generally don't get in till late."

While Overmire presided an Indian woman padded around the table ladling elk stew from a bowl carried in the crook of her arm. Bread and butter, bowls of beans, plus a big platter of hot sauerkraut were on the table and passed along by the diners.

Over the sounds of eating Overmire called, "Eat hearty, Baker, make yourself out a supper!" Clay, his mouth full, waved back.

A man seated across from Clay asked, "What's your line, Baker?"

"I'll be working in the Bank of Eagle Rock."

All the bobbing heads at the table stopped and turned to look at Clay. He saw quick smiles, dumb stares, and one frown. Clay's father would have been pleased. Heads didn't turn like that to see the man who said he was a farmer.

"I'd be ascared of gettin' held up," said a man down the table from Clay. "There's a lot of hard characters in this country."

"Banks lose a lot more money to bad loans than to bad men," said Clay. "With the railroads, the telegraph, and now this telephone comin' in, it's hard for a robber to get away. And the new steel vaults and alarms we have make it tough to steal much money in the first place."

The men fell silent, studying their coffee mugs and dipping spoons into bread pudding. Overmire spoke, "That's interestin'. We hear rumors that wanted men come through here on their way to Star Valley an' Jackson's Hole."

"Yep," a boarder said. "About a month ago onea them rumors et his supper right where you're a settin', Mr. Banker." There was a general guffaw.

Clay dismissed most of the dinner-table conversation as "dude stuffing," yet its theme was similar to the conversation he'd had with the salesmen the previous evening. Shrugging off the thought he went up to his room and began reading from a book entitled *Principles of Modern Accounting*.

Sometime after he had gone to bed, Clay's roommate, Pat Jennings, tumbled into bed beside him. Jennings smelled of whiskey, coal smoke, and sweat, and after a grunted "Howdy" he began to snore. Clay slept poorly and got up when he heard the first sounds of morning in the house. After dressing he went down to the kitchen where the Indian woman filled a tin basin with hot water for him. "Shave *every* day?" she asked, incredulous.

"Every day."

After shaving, Clay put on a clean collar, tied his tie, and buttoned his vest. He carefully brushed his suit coat before putting it on.

In the dining room he poured himself a cup of coffee and took a seat at the table. Two other men were there and they exchanged, "Mornin's."

The Indian appeared and slid a plate-full of fried mush and side pork in front of him. To Clay's surprise the food tasted better than it looked. He ate quickly, wanting to be at the bank when it opened.

He was standing in front of it when the teller raised the window shades and unlocked the front door. "Morning," said the teller, "Asahel Cannon got in from Riggs last night. I expect you'll want to meet each other."

Cannon was seated at a desk behind the tellers' cages. When Clay came in he stood and smiled. That was a change in this bank, Clay thought.

Asahel Cannon was about thirty, tall and lean with thinning blond hair and an almost angelic face. "Welcome! I'm Asahel Cannon, chief teller. Call me Asa. I've been looking forward to meeting you."

As they talked Clay was surprised at how much Cannon already knew about him. "Have you had much experience in making farm and ranch loans, Mr. Baker?"

"No. Mr. Meggs made all the loans himself."

"I see," said Cannon, frowning a little. "How did Mr. Meggs handle his defaults and foreclosures?"

"We never had a foreclosure the three years I was in Valverda. We only had one serious default. A farmer died owing the bank six hundred dollars, and his family couldn't make the payment. Mr. Meggs extended the note for another year. The widow and her sons were doing fine when I left."

"If you come with us," said Cannon, "you may find our methods a little different."

"How is that?"

"This is new country," said Cannon. "We're helping to open

it up. There's money to be made here. The trick is in knowing just where. If you irrigate some of this land the alkali comes up. We know about things like that. But it's still a gamble. And, you know emigrants; a lot of them wouldn't be here if they hadn't failed at home. They come and then they move on, some of 'em in the middle of the night. To protect the bank we have to charge a fairly high rate of interest—right now fourteen per cent."

Clay said, "At that rate the bank must own a lot of land and livestock."

"Yes, but we try to resell most of it as fast as we can. We've sold some places three and four times already. We keep a few of the best properties and use tenant farmers or run them on shares."

Clay recalled the fear that gripped his parents when a note fell due. They had nearly lost everything in the financial panics that followed the Civil War.

Cannon went on, "The land around Riggs is being taken up fast. It is good farming and grazing land. Most of the settlers are Mormons from Utah. They understand dry farming and also irrigation. Emigrants just coming out don't understand either one. Their rate of failure is much higher than the Mormons'."

"Does the bank prefer to have Mormons on places it mortgages?"

"Yes," said Cannon. "Most of them have very large families. Everyone pitches in, and they get a lot done."

At that moment a bell on the wall jangled loudly. Cannon jumped up. "That's Mr. Warburton." He almost ran into the bank president's office. Cannon returned in a moment. "He wants us both."

Warburton was behind his desk and still unsmiling. "You had a good look at our town already, eh, Baker?"

"Yes, sir."

"Well, don't believe all that ol' Marv Feltch tells you. He's been here so long he thinks he's God. He gives credit to half the squawmen in the territory. That's not the way we do business; not by a damn sight."

"I'll remember that, sir."

Warburton continued, "I'm not saying we don't take chances on people. We do. I'm takin' one on you. But I favor a solid, young white man with a strong wife and some healthy kiddies to anchor him down. They make the best risks for a loan, especially if their folks own a good farm and will cosign."

Although Warburton didn't mention it then, he also did a lucrative business with some carefully selected residents of the Hog Ranch. But even strait-laced Mr. Meggs had said, "A honky-tonk is a good investment. Just don't take your payments in kind."

Warburton asked, "How does the prospect of young Baker's coming in and eventually going out to Riggs's bank strike you, Cannon?"

Cannon looked at Clay with eyes that were suddenly cold and appraising. "It's up to you, sir. And, of course, to Mr. Baker. My recommendation is to give him the same opportunity you gave me when I started five years ago."

Warburton smiled for the first time that morning. "Baker, what Asa means is that I put him on at a small salary for a thirty-day trial. He did everything, including cleanin' out the spittoons. After a month, if both Cannon and I agree on you, I'll give you a salary increase and three per cent of the net from any new business you bring the bank. The next step, if I still like you, will be for you to go out with Mr. Cannon and clerk for him in the new Bank of Riggs."

"What would my starting salary be?"

"Thirty dollars a month."

"My room an' board here cost almost that much. I got fifty dollars in Valverda," said Clay.

Warburton flushed, his big freckles growing darker, "Thirty dollars is my offer, take it or leave it. I will raise that to forty dollars if you prove up after a month. Also, you can live in the cabin at the back of my lot until you go to Riggs."

"Thank you, sir, I'll take it."

Warburton waved his hands as if he were shooing flies. "All right, all right. Let's get some work done around here."

Clay started that day. After the bank closed he hurried to the rooming house, got his old clothes, and went back to the bank where he spent the evening cleaning the lobby.

The following night he painted the drab ceiling and walls with calcimine. On the third night Clay visited the small cabin behind Warburton's solid-looking home. The inside was reasonably tidy except for accumulated dust and a strong, almost chemical odor. Clay recognized it. "Hell! They've had chickens in here."

Clay built a fire in the stove and began cleaning. It was nearly midnight when he finished and, as he was about to leave, there was a tap on the door.

Startled, Clay opened the door cautiously and held his lamp high to see who was there. It was a woman wearing a dark cloak.

"Mr. Baker? I'm Mrs. Warburton. I saw your light and thought you might like some cookies and milk." She handed in a large, covered plate and a small pail of milk.

Clay was so surprised that he could barely mutter, "Thanks. I'm pleased to meet you, Mrs. Warburton."

Alma Warburton was past forty, but she had the well-kept look of a banker's wife, and Clay couldn't guess how much past. She said, "Enjoy the cookies. When you're finished put the plate and pail on our back porch. Good night."

Clay pushed the door shut and sat down at the table. Under the towel he found a plate filled with ginger snaps, oatmeal, and spritz cookies. They were all delicious and before he returned to the rooming house that night he ate them all and drained the pail of milk.

The following night he was polishing the cabin's one window when the door suddenly opened. Clay turned, startled and half-hoping to find Mrs. Warburton with another plate of cookies. But it was not. It was J. M. Warburton.

"Well, Baker. This place looks better."

"I'm afraid it still smells of chickens."

Warburton looked at him, smiling a bit, "What are you doing for wood?"

"I bought a dollar's worth from the half-breed. He piled it out by your back gate."

"That won't last too long. Tell you what. There's a lot of nice dry pine in my woodshed. If you'll cut it and keep my woodboxes full, you can help yourself to whatever you need. There's an ax and a buck saw in the shed. Well, keep this place cleaned up. I don't want any boar's nests on my property."

"No, sir. I like things neat myself."

The next day was Sunday and Clay worked all morning cutting then splitting firewood. He loaded a flat-bed wheelbarrow with it and trundled it to the Warburtons' back porch.

Mrs. Warburton answered his knock. Her brown hair was grayer than he'd expected. She was a smallish woman wearing a black silk dress; probably the one she'd worn to church that morning. "Hello there. I see you've brought me some wood." She smiled and when she did, she was nice looking.

Clay asked, "Did you find your plate and things? Those were the best cookies I ever ate."

"I'm glad. We never had any children to give them to, and J.M. says they give him indigestion. I'll make you a pie sometime. Please, bring in the wood. I'll show you where to put it."

It was while he was delivering the Warburtons' wood that Clay and Alma Warburton became friends. She appeared interested in his plans and ambitions, and Clay was flattered by her interest. One evening when he came home he found the cabin's door unlatched. Seizing a heavy piece of stove wood from the stack beside the door he stepped inside, "Who's here?"

"I'm not a burglar, Mr. Baker," said Alma Warburton. "I made apple pie today and thought you might like some."

"Well sure. Gosh, Mrs. Warburton, you didn't have to wait here in the dark." Clay lit the lamp. The lamplight revealed Alma Warburton sitting at the table and wearing a high-collared, alpaca overcoat.

"Is this what you read?" She picked up Clay's accounting text then let it slide from her fingers back onto the table.

"Yes, ma'am. I want to better myself."

"Well, try this pie first. I've brought you some cheese and a glass of milk." She stood and moved to the door. "I'll leave now. Come and shake hands good night." She smiled and took Clay's out-stretched hand and patted it. "I read once that it was 'mere madness, to live like a wretch and die rich.'"

"Yes, ma'am." All the wretches Clay knew seemed bound to die poor.

The following Sunday afternoon Clay was filling the War-burtons' woodbox when Alma Warburton came out on the back porch. "Clay," she said, "all I ever see you do is work."

Clay straightened the stacked wood, "I like work. Besides, Mr. Warburton and I made a deal."

"I know. My husband is famous for his deals."

Clay shrugged. "We're about even."

"I hope so," said Alma. "When you're through come in the kitchen and have some dinner. We eat early on Sundays so Mr. Warburton can drive out and look at property in the after-noon. I cooked a nice roast and there's plenty left."

And so, from then on, Clay Baker ate his Sunday dinner in the Warburtons' kitchen. He was flattered by Alma's interest in him. And he returned that interest by obviously enjoying her food and her company. He came to regard her as the only per-son to whom he could talk.

One day he said, "At home we ate out of wooden bowls my grandpa made. It was years before I knew some people had their own knife, fork, and spoon."

Alma, who had been folding napkins, stopped and looked at Clay; her normally sharp, brown eyes now inexpressibly sad. Then the look vanished and she said, "You should always re-member that, Clay. Just don't ever be proud of it."

Clay said, "Someday I'll have you to dinner in my own house. There'll be china dishes and silver rings on the nap-kins."

"We'll be pleased to come. Tell me, how do you plan to ac-quire all that luxury?"

"By working harder and being smarter than Mr. Warbur-ton." Clay hesitated, wondering if he had been too frank.

He needn't have worried. Alma's eyes were alight with inter-est. She moved toward him, then stopped, clasping her hands and smiling. "That will be something to see. I won't tell my husband your plans if you promise not to mention my being in your cabin the other night."

Clay stood up, joyful and excited to know that he now had a powerful ally. "I promise," he said. Then he went to the door. "Thank you for the fine dinner."

"You're welcome," said Alma. She walked with him out on

to the back porch and as he hurried down the steps she said quietly, "Good luck, Mr. Baker."

A few nights later Clay met a man in the hotel lobby named Charlie Richman. Richman was an Army contractor and had a contract to deliver grain and flour to the garrison at Fort Hall. But he also had a problem.

He told Clay, "You're with the bank, maybe you can help me. Your boss, Cannon, won't let me in to see Warburton." Richman explained that he was new to the area and short of cash. "Now the railroad's raised the freight rates. If I don't deliver on time the Army penalizes me. But the railroad won't give me any more credit. I've got grain and flour piling up in Nebraska. I need two thousand dollars for thirty days to get it here."

The next morning Clay read the man's Army contract and led him into Warburton's office. Later Warburton came out where Clay was working. "Well, Baker, we should net about twenty dollars on your contractor's loan.

Clay suppressed a grin. For helping him get the loan, Charlie Richman had already paid Clay twenty-five dollars.

Chapter Three

Spring in the Rocky Mountains can be a treacherous season. One sunny April morning when Clay Baker went to work he noticed a light breeze blowing from the northwest. By six that evening the breeze was a gale that had brought the town a foot of snow.

Marv Feltch, with whom Clay often lunched, had a great fund of weather yarns. "The buffalo and the moose was built for our climate. If you ever seen moose beddin' down in the meadows at midday, expect a good snow.

"The buffalo could look at a blizzard all day. But a beef cow can't. Sometimes their tails freeze and fall off.

"I used to have a big black horse that had the tips of his ears froze off. Made him look like a moose."

Feltch said this to emphasize to Clay how important the mountain climate was to business. "If we don't get a frost, the grain won't set. An' it can't be cut and threshed until it has set. If we get a late frost, it puts the harvest back and sometimes the farmers can't get in their fields for mud and snow by the time their last crops is ready. About all a man can count on is that the weather will try to flummox him."

The spring storm that hampered life in Eagle Rock buried Riggs. Work on the new bank building stopped, and Asahel Cannon was temporarily marooned by six-foot drifts that did not completely melt until June.

Nevertheless, everything needed to operate the new bank was packed in wooden crates awaiting the day when freight wagons could haul the supplies to Riggs.

Clay was going. He had proven himself to both Warburton and Cannon. Advertisements had been placed in the newspapers announcing the opening of the new bank. The Territorial Governor had sent a letter of congratulations. Warburton grumped in private that a government deposit in his new bank would have done them more good than political hot air.

His impending move excited Clay. But the only person he knew who could share his excitement was Alma Warburton. While he ate her Sunday dinners Clay told her his dreams.

"I won't be just a banker. I'll need land, too. And livestock. Not fancy stuff that'll die if it rains on 'em. But hardy animals with good bloodlines. Every farmer and rancher in the Territory is going to respect my brand and buy my bloodlines for their own herds."

Alma poured a cup of coffee then sat down at the table across from Clay. "My, you're ambitious. Will you be governor, too?"

"Why not? But I've heard tell it's better to own a governor than to be one. Politics are important. A man's got to know his way around the court house."

Alma smiled, "You've thought it all out, haven't you? I'll miss that. I've enjoyed giving you dinner and hearing all these dreams. Mr. Warburton and I don't dream much anymore. Isn't that a shame?"

Clay shrugged, "Mine aren't dreams. They're plans. I've been makin' them since I was a kid. They're gonna happen."

"I hope so," said Alma. "Just be certain you really want your plans to happen. Because they will, you know."

"I'm certain," said Clay.

"That's fine, then." Alma Warburton got up from the table and carried her cup and saucer to the sink. A tear had welled in her eye, and she did not want Clay Baker to see it.

Moving day finally arrived and Clay was assigned to handle one of the two heavy freight wagons drawn by four mules. The wagons were laden with bank furniture, supplies, plus household articles belonging to the Cannons. Some groceries were included at the last minute by Warburton who had sold them to a storekeeper in Riggs.

The other wagon was handled by a professional teamster who knew the road. It was a trip of sixty rough miles that took wagons almost three days to complete. In places the wagons passed through grass that was already halfway to the mules' bellies. The cottonwood and aspen trees were richly green. And even the grayish sagebrush was vibrant with buzzing insects and fluttering birds.

At long intervals they passed solitary homesteads. The tiny cabins had low, dirt roofs and mud and manure chinking between the logs. At one such place the ragged, barefoot children scurried and hid behind their mother's skirts like chicks hiding under a hen.

At that time the homestead laws allowed adults to file on one 160-acre homestead and a second 160 acres called a "desert land entry." Those families who could afford the fees and performed the labor required to "prove up" often filed on two more quarter-sections in the wives' names. Corruption was rife in some land offices, and children occasionally filed claims with their parents' connivance.

It was possible to advance filing fees to people who had no intention of taking up land. Later their "relinquishment" was purchased by those who had advanced the filing fees. It was one means unscrupulous land sharks used to gain control over huge tracts of western land. Water was the key, and by filing on dependable water sources thousands of surrounding acres could be controlled by those claiming the water.

In passing through the hills Clay saw many slopes that were covered with fine evergreen trees. They would make millions of saw logs, and ties for the railroad they all hoped was coming.

But not all the timber was green. They passed whole mountain sides that had been blackened by fires. Clay asked the teamster about the burns.

"A lot of it's the Injuns. They set the timber afire to drive out the game. The prospectors burn a lot, too. Some of 'em claim they can locate ore better when the trees are gone. Then, some of the fires are just get-aways. You'll see 'em burn all summer."

Riggs, when it came into view, was nestled in the curve of a long, timber-clad butte. Beyond it to the east there arose a high range of mountains with snow still covering the peaks. Lying between the mountains and the spot where Clay sat was a great basin, hazy green in the spring sunshine. Here and there in the distance tiny plumes of dust marked spring cultivation or where yet another pioneer was grubbing out sagebrush.

In Riggs itself there were fourteen permanent buildings plus some tents with wooden frames built around their walls. "I seen Eagle Rock when it looked like this," said the teamster, "but this burg will be lucky to grow that fast."

The grand opening of the Riggs State Bank was announced for the second Saturday in May 1884. J. M. Warburton himself was coming to preside. And he was also to deliver the bank's cash assets, $1,500.

"That isn't much to start on," said Clay after reading Warburton's letter.

"I wanted twice that amount," said Cannon, "but cash is scarce, especially in places like this. We can issue bank drafts though, and we'll work hard to get depositors."

Warburton traveled with two well-armed companions. The men rode fine saddle horses that were exchanged for fresh mounts halfway to Riggs. They left Eagle Rock long before dawn and by riding hard had arrived in Riggs early in the evening of the same day.

"Oh Lord!" groaned Warburton. He was reclining in Cannon's new desk chair with his feet on the packing case Clay had hastily provided. "I'll never do that again! I'll never make it back on a damn horse. Cannon, get me a wagon to ride home in. One with good springs and a box where I can lie down on a tick."

The next day, the first day of business, Mr. Warburton could scarcely move. "Pardon me not gettin' up," he said on meeting the bishop of the local Mormon church. "My horse fell with me yesterday an' I'm stiff all over."

Clay's expression didn't reveal Warburton's lie. He knew Warburton thought it embarrassing to appear unmanly before men who were not impressed by horseback trips of sixty miles in a day.

But, despite all the fanfare and work, the new bank did not thrive. Ulysses S. Grant's Wall Street firm had collapsed taking the ex-President's fortune with it. A panic ensued, and banks all over the country were failing. Warburton sent out weekly letters exhorting his men to greater effort. The bank could be closed. Cannon appeared to become paralyzed with caution, and Clay realized he would have to come up with something or lose his job.

His thoughts settled on one of the farmers who drove into town every Saturday morning. He was a well-dressed young man named Abbot Smith who was always accompanied by his equally well-dressed mother. Clay sensed wealth in this pair and made it a point to become acquainted.

"Mr. Smith, we'd like you to visit our bank some day when you're in town."

"Why?" asked Smith.

"Because I think we're all interested in the same things—making a living, preserving our capital, and building this country. We could help each other," said Clay.

He continued, "We have the latest combination safe. It is fireproof and burglarproof. It's ordnance steel and set in a half ton of concrete. We keep our own money there."

Smith said he'd think about it. And Clay spent the week in nervous anticipation. But, sure enough, the next Saturday morning Abbot Smith ushered his mother into the bank. Clay hurried to greet them.

"Mother and I want to see this safe of yours," said Smith. Clay showed them the squat, black safe with the mountain scene painted on its door. "It's kept locked at all times. Mr. Cannon and Mr. Warburton in Eagle Rock are the only ones who know the combination."

Mrs. Smith spoke for the first time. "What rate of interest do you pay?"

Clay replied, "Three per cent a year, ma'am. Compounded twice each year and paid once on January second."

"All right," Mrs. Smith nodded to her son.

Abbot Smith turned his back and opened his coat. When Smith turned around again he was holding a sheaf of yellow-back currency. "Here's five thousand dollars. Open our account."

Both Clay and Cannon barely concealed their joy. With great ceremony Cannon made out a deposit receipt while Clay inscribed a bank book with the Smiths' names.

As soon as they'd gone Cannon exclaimed, "Hallelujah! I'd

better take half of this cash to Eagle Rock. I'll go out with the mail rider Monday morning."

For all their assurances to depositors, neither Cannon nor Clay knew how long their safe could resist the efforts of a competent dynamiter.

The Smiths' deposit increased the bank's lending capacity. This, plus a substantial show of trust in the new bank, inspired other depositors. Some came from as far as the gold mines in Caribou City just south of Jackson's Hole.

By midsummer the cash reserves of the Riggs State Bank had grown to more than twelve thousand dollars. Even J. M. Warburton seemed satisfied. At Clay's suggestion the bank spent a hundred dollars to improve the road to Eagle Rock. When the work was finished several farmers agreed to take their grain to Eagle Rock. The grain sale was not especially profitable, but the quality and quantity of the crop was remarkable. The *Eagle Rock Register* headlined, "Grain Bonanza in Riggs Basin."

This publicity helped the Warburton banks to sell profitably thousands of acres of Riggs Basin land. The banks made new and larger investments, and J. M. Warburton grew ever more powerful. In the fall of 1884 everyone who knew him believed that Warburton was on his way to becoming a very rich man.

Then, early one morning in October, Alma Warburton awoke with a strong sense of foreboding. She lit the candle on her bedside table and held it up to examine the man lying on his back beside her. His mouth was open and so were his filmed eyes. J. M. Warburton was dead.

Mrs. Warburton sat in the bed for a few minutes clutching her elbows. She did not cry. Then she got up and put on her best and warmest serge dress. In the kitchen she built a fire in the stove and made coffee.

She drank two cups. Then she washed her breakfast dishes, tidied up the house, and took some papers from her late husband's desk and put them into her knitting bag. At 8:45 she put on her warm coat and new hat and walked to the Bank of Eagle Rock.

Mr. Charles, the teller, met her at the door. "Good morning, Mrs. Warburton. How are you?"

"Well, thank you," said Mrs. Warburton. "Mr. Charles, I've

come on business. My husband won't be in today. May I speak
with you in his office?"

When Alma was seated at her husband's desk she opened
her knitting bag and removed a bank book. "As you know, Mr.
Charles, my husband and I kept our personal funds in a joint
account."

The teller nodded, curious.

Mrs. Warburton continued, "We have $32,573.38 in that ac-
count, and I am withdrawing it all this morning—in cash."

"Mrs. Warburton, that's a lot of money. Have you discussed
this with Mr. Warburton?"

"I have, many times, and I am acting now on his orders."
Alma handed the teller the passbook. "Please, Mr. Charles, I'm
in something of a hurry."

"Come with me, then." Charles led Mrs. Warburton to the
bank's vault and opened it. He began removing packets of
yellowbacks and bags of gold coins. "Mrs. Warburton, won't
you reconsider and take a check for some of this? You're reduc-
ing our cash reserves below the established limits."

"Please, Mr. Charles, in cash?"

"Yes, ma'am."

When the money had been counted Mrs. Warburton put it
into her knitting bag and, thanking the nervous teller, left the
bank. Her next stop was the Eagle Rock Hardware Company
whose proprietor also served as the town's undertaker.

"Good morning, Mr. Gunderson," she said, "I'm here on an
unhappy errand. Mr. Warburton passed away in his sleep last
night."

"Oh! Mrs. Warburton, I am sorry!"

"Thank you. I would appreciate it very much if you would
handle all the details and make the funeral arrangements."

"Of course."

Mrs. Warburton ordered a plain casket and a simple funeral.
She paid the entire bill in cash.

Leaving the hardware store, Alma Warburton walked to the
railroad station and took the 11:15 for Pocatello. The conductor later remembered helping her off the train there. But he
was the last person to positively recall seeing her in Idaho Territory.

After Alma Warburton left his store, Mr. Gunderson left, too. He almost ran to the Bank of Eagle Rock, closed his small savings account, and then drew a check on his business account for the total amount on deposit. With the cash in his pocket he strolled back to his store and calmly proceeded with the funeral arrangements for the late banker.

The news that "J. M. Warburton died!" surged through the town like the waters of a flash flood. Within an hour of the first report people were lined up at the teller's window of his bank.

Teller Charles did his best to stall the run. He slowly checked and rechecked accounts that were being closed. The slightest error on a withdrawal slip caused it to be returned. And when he did pay out money he did so leisurely and in bills and coins of the smallest denominations. Transactions that normally took two minutes now required more than five. The crowd in the lobby began to murmur with impatience. And when Charles closed the teller's window they came close to rioting.

"Sorry, folks," he said, "the bank closes at three. Your money is safe. We will be here tomorrow morning to do business as usual." Somehow Charles and his assistant managed to push the anxious depositors out the front doors.

As soon as the doors were bolted Charles dispatched the assistant to the bank in Riggs. Cannon was to be told of Warburton's death and urged to send all his available cash to Eagle Rock to help stop the run.

Charles next went to the town's other bank. They were unsympathetic. Charles sent a telegram to the Pocatello bank announcing the run and urgently requesting a loan. The Pocatello banker replied, "Sorry. Regret our cash previously committed. Good luck."

It was the next morning before Asahel Cannon received the express message from Eagle Rock. When he had read it, he immediately took three thousand dollars from the safe and stuffed it into a pair of saddle bags. In an hour he was mounted on one of the best horses in town and galloping west to Eagle Rock. Thirty miles out he began meeting depositors from both his bank and the one in Eagle Rock all racing in buggies and on horseback for Riggs. One of the riders yelled, "Ol' Warburton croaked! They're runnin' his bank!" Cannon realized then it was too late. Now he must try to save his own bank.

He jerked his horse around and began a frantic race for Riggs. In five miles his horse lay down and refused to get up. Cannon abandoned the exhausted animal and began walking to Riggs. He tried to hail passing riders and buggies, but no one would stop for him.

It was early the next morning when Cannon arrived back in Riggs. He went immediately to the bank and found that heavy planks had been nailed across the front and back doors. The windows were smashed and the bank's interior was a shambles. Papers littered the floor, furniture was overturned and broken. The partition that had separated the teller's cage from the lobby had been knocked flat and splintered into kindling. Only the safe appeared intact, though it had obviously been beaten with a sledge hammer.

As he walked around the bank building someone said, "Hold it." It was the postmaster who also served as town constable. He had a shotgun under his arm. "Mr. Cannon, you'd better come with me." He took Cannon around to the back of the post office and directed him into a storeroom. When Cannon was inside the postmaster shut the door and barred it with a heavy timber.

The room was windowless, but Cannon's eyes soon became accustomed to the gloom. Someone was lying against the wall.

"Clay!"

Clay Baker was no longer the ambitious and neat banker Cannon had left in the bank the day before. His clothing was ripped and both eyes were swollen shut. One cheek was puffed to twice its normal size and his lips were split and bruised. His badly swollen left hand lay useless in his lap.

"My God, Clay! What happened?"

Clay spoke slowly. His speech had a dreamy quality that suggested a brain concussion. He described what had happened. Abbot Smith had come first and withdrawn all his money. With his account gone, the safe was nearly empty. But, in a few minutes, other depositors began arriving. All demanded their money, and Clay did not have it.

The people would not listen to his explanations. They jerked him out of the teller's cage and beat him. As he lay on the floor they kicked him and turned out his pockets. Then they wrecked the bank. Clay said that the mob would have killed him had not the postmaster come with his shotgun and forced a couple of the men to drag him into this room.

Cannon began yelling for the postmaster. He came and listened through the door. Cannon told him, "This man is badly hurt. He needs a doctor!"

"So will you if folks decide to take you outa there. You stay put until folks calm down." The postmaster went back to his office.

The next day the postmaster brought the Mormon Bishop to the storeroom. "Brother Cannon," asked the Bishop, "what have you done?"

"Bishop, I swear, I haven't done anything wrong. And neither has Baker. I'm not sure why all this should have happened."

The postmaster interrupted, "It happened because Warburton's wife cleaned out their account and skedaddled. People stampeded and busted the bank."

"Bishop," Cannon led the man into a corner, "if what he says is true, the Riggs Bank will fail, too."

"Seems to me it already has. You're broke ain't you?"

"No. Not if the brethren will trust and bear with me. I have three thousand dollars in these saddle bags. I was taking it to help the Eagle Rock Bank, but I never got there. This is just enough money to keep us going—if the people will trust me until we can re-charter the bank." Cannon was thinking as he spoke, "We can't help the Bank of Eagle Rock. But we can help ourselves."

The Bishop stroked his beard. "Maybe we can. The Lord says so. It's plain we'll lose everythin' if we don't try. But, this time, it must be an honest, Latter-day Saints bank. We'll not be deceived again."

Both men looked at Clay. He looked back, knowing he was being sacrificed. What made things worse was his knowledge that he couldn't do a thing about it.

Cannon was released, but Clay was held as "an accessory to

bank fraud." What followed were some of the most bitter hours of Clay's life. He could still see the windows breaking and the partition crashing down. But the worst had been the woman. A mousy little creature who started screaming. Her colorless lips had gaped like an open tar barrel. The more the mob wrecked, the more she shrieked.

Now, still too sore to move and being poisoned by his own anger, Clay lay alone in the dark. It was two days before he heard a wagon rattle up and stop behind the post office.

"He's in here," said the postmaster. The bar was removed from the door and it swung open.

"Well, it's about time you started doin' somethin'." Marvin Feltch stood looking down at Clay. A burly man with a heavy beard stood behind Feltch. Feltch said, "This is the one, Johnny. Maybe his pelt's worth somethin'."

The two men helped Clay to his feet. Once they had him standing they half-walked and half-carried him outside to a spring wagon. A big wool sack filled with straw was in the wagon box and Clay was helped to lie down on it.

The wagon jolted off and Feltch, looking back from the driver's seat, said, " 'Pears to me you lost that one. But, you're young. You'll heal."

The wagon rumbled through the afternoon and into the night. They stopped once at a homestead to eat and rest their horses. It was early evening of the following day before they reached Marv Feltch's large home on a farm near Eagle Rock.

"C'mon, Clay. If my poor old leg could stand this damnable ride, I think your young ones can, too." The men got Clay between them and hauled him into the kitchen. A large, portable zinc bathtub sat in the middle of the floor. An Indian woman was at the stove, heating water in big, copper boilers.

"Got enough wood?" Feltch asked her. The woman nodded.

They helped Clay into a kitchen chair and gently pulled off his boots and removed his torn and bloody clothing. Even the two men winced at the sight of his injuries. The woman tenderly examined Clay's swollen hand. "OK. It's not broken."

The two older men helped Clay into the tub and began filling it with hot water from the boilers on the stove. "This'll take out a lot of the soreness," said Feltch. The Indian woman poured leaves, dried berries, and bits of roots and bark into the water.

"You was too woozy to interduce before. This here is Mrs. Feltch. I call her Sunshine." Feltch grinned at the woman.

Clay said thickly, "How do you do, Sunshine."

The woman looked down at him and said, "Better than you, kid."

When the men finally hauled Clay out of the hot water he was weak but the terrible soreness had lessened. He was able to walk unaided to a big bed piled high with warm quilts. He found a blanket-wrapped bundle of hot stones at his feet. Feltch handed him a filled tumbler. "Kentucky Bourbon. Drink her down."

Clay was surprised at how easily he was able to swallow the whiskey. In less than five minutes he had fallen asleep.

Before daylight Feltch was back in the bedroom carrying a lamp. "Clay?"

"I'm awake."

"How ya feelin'?"

"A lot better."

"Good. The missis has made some poultices for the worsta them knots on ya. She'll put 'em on in a bit."

"Thanks, Marv. Nobody ever did for me what you have."

"Well, it was done for me. An' I think helpin' you will be worth it. But if some of the folks that got busted by your ex-bank knew you was here, we might both get hung."

"Is the bank really gone?"

"Flat busted. After Warburton kicked off, his missis got their money and flew. For a while they was talk of hangin' you an' Cannon. But now the lawyers has it. You know what that means; years of layin' the blame while they milk the assets for whatever's left. I seen it happen before. Never have trusted bankers too much. You're well out of it, to my notion. A man shouldn't wake up ever' mornin' worryin' about money."

"The banker I worked for in Colorado was honest."

"So was Warburton, more or less. I guess what his missis done was legal. But what's legal and what's right can be two different things." Feltch's voice became even more serious.

"You know you're washed up with the people in these parts— at least for a few years."

"I am?" All Clay's dreams were crumbling around him.

"Yep. You were in the bank that broke 'em."

"But I'm broke, too."

"Some folks think that's a sin, and others won't never believe you got busted, too."

Feltch told Clay that he ought to leave and the sooner the better. "Johnny Kelly—he's the fella that helped me get you outa Riggs—has a new place on the head of Snake River. There's a big valley over there, wild as hell. Not more'n a half-dozen white men in the whole place an' halfa them's renegades.

"But it's a place to get started again with no questions asked. You said once you used to trap. Well, you can trap them mountains over there till kingdom comes. There's no end to the beaver, mink, an' marten."

Feltch continued. "Kelly's willin' to take you over and let you work for your keep. You can trap on your own. He's got a pack string out at a place I own easta here. Him an' his woman wants to get goin' before the Pass gets snowed shut. What do you say?"

"I say, 'Yes.'"

Early the next morning Clay Baker left for a wild mountain valley that was a hundred miles from the nearest town. The place was called Jackson's Hole.

Chapter Four

That morning Johnny Kelly had sat at the Feltches' kitchen table forking down a huge breakfast of hotcakes, steak, and potatoes. Clay sat across from him sipping coffee.

"Better eat all ya kin, kid," Kelly said, "I can't promise when you'll eat this good again."

Kelly was a stocky man of middle age. He weighed more than two hundred pounds, but it was impossible to guess how much more because of the bulky clothing he wore. His costume was a worn mixture of homemade, Indian, and Feltch's store. Like Feltch he wore a brilliant red sash around his waist but, unlike Feltch, he anchored his baggy woolen pants with leather suspenders. Kelly's grizzled beard seemed to Clay to suit his gruff manner.

Feltch had outfitted Clay with clothing from his store. There were woolen trousers, German socks, felt pacs, heavy leather boots, and overshoes. Clay had gloves, woolen shirts, a mackinaw coat, and long woolen underwear. It all made Clay think Jackson's Hole was unheated as well as uncivilized. Besides the clothing there were three dozen traps of various sizes, a huge Winchester Model 1876 in .45-75 caliber along with ammunition reloading tools, brass cartridge cases, powder, primers, and a bullet mold.

There was also a big, rope-tied bedroll wrapped in a weatherproof tarp along with a bridle and saddle that had a pair of leather hobbles tied to its horn. On seeing all this Clay had sighed, "It looks like I'll be gone a long time. I don't know how I can ever pay you for all this."

Feltch said, "You'll find a way. If I didn't think you'd at least try, I wouldn't set you up."

All of Clay's gear was piled into an already well-loaded

wagon. There were sacks of flour, grain for the horses, sugar and salt, plus coffee, tea, horseshoes, nails together with spikes, carpenter's tools, and two scythes with their long blades removed, wrapped in sacking, and wired to the wooden snaths.

It was just getting light when Kelly shook hands with Feltch and climbed onto the wagon seat. "C'mon, kid, we got a long day ahead."

Clay clutched at Marv Feltch's hand. "Thank you. Thank Mrs. Feltch, too." His eyes watered and he had trouble swallowing. Clay climbed up beside Kelly who immediately slapped the horses' rumps with the reins and the team was off at a trot.

"Good-by!"

"Good-by!"

Clay's thoughts were a mixture of eager anticipation and gloomy misgivings. The letter he'd written his parents and given to Feltch to mail had the air of a final farewell despite his efforts to make it cheerful. Was Jackson's Hole a punishment or a reward? Clay didn't know.

Once the team settled into their collars Kelly reached into his coat pocket and pulled out a plug of tobacco. "Chew?" he asked.

"No thanks."

"You ain't in no bank now. You might as well start bein' human."

Clay didn't reply.

In an hour Kelly said, "Here we are," and swung the team through the gate of a farm. As they drove up to the small house Clay counted twenty-five horses and mules tied around the perimeter of the corral.

"Hullo the camp!" yelled Johnny.

The door of the farm house flew open and a squat little Indian woman hurried out. She was grinning. "How! How! Johnny!"

Kelly looped the reins around the brake handle and clambered down to embrace the woman. "How, how yourself, honey. How you been keepin'?"

The woman answered, partially in broken English and partially in what Clay guessed was Shoshone, "Hokay. Horses ready." The middle-aged woman was jumping around Johnny like a young girl greeting her sweetheart. Clay could not help being amused. And he could not help liking someone with so much enthusiasm.

"Clay Baker, this here is Mary. She is my true-blue partner. And she is the boss wrangler."

"Hello, Mary," said Clay.

"How, how," said Mary, smiling shyly and coming up to shake Clay's hand in that light-gripped pump peculiar to Indians. She put her hand briefly on his battered cheek and then shook her head.

All of the horses in the corral were fitted with pack saddles except two, big bays that wore riding saddles.

"Clay'll drive the wagon. Won't have ta leave it here an' pack the horses," said Johnny. "Save their backs a day's haulin' now we kin make a drive with the wagon. Mary an' me will drive the horses to where we can't go no more with the wagon. Then we pack our stuff on the horses an' hit for the Pass."

Within a few miles the road became only a track through the sagebrush. The wagon's jolting was torture for Clay. But he had to endure it for walking was impossible.

Clay noticed that when Kelly arrived at the farm he had given Mary a paper sack of hard candy. Now Mary was popping piece after piece into her mouth. No sooner had one chunk dissolved than she took another and sometimes two. Her cheeks puffed out until she resembled a bright-eyed chipmunk carrying pine nuts.

Clay also noticed that while Mary was childlike and dumpy-looking, she rode her horse with graceful and enviable ease. Mary rode astride, her cotton squaw dress pulled up to reveal buckskin leggings.

As they traveled farther east, the few isolated homesteads dwindled until there were none at all. Clay saw large numbers of sharp-tail and sage grouse in the swales and grassy uplands. Antelope were almost constantly in sight, and when the little caravan crossed a creek a doe deer and two fawns burst from the willows and bounded away.

Late in the afternoon Kelly said to Clay, "Next time we get near some antelope, plug a young one."

They had not gone a mile when four antelope appeared on

top of a knoll about 125 yards away. Clay tied the team to a clump of bushes. Then he pulled his new rifle from its fringed, Indian scabbard. His heart beat wildly. But he fought down his excitement and moved away from the wagon. The antelope stood still, watching him. Clay knelt beside a rock and rested his rifle, aiming at a black-faced buck.

Clay squeezed the trigger. There was a loud "whump!" and a cloud of white smoke rose up. When it drifted away the four antelope were still standing on the knoll, looking at him. Clay fired four more shots, emptying his rifle, with no more effect than he'd achieved with his first shot.

Kelly was sitting on his horse beside the wagon when Clay returned. "Didn't you never shoot a rifle gun afore? You shot over 'em ever' shot."

"How do you know?"

"I know," said Kelly. "You listen to me the next time we see some goats."

Clay didn't have long to wait. Another band of a half-dozen antelope appeared and ran halfway up the side of an adjacent hill. They paused there to look back at the halted caravan. Kelly rode back to the wagon. "Get your rifle, Clay. You won't miss this time."

Clay obeyed, but he was less than eager to further embarrass himself. He had never fired a rifle before, and he thought this one must be defective.

Kelly said, "Go over to that big sage bush and put your hat on it. Good. Now rest your gun on the hat." Clay followed instructions, sitting down by the bush and steadying his rifle's sights on another antelope. Kelly said, "This time hold just above the brisket and on line with the front leg."

Clay aimed exactly as Kelly ordered and squeezed the trigger. The Winchester thudded and, just as the gun smoke obscured his view, Clay saw the antelope collapse.

"That was better. Can you clean it?"

"I've butchered a lot of farm animals."

"No difference. I'll go back and help Mary with the horses. I guess you learned somethin'?"

"To aim low?"

"That ain't all there is to mountain shootin'. But when

you're shootin' sharp uphill or down, aim low. Otherwise you'll shoot over 'em."

Clay found the antelope, dead. It was a young buck with black, pronged horns eight inches long. The bullet had struck the animal where Johnny had told him to aim. Almost an hour elapsed while Clay dressed the buck and dragged it back to the wagon.

In that time the Kellys had moved far ahead and out of sight. This didn't worry Clay because he could clearly see their tracks in the trail ahead. His team shuffled along and Clay sat back on the wagon seat, enjoying the fall sunshine and his new-found prowess as a hunter.

The team had pulled the wagon all day with quiet willing-ness. And Clay was not ready when the nigh horse suddenly reared and snorted.

"Whoa! Whoa!" Clay sawed hard on the reins. The rearing pinto was too old to be fiery for long, and Clay soon got him under command. It was then that he saw the cause of the trouble. Five Indians were standing in the trail, blocking it.

In front was a man with a flat and deeply wrinkled face. He was squinting into the late afternoon sun and the result was a fierce grimace. The Indian wore a sleeveless cloak of rabbit skins and a pair of old Army pants with the seat cut out.

The other Indians were three blanket-wrapped squaws and a dirty, wild-haired little girl. She wore a gingham smock and was barefooted.

"You got 'em whiskey? Make Tom warm. God Damn!" The old man had come around to stand on the hub of the front wagon wheel from where he could stare directly into Clay's face.

"No! No whiskey!"

The man patted his scarred belly and made eating motions. He pointed to the squaws. "Eat? Eat?"

Clay nodded and waved the Indians around to the back of the wagon. When they had assembled there he crawled back and pulled up the antelope carcass. A squaw stepped forward, whipping a butcher knife from under her blanket. Clay signed for her to take off one of the buck's hind legs. The woman did this with such quick skill that Clay wondered if she could disembowel him as rapidly.

The Indians took the meat but stood looking at Clay. He waved his hands, palms down. "That's all. No more." The Indians just stood, looking. Finally Clay crawled back to his seat, unlooped the reins from the brake handle and clucked to the team. After they started he looked back. The Indians were still standing in the trail.

It was a long, unpleasant hour before Clay caught sight of the Kellys. They had stopped to camp in a large meadow. "Hella mighty, boy! Where ya been?" Kelly shouted.

"Injuns! Mr. Kelly! They scared the team. I gave 'em some meat. I don't know where they went."

"Injuns?" snorted Kelly. "Do you mean ol' Tom and his gal friends? Why, kid, that old gummer couldn't hurt you."

"How was I to know?" Clay was indignant. "They made the pinto rear. I gave 'em some meat and they never said a thing, just kept standing there, lookin' at me."

"If I hadn't seen that purple-and-yeller mug-a yourn before, I'd of looked, too."

Clay touched his still-tender cheek. He had forgotten how strange he must look. "Was it OK to give 'em the meat?"

"Sure. The chizzler squirrels is all denned up for winter. The chucks, too. Those folks probably ain't had no fresh meat in a long spell."

Kelly helped Clay unload the antelope, and Mary knelt beside it to skin some of it while the men unharnessed. Clay was impressed by how quickly and cleanly she worked.

Later, while the men brought in the horses from the meadow and tied them for the night, Mary cut the antelope meat into strips. In the process Clay thought he saw Mary gobble some of the liver raw. He tried not to think about it as the three of them sat together on their soogans broiling meat over the fire. When he could eat no more Clay said, "I'm stuffed. I'll take my bed over by those trees and turn in."

"No," said Kelly, "you sleep here with us. Put your Winchester in your blankets with ya. They claim times has changed, but I don't take no chances on this trail." Of course, given that sinister remark to sleep on, Clay hardly closed his eyes all night.

It was barely light when Kelly got up to grain the horses and begin putting pack saddles on them. Clay hurried to help. "Ever pack a horse?" asked Kelly.

"No, but I've worked them a lot."

Kelly pointed to a rangy black mule. "Put a pack saddle on him."

The pack saddles had been placed astride a downed log the night before. Some were made with stout, oaken bucks and tanned leather rigging. The rest were Indian made. Their cross bucks were formed by the clever use of elk antlers fastened with rawhide and Indian-tanned leather riggings.

"Mind this bugger," Kelly warned. "He'll kick you."

"Then I'll kick him back," said Clay, placing a blanket on the mule's back. It still hurt him to move but not like it had yesterday.

Clay gathered the rigging on top of the saddle so no dangling straps could bang into and startle the mule when the saddle was set on his back. He adjusted it until the swell of the saddle-tree merged with the hollow behind the mule's withers. "How's that, Mr. Kelly?"

"I'm just Johnny. I'm not a customer nor nothin' so don't call me 'mister' or 'sir' no more. The saddle looks good to me. Go ahead and cinch him. Not too tight. Just snug 'em up. We'll tighten cinches just before we load 'em."

Clay decided pack horses were about like farm horses. He spoke quietly to the animals, touching them firmly but not slapping them or jerking too hard or fast on the rigging. The animals took him for granted.

"Eat!" Mary called. The men finished saddling the horses they were with then went to the breakfast fire. In addition to the broiled antelope and coffee, Mary had made a sticky sourdough and wound it on green willow sticks to roast over the fire. The Kellys ate speedily, working their meat off knife blades and into their mouths Indian fashion.

"Clay," said Kelly standing up, "when you're done, roll your bed, good and tight, an' then take the tongue outa the wagon."

Clay did as he was told and Kelly helped him hang the wagon tongue in a big spruce.

"The porkypines may eat on the wagon this winter. Can't be helped. But no one's gonna steal it without a tongue."

At the camp site Mary was busy packing horses. Working alone it took about five minutes. But when Johnny and Mary worked together baggage was loaded, hitches thrown, and knots tied with a swiftness that astounded Clay. But the work slowed if an animal fought and had to have a front foot roped and tied up.

There were enough such animals that the packing job lasted into midmorning. When the last animal was packed it was led away to join the others all standing tied to trees.

"We'll tail up some of 'em," said Johnny. "Clay, you lead the ones over that I tell ya."

Kelly made up a pack string of seven animals. The leader was a trailwise mule. To his looped tail the lead rope of a less experienced animal was tied. Kelly alternated "good" and "bad" animals, thus avoiding having two troublemakers attached to each other. As soon as the string was ready Mary swung aboard her horse and took the mule's lead rope from Johnny.

"Go ahead, honey. We'll catch up." Kelly waved her up the trail. He made up a pack string of four, for Clay. "You'll prob'ly have all you can handle with these." Kelly sent Clay away leading his string and driving a half-dozen other pack animals ahead of him. Several of the loose trailed animals had large cow bells hung around their necks to help locate them by if they wandered into the timber.

Clay marveled at the two Kellys because they seemed to have no trouble managing so many animals both ahead of and behind them. Yet he, in his first hour, worked himself into a heavy sweat. He had trouble keeping the driven horses on the trail. His lead pack horse suddenly hung back and jerked the rope from Clay's hand. He tried to hurry off his saddle horse and retrieve the dragging rope but was too slow. Before he could catch them, the pack animals wound themselves around a tree. He was ten minutes getting them untangled and moving again.

Although Clay had ridden horses before, they had been draft

horses. And he had ridden them while holding onto their harness but never with his seat in a saddle and his feet in stirrups.

Kelly soon overtook the struggling beginner. "Next time you ride under a tree with a switchy limb, break it off. Use it on that pelter and make 'im walk. If you don't get a move on, you won't cross the divide before Christmas."

Clay got a switch and was pleased to discover that just holding it prompted his horse to walk faster. The steepness of the grade was increasing and for some time they rode along an old creek bed that was thick with willows and undergrowth.

Shortly before noon the party swung away from the creek bed and began winding up some heavily timbered ridges. The ground here was snow-covered, and the higher they climbed the deeper the snow became. The only trail that Clay could see was the one left by Mary and her horses. The horses began to grunt and slip as they churned up through the snow.

Just as he was wondering if he'd ever overtake her, Clay came on Mary in a forest glade. She had tied her saddle horse and was readjusting some packs and retying ropes. Clay noticed that the packs on two of his horses had been knocked askew, apparently when the animals banged into trees. Mary helped him straighten the packs, and when they finished she pointed in the direction the trail appeared to be heading. "Injun," she said.

Presently Kelly came up and Mary made the same gesture to him. He dismounted immediately and bent to examine the trail. "They're up ahead. Either last night or this mornin'. Prob'ly they're just huntin' but we can't take no chances. They like to jump you in the timber and drive off the loose horses."

Kelly consolidated the outfit by tying three more pack horses into Clay's string. He said, "I'll take lead now. Mary will be in the middle an' push the rest of the loose stock. Clay, you keep up an' holler if you have trouble." Kelly looked down at the cased rifle Clay had tied to his saddle. "The only thing worse than shootin' an Injun is not shootin' him when it's necessary. I'd rather lose a horse or two, packs an' all, than have shootin'." Kelly rode ahead.

There was no stopping now except to occasionally rest the horses on the steepest grades. Clay's eyes began to feel strained from staring so hard into the timber for lurking savages. He saw none, but his experience with Old Tom convinced him that not seeing anything might mean there was an Indian behind every tree.

At midafternoon the party crossed a divide. The steady climbing ended and the snow lessened. In another hour they reached a clearing where Kelly halted. Clay would gladly have dismounted there and not moved for an hour.

But the Kellys were bustling. Some of the stock was picketed for a couple of hours while the remainder was hobbled, then turned loose. In that time each animal was able to eat a subsistence meal before being tied to a tree for the night.

While the horses grazed Johnny asked Clay, "Think you could climb this here tree an' look around? We want to know if there's any smokes close by."

Clay said he'd try. So Kelly boosted him high enough to catch hold a lower limb. Clay's injuries made the climb laborious. But eventually he was able to look out from a place high in the tree. All that Clay saw were deep canyons and steep mountain sides. There was no smoke, only clouds hugging the peaks. Not only were there no Indians, Clay decided, there was nothing here but wilderness.

He climbed down, disheartened. "I didn't see anything."

Kelly nodded. "Likely it was just a huntin' party passin' through. But we won't take no chances. We'll have a quick, hot fire with dry aspen, then put it out."

Mary cooked and the men unrolled the soogans. Kelly sat down heavily on his. The ordinarily ruddy-faced man was pale. Clay asked, "Are you all right?"

"No," Kelly forced a brief smile. "But I will be." Mary must have recognized Johnny's attack at its onset. Because as soon as he sat down she gave him a cup of hot coffee laced with whiskey.

The drink apparently helped, and Kelly was soon himself again. He explained, "I got hurt in the War, an' ever since, when I get too tired, like today, I take these spells. Mary's been about as good as any sawbones the Army had." Kelly looked at the Indian woman humped beside her cooking fire. There was deep emotion in that look. Clay saw it, but he did not understand and it made him uncomfortable.

Clay turned in with his Winchester beside him. But despite a mental vow to awaken periodically throughout the night, he slept soundly. He awakened at dawn to find the Kellys already up. Clay hurried out of his blankets and began helping Johnny with the horses. The adventure he had envisioned in this trip over the mountains was forgotten. This was work.

Half the horses were saddled before Mary waved the men in to eat. This morning she had a little treat of bacon to go with the antelope. Mary often added some specialty to meals that would otherwise have been drearily repetitious. Sometimes it was an herb, at other times she cooked yampa roots or scoured a spring for a few sprigs of watercress.

While they ate, Clay said, "This trail's so rough, a lot of the horses have bunged up their legs."

Kelly replied, "It don't really hurt 'em much. They'll all be healed a week after we get home."

HOME! Clay wondered how anyone could call such a lonely place "home."

Their packing finished, the party set out with Kelly again in the lead. There were more miles through downed timber and rocky terrain. At one point the trail pitched down through thick stands of aspen before it broke out on an open promontory. Kelly waved for Clay to come up beside him.

A great valley lay stretched before them. Its colors were a blend of cool greens, soft tans, and buffs amid exuberantly golden cottonwood and aspen trees. Here and there Clay saw brilliant yellow patches of frosted willows. It all shimmered in the warm haze of a fall afternoon. To the north a series of jagged mountain peaks gleamed whitish gray in the sunshine. They were such mountains that Clay could shut his eyes and doubt their reality. At the foot of this towering Teton range a large river sparkled its way down a long boulevard of fall-struck cottonwoods.

Marking the valley on the east was another range of mountains. Blue-green in the distance, these mountains were less jagged than the great Tetons. There was a sense of repose in these eastern mountains and their open meadows that the Tetons lacked.

At the sight of this incomparably beautiful valley Clay's spirits soared. Living here might not be as punishing as he had feared.

Johnny Kelly noticed the young man's shining face. It pleased him and he looked off again at the wild panorama that lay below them.

"Pretty, ain't it?" he said.

Chapter Five

The Snake River that Clay saw at the base of the Tetons rises near Heart Lake in Yellowstone Park. In the fall and winter of 1876 Lieutenant Doane and a party of soldiers made a disastrous attempt to survey the river beginning at Heart Lake. The attempt nearly cost their lives. Their boat was smashed and those horses and mules that did not die from exhaustion and starvation were shot and eaten by the starving men.

Johnny Kelly learned of this misguided adventure from an old trapper named Pierce who was in the valley at that time. Pierce had saved the soldiers from starving by giving them elk meat.

After the Snake River leaves the Yellowstone country it thunders down a rocky gorge to suddenly adopt the placid character of the meadows it flows through north of Jackson Lake. Below the lake the river generally follows the contour of the harshly beautiful Teton Mountains. In the river's bottoms trappers found some of the best beaver hunting in the Rocky Mountains. And many of them also found that crossing the Tetons and reaching Jackson's Hole was not the end of their perilous journey. It still remained for them to ford the Snake.

It was chilly when Johnny Kelly led the way down to the stream. The ford was on a gravelly beach where the clear water soughed along like a lover's whisper.

"This ol' river moves around a lot," said Kelly. "I think we can push 'em across here without swimmin'. But we won't know for sure till we get out there. So, Clay, you go downstream from the stock an' keep 'em movin' as straight across as you can. Some of 'em will try an' angle downstream if we let 'em. There's holes an' fast water down there. Can't let 'em get in that."

The horses' lead ropes were untied and fastened on top of their packs. Then, with Clay on his horse and waiting downstream, Johnny and Mary began urging the pack string into the river. Some of the animals had crossed before and moved right out. The water made silvery plumes as it broke and flared around their legs. Johnny had his lariat uncoiled and was popping its end on the rumps of the less-willing animals.

The lead horse reached midstream and suddenly settled in the water. Johnny yelled, "Turn 'em up! The bottom's shifted!" His horse threw up a shower of water as Johnny charged him downstream. Clay moved farther out, then paused, not sure what to do. The swimming pack horse had already regained its feet and was striding out of the water and onto the far shore. The other animals were either following it or moving upstream, away from Kelly's whistling rope.

Clay ventured out a bit farther. The water deepened and threatened to spill into his boots before he cocked his legs up high on the saddle skirts. His horse made a gentle bobbing motion beneath him and Clay realized he was swimming. Clay gave him his head and the horse made for the opposite bank.

"What's all the fuss?" Clay wondered. Swimming a horse was fun.

Johnny interrupted this reverie by bellowing at him. Clay looked up in time to see one of the swimming pack animals flounder momentarily against the rump of the horse ahead. Finding his way blocked, the horse panicked and veered off downstream.

"Whoa! Turn him, Clay!"

Without thinking, Clay turned his own horse, jerking on the reins to keep below the pack horse which was now trying to turn around in the current and regain the bank he had left. Clay yelled and forced his horse farther downstream until the animal was caught and swept along by the powerful current.

The horse struggled and Clay, reining desperately, pulled his mount's nose under water. When the horse got his head up again water streamed from his nostrils. His buoyancy was gone, replaced by leaden fear. It infected Clay when he looked downstream and saw the channel narrowing in a rough blur of white water.

Something bumped him. It was the pack horse, white-eyed and fighting the current. The horses separated, then collided again, hard. Clay was plunged into the cold water. He gripped the reins only to have them ripped from his fingers. Clay couldn't swim and his water-logged clothing was pulling him under. He made a desperate lunge for his horse and his outstretched hand struck a floating stirrup. Clay clutched it and hung on. His horse struck him a numbing blow on the thigh with a churning hoof.

Clay gasped for air and his mouth filled with water. The cold water and fear were exhausting. Clay felt his grip on the stirrup weakening. Then something bumped his knee. For an instant he didn't realize he had been pulled out of deep water and was bumping along the river bottom.

"Whoa! Whoa!" The stirrup was torn from his fingers. Clay fell and his horse splashed out of the river and onto the shore. Clay waded after him, slipping and falling as he went on the slippery rocks. Ahead his horse was standing with its head down, nibbling grass as if nothing had happened.

Kelly galloped up. "I thought you was done. You got strong medicine." Kelly caught the reins of Clay's horse and tied them to some willows. "Did ya see where our pack horse landed?"

"Hell no." Clay sank to the river bank.

"I better see if I can find him. You rest a little. But don't lay there too long. You're soakin'. Reset your saddle and drain what water ya can outa your gun." Kelly rode away.

Clay lay still. But he soon began shaking. "I'm taking a chill!" With a furious effort he stood and walked to his horse. He pulled his rifle from its wet case and water ran from the barrel. Clay shook the Winchester, trying to remove the water from the open breech. Setting the rifle aside he reset his sodden saddle.

As he finished Kelly rode up leading the pack horse, "Hi! Sorry to tell ya. This critter had all your stuff on him."

"Is it lost?" Clay could have shot Johnny and the pack horse.

"No. The pack stayed on. Nothin' got lost, but it sure got wet. Well, we better go."

Kelly gave Clay a piece of cord to make a sling for his rifle.

He hung the weapon across his back and pulled himself wearily aboard his horse.

This time the river was forded without incident. Once across the two men dismounted again. "Take off your clothes, Clay. I'll help ya wring 'em out. It's gonna get colder all the time now."

Kelly smiled but Clay could not smile back. Kelly's eyes narrowed. "Ya know, kid, my old dad used to say, 'We all get kicked in the arse in this life. It's how a man takes it an' gits up that matters.'"

Clay pointed to the large bruise forming on his thigh where the horse had kicked him. "What did your old dad say about gettin' kicked in the leg?"

Kelly just laughed and climbed on his horse. The men rode silently for several miles before catching up to Mary and the pack horses. As soon as Johnny drew even with her she began laughing and jabbering in Shoshone.

It was gibberish to Clay, so he began studying the land. Away from the river and its moist bottoms, the grayish soil turned hard and rocky. It supported mostly sage and a scattering of short, buff-colored grasses. "Is this good land?" Clay asked, his voice doubtful.

"It's good for grazin'. An' what ain't too rocky, can be plowed for crops. Got to get water to it, though," said Kelly.

The sun cast longer and longer shadows until its rays faded beyond the Tetons. The sharp peaks were touched with delicate pinks that darkened into deep purples in the great canyons. In the gathering twilight Clay saw the telltale white flashes from the rump patches of startled antelope. Sage grouse flushed noisily at their feet. Many of the large birds did not flush but paced away, their heads held high. Mary shot several of the grouse with a bow and arrows taken from one of the packs.

Kelly saw Clay watching her. "It saves lead, an' it's just as well not to do a lot of shootin' till we get home and see who's in the valley. We been gone two months."

As they rode Clay saw the bleached bones and skulls of many wild animals. He recognized antelope, deer, and bison.

They also found a skull bearing a huge pair of antlers. "That's an elk, isn't it?"

"Yep, big ol' bull." Kelly dismounted. "Look, he's still got his tusks." Kelly reached for the hatchet hanging from his saddle. With two well-aimed chops and a tap each, he removed the rounded tusks from the upper jaw.

"Here," he said, handing the blunt, smooth teeth up to Clay. "It's your first day's profit. Those tusks are worth a dollar apiece back in Eagle Rock." Kelly said the Indian women decorated their clothing with them and jewelers made them into ornate watch fobs for members of the Elks' Lodge.

After leaving the river the party crossed some small spring runs and two good-sized creeks. Kelly called the second creek the "Little Gros Ventre," pronouncing it, "Grow Vaunt."

As the day became evening coyotes began howling. First one animal wailed and then another and another until the whole valley rang with their wild cries.

"Sounds like all the banshees of Hell, don't it?" Kelly remarked.

Another howl rose up; a deep mournful cry. "That's a wolf!" said Clay. "I heard enough of them one winter in the Dakotas."

"There's too damn many of 'em. Hard on calves an' colts. We'll poison some this winter."

After crossing the Little Gros Ventre the trail turned easterly, following the bottom of a long swale that separated a low butte from the lower slopes of the eastern mountains. The weary pack horses began to step more quickly.

"They know home's at the end of this butte," said Kelly. "I'll have to head 'em up or they'll start to runnin'." He and Mary swung their horses out to flank the herded pack animals while Clay stayed in the train. He was so tired and sore that he could barely endure his saddle. And he "goddamned" Marvin Feltch for steering him into this forsaken valley.

As the party approached the eastern end of the butte the horses trotted ahead, whinnying and ignoring the Kellys' efforts to keep them bunched. Clay's slung rifle pounded up and down on his back. He stood in his stirrups to partially escape the battering he was receiving from his trotting horse.

Johnny called, "Hi! Jack! Dutch! It's Johnny comin' in."

There was no answer and it was so dark that Clay couldn't see that they were coming into anywhere. Only after his horse stopped did Clay begin to make out the dim outlines of a low cabin. Near it were a pole corral and two large haystacks.

Mary dismounted to lower the poles on the corral gate. Johnny herded the animals inside. "C'mon, Clay," he called, "let's get these horses caught an' tied 'fore they start to rollin'."

Kelly's voice was enthusiastic. Clay spat, then dismounted, tying his horse to a long hitching rail that stood before the cabin. He unslung his rifle and leaned it against the cabin.

Kelly was at work in the corral. "Mind you don't git kicked." Clay circled warily around the corral. Mary emerged from the cabin with a lighted lantern that she hung on the corral fence. The light was a great help and in a few minutes the horses had all been caught and tied.

"Mary'll cook us somethin' while we unpack," said Johnny. In a long hour the two men unpacked the horses and piled panniers and rope-bound packs in front of the cabin. "We'll turn some of the horses out," said Kelly, "but we better keep the strange ones in the corral tonight. They might decide to go home. There should be a pitchfork in that haystack yonder. Throw some hay in here for these hungry buggers."

Clay was accustomed to hard work and long hours, but this toil seemed never to end. He thought he would just as soon go "home" with some of the corraled horses. He was damp with perspiration when he had pitched the last forkful of hay over the corral poles to the hungry horses inside.

By fire and lantern light Clay made his way to the cabin. It was a sod-roofed structure with a central, open area flanked on either end by a small room. During severe weather animals were stabled in the open area between the two rooms. Clay extinguished the lantern to save precious kerosene, guiding himself now by a tallow dip burning in one of the rooms. Clay ducked to pass through the low doorway. He entered the Kellys' "living" room; the room where the now-departed Dutch and Jack had stayed.

Kelly, looking flushed and weary, was on the low, pole bunk in one corner and resting his back against the wall. The demijohn of whiskey was beside him. Mary was sitting on a bench beside the sheet-iron stove.

Glancing around, Clay saw that Mary had unpacked his wet things and hung them around the room to dry. Johnny said, "Get your gun. We'll dry and oil her."

Clay retrieved the Winchester. Kelly explained that he had learned in the Army to disassemble a firearm by placing each part in a row in the order in which it came from the weapon. The Winchester's numerous parts were laid out on a white pack cover at their feet. Kelly did most of the work while Clay watched and dried each part with an oily rag.

When all the parts were back together and the rifle functioned as well as ever, Kelly said, "Sometimes I get a few parts left over for spares." Clay stared at the older man before realizing he was fooling him. "Here, Clay, have a drink. It's been a long day."

Clay was so weary his head swam after one pull on the jug. And he was nearly drunk by the time Mary passed around plates heaped with bannock bread and fried grouse. Kelly poured molasses on his bread and ate grandly, a hunk of bread in one dirty paw and a large chunk of grouse in the other. He grinned at Clay, "Well, it's home at last! And I for one am damn glad to be here!"

Clay tried to return Kelly's smile, but his effort was less smile than grimace. He was glad for Mary's help in carrying his blankets to the other room.

He crawled onto the hard bed and blew out the dip Mary had left burning on a block beside his bed. His soggy blankets smelled and the last sounds he heard were those of mice scurrying in the black corners of the room. The next thing he knew Mary was banging around on her side of the cabin, building a fire and cooking breakfast.

Outside Clay found Kelly beside the corral. Johnny said, "Ya see over there where the spring comes out the hill? I got a spot leveled off there. I snaked in a lotta logs last winter, an' we'll start our new cabin today."

After breakfast Kelly began hewing timbers for foundation sills while Clay, walking beside a crude sledge, drove to a place on the side of the butte where Kelly said some flat stones could be found. By nightfall the foundation stones were in place and the hewn timbers were resting squarely on top of them.

In the next days Kelly proved himself a skilled builder. "I should be," he replied when Clay admired his skills. "I built more cabins than I wanna think about. I've built 'em outa sod, rock, and even made dugouts in gullies. After I got Mary she wanted to live in a tipi. But that was too smoky and dirty, 'specially in the winter. So I made her go back to cabins."

Kelly's newest cabin was to be approximately 15 feet wide by 24 feet long. The men worked from daylight until after dark wrestling logs up angled skids and into place on the steadily rising walls. Once the ridge pole was in place Clay toiled with a froe and mallet splitting shakes from straight-grain pine. As the shakes piled up Johnny used his adz and broadax to build a wooden floor. Some nails were used for the most critical parts of the building, but pegs and rawhide bindings were the most common fasteners.

As Clay nailed his shakes to the roof Kelly cut two openings in the log walls and installed the precious glass windows that had been packed in from Eagle Rock in wooden cases. The boards and nails from the cases were later used to make a kitchen table.

Also in the packs were two sacks of lime. This was mixed with the sand Clay dug from the banks of the creek that ran down the canyon south of them. Kelly mixed the mortar and built the chimney with the flat stones Clay brought in on the sledge. A new and larger stove was reassembled and put in place. In three weeks the Kellys moved into their new home, leaving Clay their room in the old cabin. Even Mary acted pleased with her new home.

As the last of the furnishings were set in place in the new cabin Johnny drew up chairs and bid Mary and Clay be seated. From its place on a shelf he lifted the whiskey demijohn. "Here's to the new house! And here's to the gang that built her!" Kelly took a big drink from the jug and poured a generous slug into the cups held by Clay and Mary. When they had drunk, Kelly danced a clumsy but joyous jig. Then he pranced clumsily around the floor, half-carrying a giggling Mary while Clay clapped and sang. A feast of elk and roast goose followed, and when Clay went to his own cabin that night he was cheerfully tight.

He was happier than he'd been in weeks, and he fell asleep knowing that he could get up the next day when he felt like it. But habit awakened him as early as ever. He rolled over on his back and blinked, his eyes focusing on the ceiling's dim outlines. A sharp click snapped him wide awake.

"Just slide them hands out easy and put 'em on top your head."

Sitting on the bench at the foot of his bunk and aiming his own rifle at him was a filthy-looking man in a dark-blue capote. But it wasn't the man's tattered and dirty clothing or his unkempt beard and long hair that frightened Clay. It was his pale blue eyes with their snake-black pupils. In them gleamed a look from the edge of Hell.

Clay's voice was barely a whisper. "What do you want?"

The man smiled, showing a little yellow teeth. "Maybe to cut your throat."

Clay let his hands slip a fraction from the top of his head. "My God, I don't even know you." His hands slipped a fraction farther. "Why do you want to do that?"

"It pleasures me to do what I like."

Now Clay's hands were under his head, his fingers moving ever so slowly, feeling for the handle of the hunting knife he kept at the head of his bunk. His fingers curled around it.

The man stood. He wasn't tall, but he was wiry and probably mountain tough. He kept Clay's Winchester pointed at him. The man began reaching for Clay's blankets. Clay tensed.

"Hello, Jack! You there?" It was Johnny. "Where ya at?" The man turned in the direction of the call. Johnny was clumping up to the door. It opened. "Hi, Jack," Johnny smiled, ignoring the rifle and reaching out to shake hands with the man.

As Jack turned, Clay sprang, the bunk groaning under the power of his leap. Jack tried to swing the rifle, but Clay was on top of him, his left arm stripping the rifle from Jack's hands while his right drove the butt of the knife at the base of Jack's ear. The blow made a meaty sound and Jack crashed to the floor with Clay riding him down. Clay ripped back the capote's hood and set the point of his knife under the man's bearded chin. Jack was oblivious.

"Clay! Don't kill him!" Johnny Kelly stood in the doorway, pale and with his hands hanging limp.

"He was gonna cut my throat." Clay's voice was shrill.

"No! Jack's a little crazy. I don't know what's got into him. Let him be!"

Clay, wearing only long underwear, was sitting on the unconscious man's chest. His knees were spread, pinning Jack's outstretched arms to the dirt floor. He bent low, holding the knife at Jack's throat.

Jack's eyelids fluttered, then opened. They opened much wider when he saw his predicament. The murderous look in his eyes was gone, replaced by fear. His mouth worked, trying to smile.

"Feel that?" Clay set the knife point more firmly against Jack's throat.

"I feel it," Jack croaked. "Gimme a chance. I was only hoorawin' you. We do that to all the dudes, don't we, Johnny?" The man's eyes begged Johnny for confirmation.

Johnny Kelly did not answer.

"Don't ever try to hoo-raw me." Clay felt for the rifle on the floor behind him. Grasping it, he stood up. He held the rifle on Jack, stepped back and simultaneously lowered the lever. A cartridge sprang from the gun and thumped on the floor.

Johnny looked at it. "Jack, you better go up to the new house. We got your stuff there." Kelly reached down, took Jack's outstretched hand, and jerked him to his feet. After he had left, Johnny said to Clay, "He really hates you now."

"Maybe I should have cut his throat."

"No! You get dressed. Come up for breakfast an' I'll try to make it up between you two."

But it was a tense meal. Mary, sensing trouble, stayed beside her stove. Johnny did most of the talking. "Where ya got my cows, Jack?"

Jack, who had been introduced to Clay as, "Jack Gorman," replied, "We decided to take 'em back up the canyon—you know where. There was some fellers in here 'bout a month ago."

"From the Stockman's 'sociation?" asked Johnny.

"We figgered they must be. They burned Dutch's old cabin on Spread Creek. And then hung around for three days, just snoopin'. We kept clear of 'em."

Kelly said, "All you could do. Glad they didn't burn me out. We'll start up in the mornin' to get the stock. It'll storm any day, an' the quicker I can get 'em in here and settled, the better."

After he had eaten, Jack left the table, never thanking Mary or looking at Clay. With Johnny's help he packed his supplies on three horses and rode away.

Watching him go, Kelly said, "If I was you, Clay, I wouldn't ride on ridgetops or too far from cover for a while. Jack's mean, too mean for you to fool with again."

"It was Jack that tried to fool with me, remember?"

Kelly threw up his big hands, "Just be careful. I don't mean set in by the stove holdin' your gun. We got to get out and make our winter's meat, an' you want to start trappin'. But this ain't a town or even a farm. There's things you ain't never even thought of waitin' out in them hills for you to make a mistake. If you'd barred your door Jack wouldn't have got in there in the first place."

Jack suggested that while he and Mary went after the cattle Clay could do some hunting. "Stay near the place. You heard what they done to Dutch's cabin. The Injuns is prob'ly huntin' in the valley. Don't get caught out all alone somewheres an' let 'em gang up on ya."

Accordingly Clay decided to hunt in the pine-and-aspen-clad foothills near the cabin. Johnny said it was as good a place as any. As soon as Clay had ridden a mile he began seeing elk tracks in the snow.

He had shot several deer and antelope that fall but he was excited about killing his first elk. And he did not have long to hunt for in an hour's ride he came upon a big cow and two yearling elk standing in some aspen. Johnny had told him not to shoot bulls or skinny-looking cows. But these looked perfect. He tied his horse and walked a few quick steps to where he had an open shot. The cow had her head down, feeding. His first shot dropped her. The two yearlings jumped but did not run. Two more shots killed both of them.

One thing he hadn't considered in his excitement was how long it would take him to butcher three large elk. The cow weighed five hundred pounds and the two yearlings about three hundred each. Clay ended up wrestling with his kills until dark. He was able to load the hind-quarters of one of the heifers on his saddle horse but the rest of the meat had to be left. It was all neatly quartered, however, and all that remained for him to do was return early the next morning with horses and pack in the rest.

The Kellys had not returned, so Clay hung the elk meat, cared for his horse, and cooked supper alone. In the morning he returned to the kill site with two pack horses. It was a cold, clear day and Clay felt pleased with himself. The previous morning he had met his man and beaten him, and that afternoon he had killed three fine elk with three shots. Clay's pleasure lasted until he came within a hundred yards of the kill site. It was then that the first raven flew up to sit and call raucously from a bare aspen branch.

Most of the meat was ruined. The loins were nearly gone, the hams devoured to the bone by coyotes that had been abetted by ravens, magpies, camp robbers, and two eagles. What had not been ravaged was foul with bird droppings. Johnny's warning about Clay's not knowing what to be careful of rang in his burning ears. He was able to salvage a little of the meat, but the bulk of it was abandoned.

Clay returned to the ranch. As he was tying his horse he glanced out across the broad meadow. From out of the screen of cottonwoods along the Little Gros Ventre he saw cattle emerging. Johnny and Mary were driving them. There were sixteen rangy cows and eight calves. There were browns and duns and speckled reddish cattle with white flanks. The only characteristics they appeared to share were wild eyes and sharp, upturned horns. Moving with the herd was a long-bodied bull with heavy front shoulders and cow hips.

Clay met Johnny halfway across the meadow. As they rode the older man said, with considerable pride, "They got longhorn in 'em. I'm tryin' to mix in some shorthorn for milk an' more weight but still have a critter that can stand up to this country an' all the varmints. With some luck we can start trailin' a few out to sell fall after next."

The cattle obviously knew the meadow and had no trouble finding grass under the thin covering of snow. "The longer they'll feed here, the better," said Johnny. "I did my best, but there ain't one speara hay to spare. We'll need it all, startin' any day now."

It was a remark Clay would not fully understand until he had seen a winter come and go in Jackson's Hole.

Chapter Six

In the first days of December 1884 one snowstorm followed another. The snow's depth increased from a fluffy few inches to almost two feet. The cattle bunched around the hay corrals and the team was needed to pack down lanes in the snow so the hay could be distributed. All but four of the horses were driven into the marshes west of the ranch and left to fend for themselves.

Before Clay had gone to Riggs, Marv Feltch had said, "The best way to learn ranchin' is to go broke at it a few times." As Clay faced the driving snows and sub-zero temperatures to feed the stock he could now add, "Or start your ranch in Jackson's Hole."

An out-of-phase heifer had chosen mid-November to have her calf. The men had been watching her, however, and when she refused to let her calf suck they drove the sledge out to the meadow. Johnny tied the calf's legs and put it on the sledge. The cow ran bawling after the sledge all the way to the old cabin. As soon as they arrived Johnny released the calf, which ran to its mother and received a kick in welcome.

Johnny said, "All right, sister," and tossed a rope over the cow's horns then snubbed it to a post. He heeled her, using a second rope. Then, with Clay's help, they stretched the cow out until she was on the verge of falling. Johnny held his rope tight while Clay tied a third rope around the cow's barrel, just in front of her udder.

"Try kickin' with that on ya." Johnny removed his rope from the cow's hind legs and Clay steered the wobbly calf to its mother's udder. In five minutes he had the calf sucking eagerly and her reluctant mother's efforts to kick were thwarted by the paralyzing rope around her barrel.

The calf, a lop-eared little heifer, was kept penned in the shelter area of the old cabin for three weeks. The calf could not drink all her mother's milk, so twice daily Clay milked two quarters while the calf nursed from the other side.

In those three weeks the calf became a pet. Even Mary, who didn't evince much interest in the cattle, came down to rub the heifer's smooth coat. But, as all pet calves will, this one also became a nuisance. When it was judged sturdy enough to withstand an occasional kick and the bitter weather, Johnny drove it and her mother back to the feeding lanes. After several stern rebuffs the cow and her calf stopped hanging around the cabins.

The snowy days were fairly mild and the cattle fared well. But in mid-December the storm tracks shifted, the skies cleared, and temperatures began to fall. Clay awoke one morning to find the inside of his cabin glazed with frost. His breath froze in the glacial air while he speedily built a fire, then tumbled back under the covers. It took the stove several minutes to warm the room enough for Clay to get up and dress.

Outside the air was still. Condensation rose like smoke from the marsh a mile below the cabin. The cattle and horses stood motionless. Puffs of steamy breath were the only signs of life from the white-frosted creatures. Blanketing the surrounding meadows and hillsides were thousands of elk. Some were pawing the snow, others stood quietly, humped against the cold. A few were lying down. Trotting among these, hopefully inquisitive, were dozens of gray-backed coyotes.

Clay had on his warmest clothes but still shivered on his way to the Kelly cabin. Inside it was comfortable. Johnny was dressed in his usual woolens but, Clay noticed, Mary had exchanged her skirts for a pair of woolen trousers.

"Cold sure brought down the elk," said Johnny.

"I never thought I'd see so many."

"I never did either, but Little Dick Pierce told me he seen more'n twenty-five thousand go through here in a bad winter. They just keep headin' south till they find open range. We ought to get us a few while it's easy an' they're still fat."

Mary fried elk steak for breakfast and made some pancakes with the last of the milk from the reluctant cow. After breakfast Johnny put on a mink-lined vest before throwing on his heavy sheepskin.

"Fancy vest," said Clay.

"Yep, caught these last year. I wanted to sell 'em, but Mary wouldn't. I think today I'll be damned glad she kept 'em."

The cold outside was unrelenting. Clay swung his arms to keep warm while they harnessed the team and hooked it to the sledge. "Go slow, Clay, when stuff's this cold it's easy to bust. Don't make the team puff any more'n ya have to."

"I know. I once had an ax fly to pieces on a morning like this."

The cattle crowded greedily around the hay sledge. As the team moved down the feeding lane, Clay noticed that the new calf wasn't beside her mother. He mentioned this to Johnny, who was driving.

"Hell! After all the work we went to with the bugger, I'd hate to lose her. After we unload our hay get your rifle an' we'll go take a look."

In the far end of the lane the men found some blood and red-flecked hairs. There were many coyote tracks plus some larger ones. "Looks like a wolf," said Johnny. They followed the wolf tracks until Johnny began wheezing. "I can't fight this snow and cold both. You look some more if you want. The calf's dead. It's too damn cold to breathe. I'm goin' back."

Clay decided to follow the track to where it entered a clump of aspen. As Clay paused there a large gray wolf sprang running from the snow. He shot and the animal fell, kicking violently. Two more wolves bolted up out of the snow. Clay dropped one, fired again and saw the third wolf lunge out of range on three legs. In the place where the wolves had been lying Clay found a short segment of spine and a scraped, bloody skull with the remnant of one lop ear hanging from it.

Clay started back to the ranch. He was concerned about Johnny but he realized if he hurried he risked frosting his lungs. At the cabin he called, "Hello!" There was no answer. He called again and tried the door. It was barred. He knocked and Mary opened it a crack. "Johnny heap sick, no, no." She shut the door in Clay's surprised face.

Shrugging, he went to his cabin, stoked the fire and brewed

tea. While he drank it Clay chewed elk jerky and thought, "Johnny's a tough old bird. Mary'll give him a drink or two and he'll be fine." Clay decided to visit his traps that afternoon and then come back to check on Johnny.

He had made sets for mink and ermine in the marsh. He was pleased to find three dark-brown minks and one ermine. All were frozen solid. He reset the traps and trudged back to the cabin. The snow was deep and he had borrowed Johnny's homemade snowshoes. He planned to make a pair for himself and, perhaps, a pair of skis.

Clay hung his catch from a rafter in his cabin and replenished the fire. The animals would have to thaw before he could skin them.

He went outside again to carry in the night's supply of wood. Clay worked until sundown when it became too cold even for him to stay outside. He knocked at the Kellys' door. Mary admitted him.

The first thing Clay noticed was that the room was steamy and almost unbearably hot. Mary had adapted to it by wearing only an apron of calico around her hips. Lying on the bed was Johnny Kelly's whited hulk. Placed around him were Indian charms; hawks' feet, feathers, and mysterious little medicine bundles. On Johnny's chest was a brilliant smear of vermillion. He stared at Clay, his eyes filmed. "I'm damn sick, pardner." Johnny's voice was thin and reedy. Clay could scarcely believe that this was the same man who had left his cabin full of life and vigor that morning.

Suspended over the bed and forming a low canopy was a pack tarpaulin Mary had rigged to direct and hold the steam she was generating by dashing cold water on hot stones. She carried the stones in buckets between the throbbing stove and Johnny's bed.

Clay placed his hand on the older man's brow. His fever was infernal. "Tea, Mary. It'll help him sweat." She brewed a pot and Johnny drank two cups, then lapsed into a sleep or unconsciousness; Clay was not sure which.

Hour after hour the steam swirled from the fiery stones. Inside the cabin the logs glistened with moisture. The windows were thickly rimed with frost. Clay stripped to his long underwear and trousers. Sweat streamed from his forehead and made dark crescents under his arms. He and Mary began working in relays. One tended the stove and rock buckets for a while and then the other took over.

During his break Clay looked at Mary squatting beside Johnny's bed. Her attention never wavered from the sick man. Once she stood to apply more vermillion to his chest and wave a medicine bag above him. The next time she stood it was to press a cool cloth to his forehead. As the night wore on Clay became unsure which of their ministrations were superstition and which were approved, medical remedies.

Sometime during the long night Mary handed Clay a bowl of rich broth. He had not realized how hungry he was. As he ate he watched Mary trying to spoon some of the broth between Johnny's lips. But he choked on it and broke into a fit of dry coughing.

As daylight came Clay got ready to go outside. He found the cattle and horses white with frost. It was too cold to harness and work the team, so Clay pitched hay off the stack, then went outside the hay corral to spread it around. Some of the cattle had bloody noses because small veins in them had frozen and then broken open.

Hundreds of elk stood close by watching him. Clay examined each of the hay corrals to be sure no elk were getting in. He added poles to several gaps that appeared large enough to admit a determined elk. There was scarcely enough hay for the cattle and working horses and none at all for wild animals. Clay tied old rags to the corral poles in hopes that the human scent on them plus their fluttering would frighten the elk away. They did not frighten them, and Clay later found elk gnawing at the poles themselves.

His chores finished, Clay gladly got out of the cold. The scene he found in the cabin was unchanged except that Mary was now sitting on a pannier instead of squatting beside Johnny's bed. The room was oppressive with heat and steam. Fire roared in the stove and the rocks hissed angrily when cold water was dashed over them.

Johnny's eyes were open and he gave Clay a weary smile as the young man bent over him. "I got two good docs." Johnny wheezed, then broke into racking coughs that choked off further speech. Clay felt the man's forehead. His fever was unchecked.

"If this would just break out in a sweat, I think he'd get better," Clay said.

Johnny was able to drink a half-cup of the tea Mary held to his lips. When he could drink no more Mary wrapped herself in a blanket and lay down beside the wheezing Johnny. Clay took up the vigil. Sometime in the night Mary roused herself and took Clay's place at the steam bucket.

Clay immediately fell asleep and did not awaken until after daylight. The room was stifling, and although Clay had moved as far as he could from the stove, he was still damp with perspiration. Mary was sitting beside Johnny, chanting some incomprehensible Indian song.

Clay went out to bring in some wood. In the clear, frigid air the Teton peaks looked close enough to touch. Every fissure stood revealed by the lens of clear air. But, far to the west, there were faint streaks in the sky. Clouds. He hoped they were a sign that by tomorrow the awful cold would abate.

Less pleasing to Clay was finding that all the horses had come up from the marsh to stand hopefully around the hay corrals. There was no hay for these horses. With a sigh, Clay herded all the cattle into the stock corral. Then he forked hay over the fence to the cattle inside.

As he slid the hay corral poles into place the horses crowded around him. Today even a cantankerous white gelding would let himself be caught. Clay suppressed an urge to feed the horses and, instead, drove them away from the corrals.

At the woodpile he split a huge pile of stove wood. It seemed warmer, but still he worked slowly protecting his lungs. The fuel supply in the Kellys' cabin was almost gone when he carried in the first armload and dumped it in the woodbox.

"How's Johnny?" he asked Mary. The big man was asleep and had been covered with a blanket. There was a bluish tinge around his eyes. Clay felt Johnny's forehead. If anything, the fever was worse.

Clay sat down on a bench and leaned back against the wall, thinking. Before he knew it, he was fast asleep. He started when something disturbed him. It was a wail that rose and fell with awful intensity. Mary was kneeling beside Johnny's bed, her head resting on its side. Johnny was terribly pale. And then Clay saw the blood dripping from both of Mary's hands.

"Oh, Jesus!" He sprang from his seat and in two strides was beside the bed. Mary had cut off the little finger of her left hand at the first joint. And from the top of her right forearm blood ran heavily from a series of lacerations. Johnny Kelly had died.

Mary would not leave his bedside. She knelt there keening for twenty-four hours, oblivious to Clay's pleas and violently resisting his efforts to lift her and lead her away from the corpse. She would not eat and she would not drink—not even a few sips of whiskey.

Clay finally gave up trying to console Mary and went out to feed the stock. Even amid the bawling of the cattle he could hear Mary's lamentations.

But when he returned to the cabin Clay was relieved to find that she had dressed in an elk-skin shift and had not further mutilated herself. But she had rubbed ashes both on her face and hair. The hair hung down to her shoulders, unkempt and ugly.

Johnny was laid out beautifully in tanned deerskin leggings and a new woolen shirt. In his clasped hands were a quirt and a medicine bundle cased in ermine skin. His beard was brushed and his face had been painted black, which, among some tribes, was a sign of great accomplishment.

For the first time since Johnny's death Mary began to communicate with Clay. Using what little English she knew and a multitude of signs she made Clay understand what she wanted done with Johnny. It was too late to do it all that day, but Clay made what preparations he could.

Early the next morning he hooked the team to the sledge and put Johnny on it, wrapped in a big elk skin. Mary tied on some medicine, owl wings, and strips of fur wrapped around dried weed stems. Before starting out Clay had placed some short poles and a few tools on the sledge.

It was a gray morning with low clouds and chilling winds that sent many of the wild birds and animals under cover. Mary was wearing a capote made from a red blanket and had on a heavy pair of winter moccasins. Crusted blood was still on her hands and wrists.

Mary led the way. She wanted Johnny up on the butte behind their cabin. Much of the snow had blown off the windward side of the ridge and Mary walked there, stopping to puff occasionally but seemingly oblivious to Clay and the team and sledge following her.

Growing just under the top of the butte was an old, windtwisted fir tree. And it was here in the sheltering bows of the ancient tree that Mary had Clay build a burial platform.

While Clay worked, Mary walked from the tree to where the wind whipped her loose hair and set aswirl the hem of her red wrapper. She faced the great Teton range and held out her arms, gesturing first east and then west. She stood there for an hour, chanting a monotonous death song while the horses rattled their trace chains and Clay shivered. Finally she swept the sky with one hand, perhaps to trace the sun's course and came back to where Clay waited.

"Ready?"

Mary nodded. He had never thought much about it before, but now Clay realized that this simple woman had loved Johnny Kelly with all her heart. Clay had never before thought of an Indian loving anyone.

At the ranch he unhitched the team and let the cattle into the corral where he had been feeding them. The wind that had come up with the wintery red sun was blowing harder and driving a few snowflakes before it.

Clay began splitting wood. He worked until sundown, accumulating a large supply of fuel for both cabins.

Mary wasn't in her cabin when he knocked. He went in and built a fire for her. Back in his own cabin he found the three minks and the ermine still hanging from the rafter, frozen. Clay lit a tallow dip, built a fire in his stove, and put on water for tea. He drank the tea and chewed elk jerky while sitting beside his stove. He wondered where Alma Warburton was tonight? Probably in a place a lot cozier than Clay's. What was it she had said about the "rich wretch"? He couldn't remember.

Eventually the minks and ermine thawed enough to be caseskinned. He slipped their pelts over the ends of some short aspen poles to dry. Outside the wind gusted under the cabin's low eaves, rattled the door, and sent icy drafts across the floor. Clay stepped out to look at Mary's cabin. A light was flickering through her window. He assumed she was all right. Wet snow-flakes clung to Clay's coat when he returned to his cabin and prepared for bed.

The weak storm that gusted through the valley left a trace of fresh snow but, more important to the inhabitants, it brought milder temperatures. The spring behind the Kelly cabin began flowing again. And the livestock perked up.

In those first days after Johnny's death Clay did little but feed the animals and cut wood for both cabins. Mary kept to herself, not offering to cook or even have much to do with Clay beyond giving him a grunt when he brought in the wood. At those times he noticed that her cabin was disordered and dirty.

Clay reacted to this by thoroughly cleaning his own cabin, then starting to work on a pair of snowshoes. "My Christmas present," he thought. He used the trunks from chokecherry bushes to make the frames, first steaming the wood over a pan of boiling water then carefully bending the wood into shape. He made long strips of rawhide by placing an elk skin on the floor and then cutting round and around it. When his webs were finished he eagerly strapped them on and went down to the marsh.

None of his traps had been sprung, so Clay moved them to new locations and reset them. On his way back one of Clay's new snowshoes broke. He regarded the accident philosoph-ically, glad that it had not happened far from home. And, after dinner, he began making a new pair, trying to correct the faults he'd found so quickly in his first pair. As he worked Clay tried to recall the days just past. It was disturbing how easily he lost track of them. Johnny must have died about the twentieth of December. If that was true, it was almost Christmas Day.

Clay said to himself, "Tomorrow night is going to be Christ-mas Eve."

In the morning Clay roped one of the gentler cows in order to milk her. At the spring he was pleased to find over a half-pint of watercress. It might be rank, but he craved something besides meat and bannock bread. On top of the butte he found, then killed, three blue grouse.

After dressing the birds Clay hung them in the shelter area of his cabin to drain. Next Clay got a bucket of water from the spring and put it on his stove to heat. When it was hot he gave himself a bath. He also put on a clean shirt and a new suit of underwear, rubbed his teeth with a frayed aspen stick and combed his hair. Because he did not have a mirror Clay was only approximately sure of his appearance. But he did know that he smelled differently.

After dressing he took the grouse to Mary's door. "Hello!" he called and knocked loudly.

Mary came and stared out dully at him. Then her expression brightened. She saw that Clay was spruced up and that he held three fine grouse. Curious, she let him in.

The interior of her cabin was smelly. The stove was smoking and clutter was everywhere. "Mary, you old magpie, it's Christmas Eve. I'm not going to rot here. We are going to clean up this cabin. And then we are going to clean up you. When that's done we're gonna eat these birds and have a drink of whiskey—providing there's any left."

Clay adjusted the stove's damper, stoked the fire, then took a homemade broom and began sweeping. When there was hot water on the stove he washed and dried all of the kitchen utensils. Mary sat watching him from her perch on the unmade bed. She moved grudgingly when Clay, refusing to be daunted, drew her away and pulled the blankets off the tick and hung them outside to air. He took the tick to the hay corral, fed its musty contents to the team, and refilled it with fresh, sweet-smelling hay.

Returning he was delighted to find Mary on her hands and knees, scrubbing the floor. She had skinned the grouse and put them in the Dutch oven to cook. Clay remade the bed, dusted the furniture, and carefully washed the windows.

He heated more water and said to Mary in words and signs that she must take a bath, "You stink, old girl." Mary began to undress and Clay returned to his cabin. When he came back he was carrying the pail of milk and a plate of watercress.

Mary had bathed and was wearing a clean, woolen dress. She

was braiding her hair when Clay came in. He put his presents on the table and went outside again. He returned this time with a small Christmas tree fastened in a stand. He placed the tree on the table and Mary's dour expression lightened. She understood at last what had fired Clay's enthusiasm.

Clay reached into his mackinaw pockets and brought out the wild rose hips he had picked on the butte. They made a soup from some and strung the others on needle and thread and used them to trim the tree. Clay found Johnny's block plane and with it made a bright pile of pine shavings. These were impaled on their tree's branch tips and hung down in bright spirals.

After watching Clay, Mary suddenly got up and went to a parfleche hanging on the wall. Rummaging in it she produced pendant elks' teeth, brass earrings, shells, and strings of multicolored beads. She hung some of these on the tree and draped the others around her neck or used them as hair ornaments and brooches.

Clay partially filled two cups with milk and then topped them off with big measures of whiskey from the demijohn. He stirred in some sugar and each of them took a drink. They smiled.

"Happy Jesus!" said Mary.

Chapter Seven

It had been fun cleaning up and trimming the little Christmas tree. But after dinner, when Clay and Mary had no more to do but sit across the table from one another, Clay began to feel let down.

Mary was twenty years older than he. Her dark face bore the deep lines carved there by a thousand days of wind and another thousand of burning suns. It was a good face. Mary wasn't mean like a lot of squaws her age. But neither was she kindly in the sense that a white woman might be kindly. Mary was an Indian raised in aboriginal villages where heirlooms were enemy scalps and a fine dinner was liver eaten hot and raw from the bodies of freshly killed animals.

As Clay sat looking at her he realized that there was little they could share in common. They understood perhaps twenty-five of each other's words and some signs. Clay could not, as he had with Alma Warburton, tell Mary his plans and ambitions. He got up from the table and put his dishes in the pan. Then he put on his coat and hat and went home to bed.

He did not fall asleep right away. Christmas was a troublesome day. None of the jolly things he had heard about in Christmas stories ever happened to him. "I guess Christmas is a rich man's holiday. All I got out of it was a bath."

In the morning after the cattle had been fed and a supply of wood split Clay drove the team and sledge across the snowy uplands to the timbered slopes southeast of the cabins. Wherever he could, he followed the elk trails beaten into the snow. The team found it much easier going there, and Clay was not too long in reaching the timber. By late afternoon he had loaded the sledge with short logs and was on his way home. When Clay arrived he saw something new. Two pairs of long skis and two ten-foot poles were propped in the snow and leaning against the eaves of Kelly's cabin. Clay slid from the loaded sledge, taking his Winchester with him. Since the episode with Jack he never traveled without it.

Clay unharnessed and fed the team. Then, carrying the rifle in the crook of his arm, he started to the cabin.

"Hello, the house!"

A man looked out the cabin door, "Hello, yourself." It was Jack.

Clay approached him slowly, carrying his rifle easily. "This is a surprise," he said.

"No it ain't. We been plannin' to come down for Christmas dinner. Course we didn't know Johnny had cashed in, an' you was the boss now."

"I'm not," Clay replied. He was facing Jack and saw the man's narrowed eyes burning with hatred. Clay said, "I'm staying here until I know what Mary wants to do with her place."

"An Injun can't own nothin' off'n the reserve."

"Maybe not," said Clay, "but Johnny could, an' she's his widow. I'm gonna help her."

"Bully for you," said Jack, turning and leading the way into the cabin.

Clay followed warily, straining his eyes to see in the relative darkness of the cabin. "Hullo!" A second man was lounging on the bed, smoking a pipe.

Jack said, "Dutch, this here's Clay. I tol' you about him. I don't recollect your last name."

"It's Baker."

"OK then, Clay Baker, this here's my partner, Dutch Johnson."

Without moving, Clay said, "Pleased to meet you, Mr. Johnson."

"*Mister!*" Dutch shrilled. "Hear that Jack? Just call me Dutch, Clay. The last feller called me 'Mister Johnson' was a judge sendin' me away."

Clay couldn't help smiling. He put his rifle on half-cock and stood it carefully beside the door. After he'd hung up his hat and coat he looked at Mary. She was sitting behind the stove, grinning and stirring something in a pot.

Jack Gorman was as dirty as Clay remembered him, although he had combed his hair and beard. A blue silk neckerchief was knotted at his throat. Otherwise his costume was the same as it had been when they first met.

Dutch Johnson had long, brown hair. It appeared to have been slightly curled. His short beard was freshly trimmed. He wore a light, buckskin jacket brightly embroidered with twining pink roses and yellow sunflowers. Around his neck was a purple scarf caught at the throat with a big, nickel-silver concho. He had on heavy woolen trousers, still wet at the bottoms from skiing.

Both he and Jack wore red sashes at their waists and small, red ribbons around their upper right arms. Jack saw Clay looking at the ribbons. "You don't know about the union, I guess?"

"What union?"

"All the boys in the valley, they's only a couple of others now with Johnny croaked, met up and made a union. The idea bein' to look out fer each other. You know the stock 'sociation sends men in here an' they does as they pleases. Burns cabins, takes away stock, an', I've heard tell, does a little shootin' or hangin' if they don't like your looks. So we valley boys has promised to sorta stick together."

Dutch produced a quart bottle from the bedding beside him. "Damn the 'sociation. We got a couple more quartsa this brandy when this uns gone. How 'bout havin' a slug?"

Clay took the proffered bottle. It was excellent brandy and he said, "That sure is smooth."

"We got that offn a dude outfit that was in huntin' last fall. They had cases an' cases of all kinds of stuff. The dudes mostly laid around camp and got drunk or went fishin'. Their guides shot some bull elk and sheep fer 'em an' a hell of a big grizzly bear. Then they went home."

Clay got himself a cup of tea from the stove. A Dutch oven was beside the pot and emitted an excellent aroma.

"We brought some yamp root we been savin'," said Dutch, "an' there's part of a buffler hump in the Dutch oven. Jack got a fat cow a couple weeks ago."

"Sure smells good," said Clay. "Where'd you get the fish?"

He was looking at a large pan on the floor that held several handsome trout.

"We got them salmon-trout out'n a spring hole in the crick. Ever' winter some big fish moves in there an' we shoot 'em. They're real sweet this time of year," said Jack.

The conversation turned to the long cold spell that had killed Johnny Kelly. Jackson's Hole weather always is good for a discussion. As they talked, they passed the brandy bottle. Clay was afraid to drink too much with these companions, so he sipped tea, listened, and asked an occasional question.

Once he asked the men, "Where do you come from?"

The pair fell silent, both staring at him. Jack said, "One rule here is not to ask too damn many questions. We let a man tell what *he* wants to about hisself." Jack smiled. "You know how gossip gets around in a little place."

Mary took her full share of the brandy while she filleted the trout, then dropped the fish into her hot frying pan. She was also boiling the yampa roots preparatory to serving them with the rich juices off the buffalo hump.

Jack retrieved a tall bottle of wine from the snowbank outside, "All the way from Germany. We got this from them dudes, too." He produced a large clasp knife and lifted the corkscrew that lay along the handle. When he had popped out the cork Jack filled everyone's cup brimful of white wine.

"I thought wine was red," said Dutch. "Maybe it's gone bad." But a taste dispelled that fear.

"It's a little like beer, but it ain't quite as good," said Jack. "I thought there would be more snap to it." Clay had to agree. The pleasant table wine did not seem to him like a manly drink.

When the wine was gone another bottle of brandy appeared. As the cups were filled Clay saw that Mary was tipsy. She giggled, grinned, and spoke at length in Shoshone. None of the men understood her.

But they roared anyway. And Clay was glad to see her having a good time. The first really good time since Johnny's death. Dutch grinned, "Nothin' like a little drink to get a woman talkin'."

Clay said, "Mary took Johnny's death awful hard. I thought

she might kill herself, too. It was only yesterday that I got her to clean up."

No one replied, but Jack belched and Clay accepted that as his reply. He changed the subject. "I didn't know there were any buffalo left in the country."

Dutch, turning professorial, said, "Oh, yass. You look aroun' the warm springs right now, you'll find buffs. They ain't wiped out like some are claimin'. You know there's plains buffs an' mountain buffs. The mountain buffs is bigger. But they's too scattered and hard to find for the hide outfits. Injuns brings 'em in, though."

Despite the location and the strange guests, it was a good Christmas dinner. Mary beamed as the men took second, then third helpings. For dessert Dutch reached into his pocket and tossed a dozen wrapped pieces of candy onto the table. Mary squealed, grabbing at the candy with both hands. The men laughed as she began to hastily unwrap and pop the pieces into her mouth.

Dutch next got up and went over to the bed. With a loud, "Ahhh!" he flopped down on it. "I been asavin' this all fall." From inside his gaudy jacket he produced a cigar. He struck a match on the wall, lit the cigar and tossed the smoking match toward the stove. Jack also had a cigar. He licked it wetly from one end to the other then bit off the tip and spat it out on the floor.

"Sorry, kid," said Dutch, "we ain't got no cigars to go 'round. I won't smoke this 'un all the way down, though."

Clay realized that Dutch was trying to be generous so he said, "You go ahead. I never smoked much. Johnny had some plug tobacco here, an' I haven't even sniffed it."

"We can take carea that fer ya," said Jack. "Come 'ere, Mary, an' take a drag on this ceegar." Jack beckoned to the Indian woman who came and stood by his side while he held the cigar out to her. Mary took a big puff and exhaled, grinning. Jack laughed and roughly patted her.

Dutch interrupted him, calling, "Come on ol' girl, let's have a dance." He began clapping his hands in rhythm to the tap of his toe on the floor. Jack took a mouth harp from his shirt

pocket and, to Clay's surprise, began playing it most compe-
tently.

For her part Mary moved to the center of the room where
she began shuffling back and forth in approximate time to
Jack's music and Dutch's clapping.

"Do the ol' sage chicken!" Dutch called, jumping to his feet
and clumping to and fro beside and then around Mary. Next
Dutch seized her around the waist and began swinging her
around the floor. Mary was enjoying it. She laughed and Jack
played all the more gaily, stamping a foot in time to his music.
Clay stood by the stove feeling somehow debauched but enjoying it. He was nevertheless aware that as Jack played and
stamped his foot, his coyote-cold eyes seldom left him.

Dutch gave Mary a final twirl, then tried to throw her on the
bed. But Mary spun away and let him fall there by himself. As
Dutch lay laughing and panting for breath, Mary crossed the
room to Clay.

Seizing both of his hands, she forced him to lumber across
the room with her, half-hopping, half-waltzing. When they
were passing the door, Mary snatched Clay's cap from the wall
and slapped it on his head. In the same instant she was throwing his mackinaw around his shoulders and handing him his
Winchester. She spun him around once more then cocked her
head to one side and rested it on her hands, mimicking sleep.
Clay flushed, Mary was laughingly telling him to go home and
go to bed. He walked in a daze to his cabin, the sounds of
revelry roaring in his ears.

Despite his bruised feelings and his hatred of Jack, Clay was
too tired to lie awake brooding. It had grown quiet again and
there was nothing left to interrupt the stillness but a few
coyote howls and the coughing barks of some cow elk having
the last word.

Clay did not awaken until the first, weak shafts of sunlight
slanted into the valley. He dressed, fed the cattle, then went to
Mary's cabin and knocked, "It's me, Clay."

"Door's open."

Jack was sitting at the table, leaning on one elbow. His eyes
were bloodshot and one grimy hand encircled a steaming mug
of coffee. Mary was on her bench beside the stove, looking lit-

tle the worse for the festivities. Dutch, wearing his trousers but no shirt, exposed his red woolen underwear. He was holding a revolver.

"Mornin', kid," he said, lowering the gun.

Clay helped himself to a cup of coffee. "Looks like everybody survived the good time."

"What's that s'posed to mean?" Jack asked.

Clay ignored him and Dutch said, "We gotta leave in a little bit."

"Yeah," Jack agreed. "We're feedin' thirty-five heada horses, an' they'll be lookin' for us. We won't get back now till dark."

After a quiet but not unfriendly send-off from Mary, the two men put on coats and caps, then went out and fastened on their long skis. Each seized his pole and, using it alternately for support or propulsion, they slid away toward the east.

Clay was impressed by the ease with which Jack and Dutch poled across the snow on their skis. After the pair had gone he got two long poles and began to make a pair of skis of his own. After he had thinned the wood as much as he dared with adz and broadax, Clay took the rough slats to the shelter area of his cabin. Fastening the boards to a pair of saw horses he began planing the boards to their final dimensions.

During his spare time for the next couple of days Clay worked on his skis. But in spite of his pains one of the new skis cracked the first time he put his weight on it. With angry determination he made a replacement, then skied around the meadow learning to use his new contraptions.

Skiing gave him something else to think about but caring for the cattle. He was doing all the work and had developed a proprietary interest in the stock. Mary was willing to help him doctor sick calves, but she had no real interest in the herd. She never considered it necessary to milk a cow night and morning. And such things as planning the breeding, nursing orphaned calves, summer haying, and winter feeding were activities that never occurred to her.

Nor did it seem to enter her head that the cattle had value beyond the fact that she could eat one if she was hungry. No, the cattle were Clay's responsibility. But she was interested in his trapping ventures. He had trapped mink and beaver before, but it was Mary who had shown him how to prepare the baits and set his traps on tree limbs for pine marten. When the freeze-up had made the beaver and mink trapping impossible Clay turned to marten.

Jackson's Hole had been trapped since the early 1800s, but the interest had long ago waned and Clay had much of the area to himself. One morning he finished his chores early in order to have time to establish a new marten trapline on a high ridge southeast of the ranch. But when he reached the ridge top he was startled to find a fresh trail in the deep snow made by someone on snowshoes. Fearing that it might be Jack's trail and that Jack might now be hidden and drawing a bead on his chest, Clay turned and skied off the ridge as fast as he dared.

Later he told Mary about finding the tracks. They didn't alarm her. She said they were probably made by someone she called, "Pree." Nevertheless, Clay found other ridges on which to trap marten. He encountered no more mysterious snowshoe tracks and tended to forget the incident.

By late February he had become a competent skier. Clay could swish over the packed snow, while his balancing pole dipped occasionally to maintain his equilibrium and adjust speed. The motions became automatic and Clay learned to scan the forest ahead for signs of marten and his traps.

While doing this one day he came whizzing around a large fir to nearly collide with a strange man dressed in a long, wolf-skin parka. "Damn!"

When he had stopped himself Clay was looking down the big bore of a Winchester carbine. The man holding the rifle had a thin gray beard and yellow eyes that burned into Clay.

"Who be you?" breathed the stranger.

"I'm Clay Baker. I live on the Kelly place."

"Oooh? What does Johnny call his big bay horse?" The rifle muzzle never wavered.

"He calls him, 'Jinks.' But Johnny's dead. He died before Christmas."

"No! The hell he did?" said the man, lowering the carbine, then suddenly aiming it again. "Did you do it?"

"No," said Clay. But before he could elaborate, the man asked a strange question.

"Was it the speerits then? They was all riled up a while back. I was askeered they'd git me, too."

"No," said Clay who was growing increasingly apprehensive from looking into the rifle's muzzle and the wild, yellow eyes behind it. "It was his lungs, the cold settled there. We tried to sweat it out, but his fever wouldn't break."

"Did you use charms?"

"Mary used a lot of them. But there was nothing that we could do to help him."

"You needed a medicine man. I never knowed a woman that could call up the right spell. I wisht I'da knowed. I might of been able to help ol' Johnny."

"We did our best."

"Sooo," said the man, lowering his carbine and looking Clay over carefully. "You're new to this country. You know that Dirty Jack Gorman an' Dutch Johnson?"

"Yes. They came in for Christmas."

"Wonder they didn't kill a young chicken like you. Pair of thieves, too. Jack's the worst, but that Dutch will foller behind him like a coyote follerin' a badger."

"I had trouble with Jack before," said Clay, "but I put a knife under his chin, and he knew I wasn't foolin'."

The yellow-eyed old man yelped with glee. "Gawd a'mighty! What I'da give to see that. I jus' wisht that you'da rubbed him out when ya had the chanct. He'll be watchin' now. Ya might not git another shot at 'im."

"I'm happy now I didn't kill him. Johnny begged me not to and I wasn't raised that way. My folks were good Christians."

"A Christian!" the man exclaimed, raising his rifle again. "I oughta cut loose an' string your guts through these trees. It's you damn Christians that have ruint the country. Don't ya know what ya done to the Injuns? It was Christians give 'em the smallpox an' the French pox."

"Wait," said Clay. "I think what a man believes is his own business. When I was in Eagle Rock they tried to get me in the churches. But I only went when I felt like it. I got too much Bible thumpin' when I was a kid."

"Eagle Rock?" asked the man. "Is she still there?"

"It was last October."

"It can't last much longer. I seen all them forts come an' go. They move up the rivers ya know. Kill off the buffler an' the other game an' clean out the easy fur. Give the Injuns some sickness, then they go up the river agin. Eagle Rock will move. The game was all gone in there five winters back."

"Maybe, but they're puttin' in a lot of farms."

"Oooh, I know, I been there. But this ain't farmin' country. They'll fail after they've ruint it all."

"Do you know Marv Feltch in Eagle Rock?" asked Clay.

"Hell yes! That there Marv is the whitest man outdoors. Is he well? Has he got both his eyes yet?"

"He did in October," said Clay, sticking one end of his ski pole into the snow and leaning on it. The trapper lowered his rifle.

"Oooh, I am deelighted to hear that. Did Marv sell you your outfit?"

"Yes." Clay was beginning to enjoy the old man now that he seemed less eager to shoot him. "He helped me. He's been a real friend."

"What was your trouble?" The yellow eyes narrowed.

"I got hurt, and Marv and Johnny and their women helped me come here. Sometimes, though, I wonder if getting steered here was much of a favor."

"Oooh, that's wrong to say! This here is the last real country left. All the good medicine left is here. Whenever I go out the valley I kin hear the speerits cryin'. It ain't good fer me to go out, but sometimes a man got to go. Ain't you heerd the speerits acryin' yet?"

"Not yet," said Clay.

"Too much Christian in ya. You stay out awhile, you'll hear 'em. Didn't they tell ya not to trap my country?"

"No. But I saw your tracks east of here and moved out. You were here first, but isn't there room enough for all?"

Yellow eyes had a peculiar habit of "ooohing" before he spoke. "Oooh, there ain't no such a thing as room fer all. They used ta say that forty years back. An' the fur was gone then, the *real* fur. They was jus' lyin' ta get us out here an' bring 'em in whatever scraps was left."

"My name's Clay Baker. I won't crowd you."

"No, for if'n ya did, I'd plunk a ball just under your right ear."

"No need for that," Clay smiled.

"Oooh, I ain't decided 'bout ya yet. My name's Dick Pierce. 'Little Dick,' but some calls me 'Yellow Dick' since my liver's gone bad. I seen a feller some years back was yeller like me. Said it was his liver. Did ya ever see such a person?"

"Not for sure. I'm sorry you're ailin'. Why don't you come down and have supper?"

"Have ya got any m'lasses?"

"A gallon or more. We got sweet cream and butter, too."

"Ya got any whiskey?" Little Dick was squinting.

"Enough for both of us to have a drink."

"I beelieve that would be good for my ol' liver. I seen ya buildin' the new cabin."

"You did?" Clay was surprised.

"Oooh, you bet I did. I laid out onta ledge above ya when ya was gatherin' up them flat rocks. The speerits was in my ears, buzzin' an' cryin'. Then I heerd 'em say, 'Not shoot,' so I din't shoot ya."

"I'm glad you didn't, Dick. Maybe I should thank your speerits, too."

"Don't mock 'em. I think you think I'm a little touched. Well, maybe I am. I got a good right ta be. But I think maybe I'm glad I never shot ya." Dick slung his carbine over his shoulder. "Let's check your traps an' git on down ta that whiskey. Do ya think I might have two drinks of 'er?"

"I think you might," said Clay, sliding ahead on his skis.

Chapter Eight

Clay skied slowly, making sure Little Dick Pierce could keep up on his snowshoes. When they paused to rest Dick said, "Oooh, skis is faster, I give ya that. But if'n ya bust one way back in the hills, ya'll have ta stop and make a paira brush webs. If'n ya kin find the brush. I've broke many a web, but I kin fix 'em like that." Little Dick waved his furry mitten, apparently snapping his fingers inside.

"C'mon," said the trapper. "I can keep up an' I've pushed all day many a day on webs 'thout restin'—too much."

The men reached the ranch late in the afternoon. Mary greeted Dick with a grin and a pumping handshake that was accompanied by a torrent of Shoshone. She called him, "Pree." Dick replied with obvious fluency in her tongue, and the two were immediately off on an animated visit that Clay could not understand. After a few minutes of frustrated listening Clay gave up, poured the old man a drink of whiskey, and went out to milk the cow that had lost her calf.

He let the milk cool while he split and carried wood into the cabins. Inside, Dick was sitting at the table wearing a lop-sided smile that was at least partially induced by the liquor. "Fresh milk!" exclaimed the old man. "The valley is settlin' up when a man can bring a bucketa cow's milk inside. Never thought I'd live to see it. Never thought I'd want to."

Mary left the pot she had been stirring on the stove and sat down at the table with the men. Clay poured them all a drink from the demijohn. "Mary showed me how to trap marten," said Clay. "I'm getting some, but I don't think as many as I should."

Dick grinned, "You ain't, my boy. Oooh, no. I seen yer sets, never robbed you, mind, just looked. Sometimes ya set yer trap too far out on a limb. Sometimes ya sets her on the wrong limb or bait wrong. Oooh, there's more to catchin' marten than a lot thinks, yessiree."

Dick's arm stretched across the table and Clay happened to glance down at the cuff of Dick's woolen shirt. Clay was sure he saw a gray-backed louse scoot across it. Later, as they ate a rich elk stew, Dick began to scratch.

The trapper grinned, "Oooh, I got me a flocka body rabbits when I went out the valley las' summer. They git to racin' when they're warmed up. Not too bad when it's cold, though. I'll strip down an' put my old rags on a ant bed soon's the snow goes off. Them ants sure do like body rabbits."

Clay couldn't help cringing. Body lice were hard to get rid of, especially in the winter when bathing was difficult and infrequent. He hoped Dick would not stay the night.

After supper Dick invited Clay to come along with him when he ran some of his traplines. "Mebbe I kin teach ya somethin'. I been at this show goin' on fifty years I guess." Then, without warning, Dick stood up, "I'm goin' now. Thanks fer the vittles."

The old man put on his parka and retrieved his carbine from where he had left it outside the door. Clay was relieved. He liked the trapper, but Dick was just too lousy to keep overnight.

Later that evening when Mary and Clay were sitting over last cups of tea she said, "Pree," and ran her fingers lightly up and down Clay's arm. She stopped to pinch him and then giggling, scratched herself. Clay couldn't help laughing.

When Clay saw the old trapper again the men were high in the mountains east of the ranch. As they had planned, Clay was to see how Pierce trapped marten.

Dick said, "Ya got the right idee, but I know this marten show." Dick had Clay make several sets, then corrected what the older man considered mistakes in technique. "Them ol' tom martens is cunnin'. Ya gotta be as cunnin' as them if ya gonna ketch any."

Clay never heard spirits whispering in his ears as Little Dick said he did. But, following the old man's advice enabled him to increase his catches by a third. And, as the winter ground on,

Clay began to anticipate the price his pelts would bring. The rafters in the unused room in his cabin were beginning to fill with hanging furs. He believed they would more than pay the bill he had with Marv Feltch. He knew it was wishful thinking, but he hoped there would be enough money to get out of Jackson's Hole; at least for a few weeks.

Such dreams helped make the long winter pass. Clay's work filled the daylight hours, and he went to bed soon after supper and fell asleep immediately. Part of it was weariness but an even larger part was because of boredom.

Mary cooked and kept Clay's clothes mended. She made him a few new garments and moccasins from skins she prepared herself. The food she cooked was as interesting as the limits of her simple larder could make it. But Clay learned that when Mary's culinary imagination failed her, she resorted to molasses.

One evening Clay explained to Mary about the sugar cane that was sometimes sold at stores. He succeeded sufficiently to have her suggest that they plant sugar cane in Jackson's Hole.

"No, too cold. But, maybe, sugar maple trees would grow here. Then we'd have maple syrup." Clay described to Mary in words and signs how sugar maples were tapped.

"Tree pee?" she asked.

Later Mary gave Clay a pleasant surprise by making some spruce honey, derived by boiling spruce buds clipped from the tips of the tree branches. She also showed him how to collect the inner, cambium layer from the bark of the lodgepole pines. Clay didn't like it but had to admit it was edible. He much preferred the tea that Mary brewed from rose hips. Served steaming hot and sweetened with molasses it was an invigorating drink.

Still, there were many times during the long winter when Clay ached for more human companionship than Mary was either willing or capable of giving him. Unconsciously he wished she could be more interested in him, as Alma Warburton had been. Such feelings led to prolonged silences.

Later Clay would feel ashamed of himself and try to be kind to her. He taught Mary the English alphabet. She learned eagerly. And she loved it when, together, they sang the simple, children's song designed to teach them their A,B,Cs:

"ABCDEFG!
HIJKLMNOP!
QRSTUVW
XYZ!"

For a period Mary repeated the song so often that Clay regretted ever teaching it to her. "Mary!" he exclaimed one evening, "hush up! I'm gonna teach you 'Buffalo Gals.' I hope to hell I can remember it!"

Somehow gray, cold February ended and March came roaring in, bringing with it wet, heavy snow. Its weight on the roof of Clay's cabin became so great that he was compelled to shovel it off. The pitch of the new cabin's roof was steeper, however, and most of the snow slid off it. But in sliding, the snow built up drifts around the cabin that came within inches of touching the eaves. Travel around the ranch was via a series of communication trenches.

One morning Clay went to the corrals and found ten elk in the hay corral hungrily consuming the dwindling supply of hay. Clay dropped the gate poles and chased the elk out. The accumulating snow had become high enough around the corral to allow the elk to jump over the poles. Clay spent the day shoveling snow away from the corrals.

Most of the great elk herd had moved south. Those animals that remained in the valley scoured the marsh and stream banks for food or pecked for existence on the wind-swept ridges. Not all of them succeeded. On the buttes and in the meadows, elk were beginning to die from sickness and starvation. The wolves and coyotes traveled constantly and black smudges against the white snow marked magpies and ravens crowding greedily over a carcass.

The horses were Mary's only real concern. They mattered far more to her than the cattle did. When Clay told her the horses were wintering on the butte west of the creek she appeared satisfied. But she made him understand that if the stormy weather continued they would have to drive the horses off the butte to the river. In the river bottoms they could fell cottonwoods so that the horses could feed on the bark and twigs. It was not a task that Clay could look forward to; pushing the emaciated horses through the deep snow would surely kill some of them.

Snow was still falling when he fell into bed that night. He was too tired to go to sleep, and his many worries grew as the terrible weather gripped them ever more tightly. Clay got up several times to peer out at the gray-black sky. The last time he looked, he saw something. In the western sky there was a small, black hole. And in that hole a star twinkled.

By morning the skies had cleared and the sun shone brightly on the snow. It dazzled Clay when he fed the stock. He mentioned the brightness to Mary and she rummaged in a parfleche until she found a pair of goggles. They were Indian-made with loosely woven horsehair in place of glass lenses. These hair lenses made a screen that allowed the wearer to see while protecting his eyes from the blinding glare.

Wearing the horsehair goggles, Clay set off on his skis to examine his neglected trapline. On the timbered crest of the ridge Clay found his efforts heavily rewarded. He had set fifteen traps and all but one of them contained a marten. The single, unproductive trap had been sprung by an unfortunate jay. Never before had Clay made such a catch, and his elation grew as each carcass was added to the others in his bulging knapsack.

After resetting his traps and renewing the baits Clay decided to ski around the ridge tops looking for new places to trap and also for some sign of Little Dick Pierce. He realized the old man had weathered dozens of such storms, but he wasn't well, and Clay would feel better himself if he knew the old man was safe.

But there was no sign of Dick and after looking for a couple of hours Clay turned for home. It was midafternoon and the sooner he returned, the sooner he could do his chores and skin his catch. He could hardly believe it. In this one day he had earned over three hundred dollars!

But Clay didn't allow his elation to affect his downhill skiing. Only on the gentler slopes did he dare crouch down on his skis and make a swift run, using his pole as a combination rudder and brake. In this way he could cover in seconds distances that would require minutes to descend one ski-length at a time.

In addition to saving time, Clay found fast skiing fun, and certainly, he had not known much of that in his lifetime.

The last open slope was nearly a half mile above the valley floor. Clay had skied this slope before. It was a gentle grade that tailed smoothly into the meadows below. The only hazards were the deep draws that broke away on either side of the open slope. But there was little danger of getting so far out of control that he might fall into one of them. Even if he lost control, Clay knew he could always fall down to stop himself.

Standing at the top center of the slope he hitched his laden knapsack squarely on his back and crouched low over his skis. With a vigorous push of his pole he started down. His skis ran easily, and he rapidly picked up speed. Cold air rushed over his face, adding spice to the adventure of speed.

Before him loomed a small rise. Clay shot over the top of it, sailed a yard through the air and landed perfectly, gaining still more speed and laughing aloud. He braked himself with his long pole then steered for another small rise. He flashed over that, spraying snow and sailing even farther. But this time he landed off balance. Clay tried to correct by dragging his pole. That failed. Clay fell in a great puff of powdery snow. He wasn't hurt and he couldn't help laughing.

But it was a laugh that died in his throat, for as he fell, there was a sharp tug at his left foot. He looked down. His left ski had broken loose and was now streaking across the slope like an arrow. As Clay watched, the runaway ski tipped and plunged into the snow-clogged draw on his left. He gasped. The realization of what had happened struck like a massive stroke. And, for a moment, he was paralyzed.

Then, using his pole for support, Clay raised himself to a standing position. Could he ski on one slat? No. On his first try he fell again, sinking to his waist. The fun had vanished. There were nearly five miles between Clay and the cabin. The temperature was dropping.

Clay stood up again, balancing himself and pushing on his pole. His clothes were damp and the growing cold probed at him. He looked around; Little Dick had mentioned making snowshoes from brush. *"If'n ya kin find the brush,"* that's what the old man had said.

He saw now exactly what Dick had meant. This ridge was bare of any useful bushes. If there were any, they were buried under five feet of snow. There were, however, hundreds of snow-laden evergreen trees just below the ridge top on the slopes of the draws.

Clay's hatchet was in his knapsack. His Winchester was slung across his back. He remembered the rifle now and carefully brushed the snow from it, making sure the barrel and breech were clear. He removed his remaining ski and stamped a place for himself to stand in the snow. Across the frozen valley the jagged peaks of the Tetons rose up before him like the teeth in a gigantic trap.

Clay began wallowing through the deep snow to the edge of the ridge. He knew he must be careful; one misstep and he could go plunging after his lost ski. He could not fall!

The trees were alpine firs and their limbs were densely filled with needles. If anything would make snowshoes, these fir branches should. Clay edged farther down the slope, probing ahead with his pole. When he was near enough to one of the firs he began beating the branches with his pole. He wanted to knock off as much of the snow as possible before he began chopping off limbs.

Once the tree limbs he needed were relatively free of snow, Clay packed down a place to stand and to put his knapsack and rifle. The snow was up to his waist. Farther down the slope he knew it would be over his head.

Clay moved close to the tree and began cutting its lower limbs. As he cut each one he tossed it up beside his knapsack and in less than five minutes he had an ample supply. It was only a few steps back to where the limbs and his knapsack lay, but he took each step with careful deliberation.

Clay had almost made it back when a foothold in the snow collapsed. He swung down with his hatchet, trying to anchor himself to the hillside. But there was nothing to anchor to. All around him yards of snow were cascading down. Clay fell with it, his hands clawing wildly in a futile effort to stop himself. The slide rushed over him, nearly burying him in a torrent of deadly white.

His goggles filled with snow. It filled his ears and nose. The whiteout turned black as Clay was buried ever more deeply. He struck out with his hands, trying to keep the snow from covering his face with its suffocating pressure. Terror blotted out his last rational thought.

And then he struck something hard. A tree! He had hit a tree. Much of the snow shot around the tree's trunk and tumbled into the bottom of the canyon. The snow burying Clay wasn't too deep. He braced himself against the tree and dug frantically at the snow. When his head came clear it was like a sunrise bursting over him. Clay pushed his goggles up on his forehead. There was something in the snow in front of him. Miraculously, it was his hatchet. And beyond the hatchet he saw the slide that had carried him into the tree. As he fell Clay knew he was being carried hundreds of feet down the hill. But now he saw that he had fallen only twenty feet below his pack and supply of limbs.

Still, he was buried to his neck in snow. If he had not had one arm raised and free when he hit the tree, Clay might not have been able to dig himself out. As it was, it was tedious work and nearly an hour passed before he had freed himself.

Being saved by the tree and digging himself free had been a miracle. It was a second miracle to recover his hatchet. Now Clay needed a third miracle. He needed to cut himself a series of slip-proof toe holds back up the frozen hillside. Only a few hand and foot holds were necessary but not one could fail or he would plummet down again and this time most likely be buried alive in the deep snow at the bottom of the canyon.

Inch by inch Clay cut his way up the treacherous slope. Once his foot broke out of a step, but he caught himself by grabbing a bush. He was streaming sweat when he finally breasted himself up and onto the small, snowy platform he had tramped out earlier. He knelt there, nervously, knowing the platform could collapse under him at any moment. His damp clothing was beginning to freeze.

After donning his knapsack and slinging his rifle, Clay took a long, leather thong from his pocket and made a parcel of the fir boughs. He pulled them up after himself as he inched his way back to the ridge top. "Whew!" Clay grinned helplessly when he finally stood on level ground again.

His joy was brief. A wind was cutting across the ridge, carrying with it hard crystals of snow that stung his cheeks. Turning his back to it Clay tramped out a working area and knelt there to try making a snowshoe.

He first laid three of the heavier branches lengthwise and cut off their tips. To this framework he wove the other branches and tied them in place with thongs. It was slow, unfamiliar work that was made even slower by the coldness in Clay's fingers. He had to stop often and hold his hands under his arm pits to warm his fingers enough to continue working.

There were moments when Clay was almost prayerful. But he was angry, too; at himself and the valley. It was this anger that forged his determination. This damned place wasn't going to get him, it was never going to get him!

Clay tied the last of the limbs together and used his remaining thong to fasten the mat to his boot. It was fully dark when he began shuffling toward home, a ski on one foot and a heavy, unwieldy mat of fir boughs on the other. The snowshoe worked. It didn't work as well as one made on a hardwood frame with rawhide webbing, but it was working well enough to carry Clay home.

Getting down the ridge was the worst part but once he was on the valley floor Clay moved with more speed. He was so intent upon the functioning of his snowshoe that the crack of a rifle made him jump. He quickly realized that it was a signal, not an attack. Clay stopped, shrugged off his knapsack and unstrapped his rifle from it.

The lever action moved sluggishly as he put a cartridge into the firing chamber. He feared that the rifle's main spring was so stiff with cold that it would not fire. He pointed the rifle up and pulled the trigger. There was a muted "click." Clay repeatedly raised and lowered the rifle's hammer until it swung easily. Again he pulled the trigger and this time the rifle fired, jabbing a brilliant yellow-orange finger into the night sky.

A second shot thudded in reply. "Hi!" Clay shouted, "I'm here! Over here!" He started toward the shots, then paused. He thought he'd heard an answering shout. Yes! It came again, "Claay!"

It was Mary. Bless her old heart! She had come looking for

him. No need to, he'd have made it. But Clay could not suppress the joy he felt. He was discovering the simple yet rare privilege of having someone care about him.

Clay Baker would not know many other times in his life when he would be so happy to see another human being. And almost as welcome was the sight of his own snowshoes strapped to Mary's stout back. Even as they met she was taking them off and throwing them down on the snow for Clay to step into. Both of them were talking, neither paying much attention to what the other said, except that they both repeated again and again the word, "Cold!"

Wearing his own snowshoes, Clay shouldered his ski, tossed away the mat of fir boughs and set their course for the ranch. In an hour they reached Mary's cabin and Clay paused outside only long enough to throw off his snowshoes and jab their tails down into the snow. He burst into the warm cabin and began peeling off his clothing. Some of it was frozen hard and some was soggy with water and perspiration. His leather boots were so rigid that Mary had to kneel at his feet and literally pry them off. After she did that and Clay removed his sodden stockings, his bare feet steamed. Across his toes were raw sores where the half-frozen boot leather had cut into the flesh.

Clay had small, white spots of frostbite on the tips of some of his fingers and another, larger one on the end of his nose. Mary bathed these in warm water and smeared elk tallow on them.

Mary put wood in the stove; then, as Clay sat beside it in his long, woolen underwear, she filled a cup with hot tea. Clay sipped the tea while Mary went to his cabin and returned with a change of dry clothing.

Clay had dressed and was finishing his third cup of tea when Mary asked, "Milk cow?"

Clay made a wry face. Why on this of all nights would she have to remember the cow? The cow didn't give enough milk to strain her furry little bag if she wasn't milked until morning. But it was Clay's own rule that she be milked. He arose wearily, took the pail down from its peg and, throwing on an old parka, set out for the corral.

He returned to find Mary humming happily and skinning his

marten. Clay placed the milk by the door to cool and sat down to help her. "I sure earned these," he said. "They're like gold now." Mary said nothing. She continued to pull the rich fur from the long-bodied carcasses. Periodically she reached down and wiped the grease from her fingers onto a rag at her feet.

Clay said, "I wonder if the rich woman that hangs these around her neck knows how much they stink? You can bet her old man couldn't catch an' skin 'em for her."

Mary smiled. "Stink! All time stink!"

"Yeah, I don't know how you folks stand it and eat some of the stuff you do."

Mary did not reply. And they worked silently for several minutes before she said, "Injun people more hungry than white people."

The last marten was skinned and stretched and Clay stood up, weaving a little. He was light-headed and had to stand still for a moment before getting some hot water to wash his hands. "I'm even tireder than I thought."

Mary, to Clay's silent chagrin, did not wash but just wiped her hands on the greasy rag and began preparing supper. After she had beaten up a batch of bannock and placed it in a covered, cast-iron frying pan to bake, she took down the whiskey demijohn. She held the big jug beside her ear and swirled it, gauging the contents.

Mary grinned when she poured a generous drink into Clay's cup. "One more freeze."

"I'll remember." He added hot water to the liquor then noticed Mary was putting the jug away without taking a drink for herself. "Hey, you take one, too. You earned it."

But Mary shook her head, no. As Clay was finishing his toddy she placed before him a steaming plate of elk steak and bannock. Clay spread spruce honey over the bread and began to eat. It was delicious even if Mary hadn't washed her hands before she cooked it.

Chapter Nine

So absorbed was Clay with trapping and keeping the stock alive that he failed to notice the first cracks in winter's icy walls. Canada geese honked noisily across the snowy fields, then landed in the marsh. Female coyotes, growing heavy with pups, hunted rodents intensely. The spring behind Mary's cabin flowed again, forcing Clay to divert the water away from the buildings.

Avalanches in the canyons convinced Clay to gather in his marten sets and return to the valley's marshes and streams for mink and beaver.

One afternoon when it was unusually warm Clay got Mary to give him a haircut. He sat on a bench in front of the cabin while she grunted and "hmm'd" and whacked out what she thought was a white man's haircut. It wasn't a stylish job, and after she finished, several splotches of white scalp gleamed through Clay's brown hair, Still, he felt more comfortable without the mop. He trimmed his beard short to compliment his haircut.

Near the end of March a warm wind began to blow. It was not a Chinook, but it was warmer than the frozen land and it began scouring the snow away. It rained. More snow melted and the resulting water formed great pools on top of the remaining snow. As he was feeding the cattle one morning Clay looked out to see most of the horse herd straggling back to the pastures below the cabins. There were even a couple of colts in the band. They delighted Mary and amazed Clay at their ability to be born and survive in such a climate.

Those elk that had remained in the valley became more active and herded eagerly on the ridge tops where the snow had gone. But many were thin, woebegone creatures, bedeviled by ticks and some malady that occasionally infected some of their jaws and caused painful-looking swellings. Despite the solid evidence of spring, the elk began to die in greater numbers than they had during the worst of the winter. The scavenging birds and animals feasted and Clay often saw bald eagles so gorged with carrion that they could not fly but had to hop ludicrously along on the ground.

There was, however, a certain benefit to be had from the elks' plight. Mary took Clay around to a few of the many carcasses and showed him how to extract the flattened "tusks" from the animals' upper jaws. The bulls' tusks were by far the most desirable, being golden to rich brown in color and displaying annular rings on their crowns similar to the rings on a tree trunk.

Not only did members of the Elks' Lodge covet these tusks to adorn their watch fobs, but Indians also sought them as decorations for their clothing. An exceptionally fine pair of bull's tusks might bring from five to ten dollars while the more common specimens were worth from twenty-five cents to a dollar a pair. Clay and Mary rode from dawn to dark, combing the valley for elk carcasses. When they quit they had nearly five hundred pairs of tusks all carefully packed in soft leather bags.

It was during this quest for teeth that Clay happened to be riding along the banks of the Little Gros Ventre. The creek was clear and not too high. Its gravel bottom would have been easily discernable except for the numbers of large trout gathered there.

The next day Clay returned to the creek with Mary who had a large bag hanging from her saddle. The bag contained light-colored dirt collected, Mary said, in the big valley to the south. In addition to their saddle horses, the pair had brought with them two pack horses.

After she had helped Clay weave a weir of willows and place it across a narrow part of the stream, Mary went upstream a hundred yards and began sifting some of her dirt into the stream. For a few minutes nothing happened. Then, as Clay, standing barefooted and with basket in hand, waited, cutthroat trout came down the stream. The fish were writhing and rolling over and over. They lodged against the weir and Clay began scooping the fish out onto the bank with his basket. For a few minutes the trout came so fast that he feared their weight against the weir would carry it away. But Mary jumped into the creek beside him and her efforts helped turn the whole tide of fish out onto the bank. In a few minutes the shoals of stunned trout diminished enough so that Mary could get out of the water and begin gutting fish. When the trout stopped coming, Clay threw the weir out of the creek and helped Mary. They filled four large panniers with trout.

"That's the best fishing I ever did," said Clay. "What's in that dirt you put in the water?"

"Med'cine, heap med'cine. Make 'em heap fish."

At the cabin Clay built low drying racks. Mary split each trout down the back, sprinkled a bit of salt on each, then laid the meat on the rack. Clay built a smudgy fire under the racks and kept it smoldering for twenty-four hours.

For two days they feasted on fresh trout—fried and also cooked into a big stew. At the end of those two days, however, Clay announced he was "fish foundered" and had to have some red meat. The last of their elk meat was getting measly, but Clay said he could enjoy even that in preference to another meal of fish.

Mary's preferences were far less choosy. And when she suggested to Clay that he shoot a big bull elk, he expected the meat to be strong and tough. Nevertheless, he shot the elk, a thin bull that had recently shed its antlers. To his surprise the meat was excellent. Because, Mary explained, the meat was "new."

By early April most of the snow had gone from the ranch meadows. Every afternoon the snow on the hillsides glowed blue with melt water. The bare ground turned to gumbo mud and ponds formed in the swales attracting the ducks that were migrating north through the valley.

On the tenth of April a strong north wind began to blow. It had started early and by late afternoon the sky was ominously gray. The mountains were smothered in clouds and large snow flakes blew by occasionally. The livestock came in from the soggy meadows to stand around the corrals.

Mary was outside gathering all the elk jerky from the drying racks and Clay came to help her. "No," she said, "cut wood."

Clay did cut wood. And as he carried it to the cabins he saw a peculiar, white cloud approaching from the north. It appeared to be running low along the ground. He thought it might be fog. But as he knelt to fill his arms with wood the cloud overtook him. Before Clay could reach the cabin he was plastered with wet snow. And by the time he had put the wood on the stack outside Mary's door the cabin was engulfed in a blizzard.

Clay didn't even try to get back to his own cabin. Periodically he rose to peer out and gauge the severity of the storm. And each time he returned to his chair saying, "It's still comin'. I don't think it's let up a bit."

The wind beat furiously at the cabin, drawing from it ominous groans and bangings. Fine particles of snow filtered in through cracks to form melting drifts on the floor and window sills. Mary shrugged when he told her, "We're nearly out of hay. I should have penned up the stock; there's no tellin' how far they may drift in front of this storm."

Toward morning the wind began to subside. Clay heard it smash at the house with one final gust and then die. The ensuing quiet was almost eerie. When Clay tried to see outside he found the window panes caked with snow. Clay went to the door and opened it cautiously. Standing in the doorway was a waist-high drift of snow. Clay shoveled it away and continued shoveling until he reached the corrals.

In a few places the wind had swept the ground bare, while in others the snow had drifted to depths of six feet. The cattle had all taken shelter on one side of the corral where he fed them. All but three of the horses were bunched unhappily beside the hay corral. Clay shoveled out the mangers and fed the cattle a scant ration of hay. The horses stood by and watched with such soft-eyed longing that he felt compelled to fork out a tiny mite for them, too.

The mystery of the three missing horses was solved when Clay found them trapped behind Mary's cabin. The animals were completely encircled by great drifts. He dug them a path out and the horses nearly trampled him in their haste to reach the hay corral.

Clay shoveled wet snow until afternoon. When he quit, his

back felt as if he had been knifed above the hips and his fore-
arms were leaden. But after eating some elk stew, he was ready
to resume shoveling. As he was clearing the snow from his
cabin's roof he looked far out to the north and saw two tiny
figures. They were snowshoeing toward him.

He dreaded a visit from Dutch and Jack Gorman. But, he
thought, if it is Dutch and Jack, why aren't they on skis? He
kept shoveling with one eye on the snowshoers. Their pace was
relentless.

"Somebody's comin'," he told Mary as he entered her cabin.
Clay took his Winchester from its place in the corner and
levered a cartridge into the chamber. He lowered the hammer
to half-cock and stepped to the window to watch.

Mary was already there. "Maybe Jack, Dutch?"

Clay leaned the rifle against the wall within easy reach. "I
hope not."

The figures were now much closer and Clay saw that they
were both white men carrying big knapsacks on their backs.
The pair halted within hailing distance of the cabin. "Helloo!"

Clay opened the door but stood back from the doorway.
"Hello!"

"Comin' in. All right?"

Clay looked at Mary who was watching from the window,
"You know 'em?"

Mary shook her head, no.

"Come ahead," called Clay.

Both men wore heavy mackinaws, woolen caps, and mittens.
Clay made note of the Winchester carbines slung over their
shoulders.

The men were fifteen feet from the cabin when one asked,
"Are you John Kelly?"

"No. He died three months ago." Clay still did not fully ex-
pose himself in the doorway.

The men stepped to the path Clay had shoveled and removed their snowshoes. One said, "Sorry to hear that. We
know from Marv Feltch in Eagle Rock that Kelly had a place
here."

"Did Marv send you?"

"Not exactly. I'm J. J. Parker, deputy U.S. marshal from

Miles City, Montana. This here," said Parker, pointing to the tall man beside him, "is Abner Duckett. I depitized him. Mr. Duckett is also repping for the Ellett an' Summersby Ranch out of Miles."

Clay glanced at Mary, who shrugged. "Well, men," he said, "you better come in."

The pair stuck their snowshoes into the snow. "We'll leave these outside, too," Parker said unslinging his carbine and leaning it beside the door. Duckett stood his weapon beside the marshal's.

The men stamped into the cabin, swinging their heavy knapsacks down onto the floor, and pulling off their mackinaws and caps.

Mary stood by the window. "This is Mary Kelly," said Clay.

"How do?" said Parker, nodding slightly. Parker was about thirty-five with black hair and a thick, black mustache. He was big and appeared trim for a marshal.

Abner Duckett was tall and slim; a cowboy with graying, brown hair and a lantern jaw now covered with a stubbly beard. When he spoke to Mary it was in Shoshone.

Clay listened for a moment, then shrugged, saying to Parker, "Members of the same tribe, I guess."

Parker smiled then bent down and removed a brown quart bottle from his knapsack, "This is genuine Hudson's Bay Rum, 150 proof. Goes down real well with some hot water."

Clay got hot water from the stove and placed four cups on the table. The officers took seats and were joined by their hosts. It was good rum. Parker refilled their cups. But before tasting his second drink the marshal went to his knapsack and returned this time with a box of cigars and a large black folder. He passed the cigars around and put the folder on the table in front of him. The deputies each took a cigar; Clay abstained but could not help smiling when Mary took one.

Once the cigars were lit Parker said, "We've been losin' a lot of stock. Ellett and Summersby has lost over fifty head of horses this past year. That's why Ab here come along. We know a lot of this stock gets moved into your country. They change the brands then trail 'em southeast. Sometimes they sell 'em right onto the cars at the railroad sidings."

"We're not rustlers," said Clay.

Parker smiled and puffed on his cigar. "Never said you was." He opened the folder, revealing a number of circulars. The top one illustrated a series of livestock brands. "Ever see any of these brands?" asked Parker.

Abner Duckett watched intently as Clay studied the circular. All of the brands were from Montana ranches and he didn't recognize any of them. "No," said Clay, returning the paper, "I've never seen any of these."

Parker slid off another sheet, handed it to Clay and passed the first one to Mary. "Try these."

Mary glanced at her sheet then looked away, obviously uninterested. Clay examined the next sheet for a minute or two, then his face reddened.

Duckett said, "See somethin'?"

"That big, red cow of ours. She's got this brand on her." Clay put his finger on the brand.

"Double D Bar," said Parker. "Outfit up near Havre." Then, to Clay, "You got the bill of sale for that critter?"

"I don't know. Mary understands you, Mr. Duckett, ask her if Johnny had any papers."

Duckett did ask and Mary rummaged in a duffel bag until she found a manila folder tied with string. She gave the folder to Clay, who opened it and found some papers. Clay examined them for a few minutes. "Here's the receipt for that cow."

He passed a grubby sheet of notebook paper to the two men. Parker said, "It's for the cow he's talkin' about. You know Mick Nichols? He signed the bill of sale."

Duckett took the paper. "I only know him by reputation. Ain't he on the blacklist? I never heard of him ranchin'."

Parker consulted his folder. "Here's the Stockgrowers' list. Mick Nichols' name is on it."

Clay had learned of this list when he worked in the Warburton banks. It was often used to check on a new account. Anyone listed could not get a job on any Wyoming ranch run by a member of the Association. Some listed were blackballed because they were rustlers or rustling suspects. Other men were named because they had homesteaded land on some big outfit's range.

Duckett said, "Mick Nichols comes to my mind as a gambler an' saloon bum. I think he sold Kelly a stolen cow."

"You haven't any proof of that," said Clay. "The bill of sale shows Johnny paid twelve dollars for that cow."

Duckett replied, "That's why it's a good idea to know who you're dealin' with an' that he really owns the critters he's sellin'."

"But you can't claim our cow just because you think she might be stolen."

"We're not," said Parker. "Course I could impound her till we find out who really owns her."

"Johnny already bought her." Clay was angry.

"Maybe Mick Nichols gypped him," said Duckett. "Don't worry, if she's stolen I think the owners'll sell her to you cheap."

"Meantime," said Parker, "you keep her here, but don't butcher her or nothin'."

The deputies looked at the remaining bills of sale in Johnny's papers. They murmured occasionally and Clay was sure it was mostly a performance to unnerve him. If it was a performance, it succeeded.

Parker relit his cigar. "I guess in this country a man has to scratch for his livin'." He riffled his circulars and pulled out several descriptions of wanted men. "Ever seen any of these boys?" he asked, pushing the circulars across the table to Clay.

Leafing through the papers, Clay felt his interest soon turning to disgust. The picturesque western bad man was more realistically an ignorant Indian or some dull-witted white scum.

Clay took another circular and, suddenly, there it was, a photograph of Jack Gorman. Only the name given was John Garrity. He was wanted for larceny in several railroad towns along the UP line. He had been in the Colorado Penetentiary. Montana Territory now sought him for larceny involving livestock. The circular further warned that John Garrity was dangerous and had "Loathsome and Unnatural Habits."

Parker noticed Clay lingering over the Garrity circular. "Know that feller?"

"Maybe. He could have been in Eagle Rock or on the train

from Cheyenne. But this picture isn't too clear, and the man I'm thinkin' of had a beard."

Parker handed the circular to Mary. She glanced at it, then slid it back, shaking her head, no.

Clay hoped that he was concealing his emotions as well as Mary had. Because at the top of the circular was printed, "$300 Dead or Alive."

More circulars were passed to Clay. He read these slowly, trying to throw off the officers' suspicions about his interest in the Garrity circular.

Accordingly, when he came to a picture of Dutch Johnson he tried not to appear interested. "Dutch's" real name was Oscar Johnson. He was an Army deserter and had been in several jails. Dutch was currently sought in two territories for rustling and burglary. The reward for Oscar Johnson was only $100.

Marshal Parker had ignored Mary's disinterest in the circulars, but he watched her intently as he handed her the last sheet in his folder. Mary took it, then looked pleadingly at Clay, her eyes filled with tears. She handed him the circular.

It read, "WANTED—John Kelly." Below the name was a prison picture of Johnny; recognizable even without his beard. Johnny's head was shaven and he looked pale and puffy-eyed. The paper declared Johnny a convicted rustler who was now sought for questioning regarding the receiving of stolen livestock.

Numbed by what he had read, Clay pushed the circular back to Parker. "You can burn this. We put Johnny in an Injun grave last winter. I'll show it to you if you want."

"Oh, kid, your word's good enough for us. Now what do you say we forget all this business and have some of that elk stew. We'll look at your stock in the mornin' and be on our way." Parker puffed on his cigar.

Clay and Mary hardly touched their food, but the officers ate heartily. When they had finished Parker put the half-empty rum bottle on the shelf beside the whiskey demijohn. "Little present for ya," he said.

The two lawmen bunked in Clay's room while he rolled up in his soogans in the room at the other end of the cabin. He slept poorly and was out at daylight, feeding the cattle. It was while he was milking that Parker and Duckett came to see him.

"Mornin'."

"Mornin'," said Clay. "Don't get too close. This old cow's not used to strangers."

The men stepped back, smoking and looking at the cattle. "After breakfast we'd like to run your stuff in and look at the brands; horses, too."

"It'll be a job," said Clay. "They're wild and their hair's long and grown over the brands."

"We can handle it," said Duckett.

Following an almost silent breakfast the men returned to the corral and began examining all the livestock. Several cows and horses appeared to be of questionable ownership.

After the last horse was released and choused from the corral Parker said, "Kid, I think we better talk."

"What about?"

"You're what we call an 'accessory,'" said Parker.

"The hell I am! You haven't any proof that these critters are stolen. Our word is just as good as yours."

"No, it ain't, Clay. How'd you like to go back to Riggs or Eagle Rock an' tell those good folks what happened to their savin's?"

"You bastard! I lost every cent I had in those banks."

"Now be careful. You may be tellin' the truth, but those farmers don't know it. There's still some paper over there with your name on it," Parker was grinning.

Clay was angry and trying to sort out his thoughts. "I haven't done anything. I think this is all smoke. What do you really want?"

Parker stopped grinning. "OK. We really want Dirty Jack Garrity an' Dutch Johnson. We know they're in here, and we think you know where."

Duckett now spoke. "We're pretty sure you know where these two birds are, Clay. Don't make yourself more trouble than you can handle."

Clay stood silent for a long moment, then slapped his hands against his sides. "I know 'em. Jack's been here twice and Dutch once, at Christmas."

"Where are they?" Parker was intent.

"I don't know exactly. But I do know it's in a place where the U. S. Cavalry couldn't go if Jack and Dutch didn't want 'em to. Johnny told me that much."

"Listen, Clay," said Duckett, "I'm not a regular marshal. I'm a workin' cowman just like you. But I do know that the law can plague you forever if they've a mind to. This whole country is a nest for rustlers and men on the dodge. You don't want that kind here. The judges don't give a damn what we do just so's we clean out this country an' get the ranchers an' big shots off their necks."

"How long do you think I'd last if the men in here knew I was turnin' 'em in?" Clay asked.

Parker answered, "How long would you last in Riggs?"

Clay didn't answer.

Parker continued, "There's a reward of four hundred out for those two. They ain't nothin' but a determent to the country. Now smarten up an' help us. There's a hundred in it for you if we take 'em."

"How long would it take you to make that much money pullin' teeth outa rotten elk?" asked Duckett.

"I have to get in some wood," Clay said leaving the corral.

When he dumped the first arm load in Mary's woodbox she asked him, "Heap bad?"

"Yeah, 'heap bad.' Three cows and five horses may be stolen. Where did you get those horses?"

Mary understood. "Jacky, Dutch give horses." Mary held up six fingers. "One lost."

"Damn! I was afraid of that. Those deputies have the goods on us. You and me." Clay pointed at Mary and then at himself.

"Kill 'em," said Mary.

"No!" Clay almost shouted. "Do that and heap, heap bad trouble!" He raked his index finger across his throat.

Mary slumped in her chair and said nothing.

Clay left, slamming the door and muttering, "Kill 'em! Lordy! There's a brilliant mind for you. Kill 'em!"

The deputies were at the wood pile splitting wood. Parker sunk the ax into the chopping block. "What do you think now, kid?"

"That's a good woman up there. This place and the stock are all she's got."

"She'd be better off over on the Reservation where she belongs," said Duckett.

"Be reasonable. You know those reservation squaws would pick her clean and toss her out."

"I got tears as big as road apples runnin' down my cheeks," said Parker. "You wanta help that squaw, you come clean on Jack Garrity and the Dutchman."

"They've got a place up the Little Gros Ventre, in the canyon. Johnny told me it's a natural fort."

"Can you get in?" asked Duckett.

"I don't know. Jack might shoot me as quick as he'd shoot you."

"I guess we'll have to see," said Parker.

The men were up at three the next morning. While Clay fed the stock and milked, Mary cooked breakfast and filled a sack with elk jerky and dried trout. She was told that Clay was going to guide the officers north to the Yellowstone trail.

"Heap snow," Mary said.

"That's their lookout," Clay told her. "All I want to do is get rid of 'em."

The snow was scratchy hard when the men set out. Clay was using skis but had his snowshoes and rifle tied to his knapsack. The two officers almost had to run to keep up with him. From time to time Clay glanced back and was chagrined each time to see them loping along with apparent ease. They were tough, he gave them that.

The men paused inside the mouth of the canyon. "We'll give you a half hour," said Parker. "When you get with 'em don't stand too close to either feller."

Clay nodded and started up the canyon. Its rough walls closed in and often there was just room enough for one traveler at a time on the narrow trail. He looked at the towering cliffs. It was a perfect place for an ambush. Clay stopped and tied a red ribbon around his upper right arm.

In a mile the canyon began to widen. There were dense pines ahead and Clay saw smoke rising through their tops. He rounded a sharp turn in the trail and nearly bumped into a pole fence. It had been built across the trail and extended far enough up each canyon wall to effectively seal off the area ahead.

Clay removed his skis, clambered over the fence, then paused to replace his skis. "Hello!" he called. "It's me, Clay Baker from Kelly's." He moved ahead slowly and calling repeatedly.

Then Jack Gorman was standing beside him. "I hear you, kid. There's no need to holler so loud." Gorman had slipped from behind a tree like a hungry weasel and was pointing a rifle at Clay's head. "You get tired of tendin' that squaw?"

"I came up to do you a favor."

"You wouldn't like doin' my kind of favor," said Jack.

"The law was in here. They found some rustled stock in our herd. They're comin' back as soon as the Pass opens. We figured you should be warned."

"There's always rustled stock in Jackson's Hole. Your ol' pal Johnny done time for keepin' it. The law usually waits for the thaw before they come in. You sure you're alone? Those law boys didn't lay back an' foller ya?"

"No, they headed out east before the big storm."

"Who was they?" Jack was motioning for Clay to lead the way up the trail.

"One was J. J. Parker. He's a deputy U.S. marshal. The other fellow rides for the Ellett and Summersby Ranch in Montana. His name was Abner Duckett."

"I know of Duckett. He's no cowpuncher. He's a hired regulator."

Clay followed tracks in the snow and soon reached a small cabin almost hidden in the pines.

"Hey! Dutch!" Jack called, "looky what's here. Fresh meat from the farm!"

The cabin door opened and a rifle barrel appeared, "You alone, kid?" It was Dutch.

"I'm alone."

The rifle barrel was lowered and the door opened wider. "Go on in, kid," Jack motioned with his rifle barrel.

The low-roofed cabin was cramped and gloomy inside. There was a stench of rancid grease and filthy bodies. Food had been dropped or thrown on the dirt floor and then walked on.

Clay began to unsling his rifle, but it was grabbed by Jack. "Lemme help you." Jack took the rifle and flipped down the lever. "Not loaded," he said.

"What's this word you brung us?" asked Dutch.

Jack answered, "He claims the law was in here, two of 'em. They found some rustled stuff in Johnny's corral. Said they was comin' back."

Dutch began pacing. "God, Jack! We better get outa here as soon as we can!"

"That's just what we're gonna do. But we're not leavin' two thousan' dollars' wortha horses here for Clay boy to sell. We ain't even sure he's tellin' the truth."

"Why would I come up here to tell you a story?"

"The reward," said Jack. "Those deputies might of told you there was money up for us. But it ain't true."

Clay said, "I came up here with the red band on my arm. I know now that if we don't help each other, the law will do whatever it pleases in here."

"You sure you didn't tell those fellers where we was?" Jack asked.

"How could I? I didn't know myself till now. But to hell with you. Gimme my rifle, I'm leavin'." Clay stepped toward the door.

"Stop right there," Jack ordered. "Now you take off your coat an' trade me." Jack was slipping off his blanket capote and holding it out to Clay. "Put this on an' go out back an' carry us in some wood."

Clay was so tense he could scarcely talk. "I don't want to trade."

"How'd ya like to get shot in the belly?" Dutch leveled his rifle.

Slowly, Clay unbuttoned his heavy mackinaw. Jack grinned as he tossed Clay's coat on the bunk. "Remember, we both got our sights on you."

For a moment Clay did not think his legs would move. He was horror-struck at the thought of stepping outside wearing Jack's capote. But one glance at the outlaws' faces told him he had no choice. "Where's your wood pile?"

"Behind the cabin. Just foller the path."

Clay went to the door. He paused, then threw it open. "Don't shoot!" In the same instant he dove to his right, plowing into the snowbank beside the cabin.

Almost simultaneously a bullet sped through the space where he had been standing. Clay scrambled wildly around the corner of the cabin and out of range.

Jack had been standing half-exposed in the open doorway. The slug intended for Clay struck the outlaw just below the navel. It passed through his body and shattered his spine.

More shots were fired and Clay, wincing at every one, heard the slugs plunking into the log walls. And over this he heard the terrible screams of Jack Garrity.

Clay heard another voice. "Come on out, boys!" It was Parker. "We got you surrounded. In three minutes we fire the cabin. Come out, you have our word."

There was a pause and then the rifle fire resumed. The officers had slipped in through the trees and were firing from point-blank range. Clay was never sure that their fire was ever answered from inside the cabin.

Clay heard Jack beg, "Dutch, help me."

Dutch replied, "I am. I'm givin' up."

Clay couldn't see Dutch when he came out of the cabin, his hands raised above his head. But he heard him calling, "I give up! Ya got Jack, he's the one ya want. Don't shoot no more!"

His plea was clipped off by two more rifle shots. Clay heard the bullets strike. They made a hollow, plunking sound.

Clay lay still. Several more shots rang out and he heard the slugs thud into the building and smash among its simple furnishings. Finally, the shooting stopped and J. J. Parker shouted, "Clay Baker! Come out, we won't shoot no more."

Chapter Ten

Clay stood pressed against the cabin wall and peeked around the corner. "Here!" he shouted. "Don't shoot!"

Parker came toward him, his carbine ready. "By Gawd, kid. I didn't know that was you in the old coat!"

"You didn't give me any time to explain."

"No," said Parker, "you can't take no chances with that kind. You got to surprise 'em."

"I think Jack's still alive inside," Clay said.

Jack Garrity was alive, but he was unconscious and bleeding heavily. Parker and Clay carried him to the bunk where Parker pulled open Jack's trousers. "Whew! He's shot in the belly." The marshal pulled a rag from a nail in the wall and gingerly spread it over Jack's wound. "He's about run his string."

Going to the door Parker called, "Ab! We got 'em. Come on in." Clay saw Duckett slip from behind a tree and start for the cabin. When he reached Dutch's sprawled body he stopped, ripped open the dead man's clothing and pulled a money belt from around his waist. Then he turned out Dutch's pockets, finding a small revolver which he slipped into his own pocket.

Parker had already begun searching the cabin. Beginning under the eaves at the top of the wall he was feeling with his fingers for anything that might have been hidden there. Duckett entered and asked, "Findin' anything?"

"Not yet."

"The one outside had a hundred an' twenty in his money belt." Duckett looked over at Jack on the bunk. "That one still alive?"

"Not for long," said Parker.

Duckett grinned at Clay. "Seen somethin' this mornin' didn't ya? Did they make you put on that other coat?"

"Yeah, they were goin' to shoot me if I didn't."

Parker spoke without stopping his search, "Bet you never saw anybody shot in the guts before. They'da treated you the same way."

At that moment Clay had to step outside and get some fresh air. He heard Duckett say to Parker, "Come help me get ol' Jack off'n the bed so's I can turn it out."

The deputies emptied Jack's pockets. Next they grabbed his clothing at the ankles and shoulders and heaved him up out of the bunk. Jack moaned but did not move. The officers placed him outside on a hard-crusted snow bank.

As much as Clay detested Jack he could not just leave him there on the snow. He got the tattered bear skin that had been on the bunk and covered him with it. As he was doing this Jack opened his eyes, but Clay doubted that he saw anything.

In the cabin the bedding had been thrown off the bunk and the straw tick ripped open, scattering its moldy contents. Containers of flour, beans, and sugar had also been dumped out on the floor.

"What are you hunting for?" Clay asked.

"Loot," said J. J. Parker. "The swag from their jobs. It oughta be around here somewheres. Say, kid, go find their horses. Count 'em an' feed 'em if they need it. I s'pose there's hay out there. Then write me a list of what's there; brands, colors, you know."

Clay was relieved to get away from the cabin. He was appalled by the deputies' ruthlessness and his own lack of conscience. He would feel better in the company of some horses. They were in a large, snow-clad meadow just beyond the trees that surrounded the cabin.

There were thirty-one horses and mules standing around a make-shift hay corral. All the animals were rail thin. Some had runny, half-closed eyes while others wheezed from congestion in their lungs. After feeding the starving horses Clay returned to the cabin and found the deputies busily digging up the cabin's dirt floor.

"Here's the list of horses and mules." He gave a piece of note paper to Parker. "Findin' anything?" Clay asked.

Duckett straightened up and pointed to a rusty baking

powder can lying by the door, "They had two hundred in gold and some bills in that."

"Jack looks dead," said Clay.

"No loss," said Parker. "Go out an' pull the boots off'n them two. Might find somethin'. Don't forget to pry off the heels."

Dutch's corpse had stiffened and Clay, reluctant to touch him anyway, had difficulty removing his boots. The stench from the dead man's ragged socks and dirty feet made Clay hold his breath. He shook out each of the boots and pried the heels loose with his knife. He found nothing. Jack had been wearing Indian-made winter moccasins and in one of them Clay found two, yellowbacked twenty-dollar bills. He took them to Parker.

"Put 'em in your pocket. We'll count that against the hundred we owe ya."

"But it may be stolen money. They keep track of the numbers."

Parker threw down the ax he had been using to root up the floor. "For hell sakes, preacher! Gimme them bills." Parker took the yellowbacks and gave Clay two twenty-dollar gold pieces in exchange. "Now we only owe you sixty, right?"

"Right," said Clay, putting the coins into his shirt pocket and carefully buttoning the flap. "I fed the horses. There's seventeen horses and fourteen mules back there. Five of the horses are in real bad shape. I underlined them on your list. It'd be kinder to shoot 'em than to let 'em go on."

"Go shoot 'em then," said Duckett.

Clay got his rifle, loaded it, and returned to the horse pasture. He stopped in front of the first animal underlined on his list. A gaunt bay with broken hooves and dull, mattery eyes. The animal didn't react as Clay took aim with his rifle. At the shot the horse collapsed, dead when it hit the ground. In fifteen minutes all five sick horses lay scattered about the meadow, blood staining the snow.

Parker and Duckett were still digging when Clay returned to the cabin. "Did you find anything more?" he asked.

"Yep, Ab dug up a jar over yonder that had five hundred dollars in it, all in them yellowbacks you don't like."

"What're you gonna do about the stock?" asked Clay.

"Best thing's for you to take care of 'em. You can either charge their owners a board bill when they claim 'em or buy 'em damn cheap."

"That's fine," said Clay. "Give me a note authorizing me to take care of the horses and mules, twenty-six now."

"Done," said Parker, scribbling in a pocket notebook.

"I'd like to get the rest of my money and leave," said Clay.

"Sure. But, before you go," said Parker, "I wrote out a paper I want you to sign." The marshal handed Clay a sheet of note paper on which was crudely printed an account of the shooting. The paper said that the outlaws had resisted and the officers were forced to fire.

"This isn't exactly the way I thought it happened," said Clay. "Wasn't Dutch tryin' to give up when you shot him?"

"That was a trick," said Parker. "He had that pistol in his pocket. He'd a plugged us all if he'd got the chance." Parker took a roll of bills from his pocket. "Here's the rest of your pay." Then he shoved his hand into his pocket again and withdrew it filled with change. "This silver must make five or ten dollars." He poured it into Clay's cupped hands saying, "Now you got your money plus a nice bonus. You remember that if anyone wants to know how those fellers tried to shoot it out."

Clay signed the statement and gave it to Parker. "How do you figure to get the bodies out to collect the reward?"

Duckett replied, "Over in Idaho they chopped off a feller's head an' brought it in, in a feed sack. He was froze so it warn't as bad as ya might think."

"Your affydavid should do the trick," said Parker. "I got the list of stock, too. But if they won't pay off, we still done OK."

Clay was sure then that the deputies were hunting so hard for "swag" because they planned to keep it. He stared briefly at the pair who scarcely looked up when he left.

As he knelt to fasten on his skis Clay glanced at the two corpses. Dutch had fallen on his face, his arms still half-raised. Clay remembered Dutch had held his arms just like that when he danced at the Christmas party.

In the surrounding trees Canada jays had begun to gather and one of the black-eyed birds was already walking appraisingly around the two bodies. Clay rolled Jack over on his face to protect it from the birds. Then he began to ski rapidly down the canyon.

Clay returned two days later to feed the horses. He found that the outlaws' cabin had been burned. There were marks in the snow that suggested the outlaws' bodies had been dragged back into the cabin before it was set on fire.

Clay made the long trip back and forth to the remote horse pasture to feed the horses there several times. But as soon as the spring snow had started to melt he and Mary rode up and drove the horses out of the canyon.

Beyond the shaded canyon the sun shone brightly. In the open meadows on the valley floor the first spring flowers, tiny buttercups, had blossomed. The sun was almost hot. And as they rode Clay removed his mackinaw and spread it across his lap. He looked at Mary riding beside him. A spontaneous grin spread across both their faces.

Clay looked at the valley around him. There was a show of green on the brown hillsides. On the steep flanks of the Tetons Clay saw brilliant pinpoints of flashing light. Perhaps they were minerals gleaming? Although the awakening valley was inhospitable and isolated, especially in winter, it was also rich in good water, timber, and grass. Clay knew men had already been here prospecting for gold. Someday someone would strike the lode. Meanwhile, the trapping was good and the elk were plentiful enough to feed an army. The streams teemed with fish, and waterfowl crowded the marshes. Even now big Canada geese were nesting in the marsh and along the stream banks.

Clay remembered arriving in Eagle Rock and how he had talked of making the country grow up with him. It wasn't that way here. This was a country that made you grow up—or it killed you.

That night Clay asked Mary what Johnny's plans had been for the valley. She tried to answer but was most eloquent when she got out the bags of vegetable seeds they had brought from Eagle Rock the previous fall. There were seeds for carrots, beets, and turnips along with lettuce and spinach seeds. Clay's mouth actually watered when he thought of eating such things again. He was anxious to plant a garden, although Mary warned it would be freezing for many nights to come.

The arrival of spring meant an end to trapping and feeding stock. On the farms where Clay had worked he would now have been plowing. But he had no plow here; in fact, no horse-drawn implements except the handmade sledge.

Clay missed a plow most when he began preparing a garden plot. He estimated it at a quarter-acre and set large stones to mark the corners. The resistant turf had to be attacked with a mattock, and Clay was three days cutting the sod and turning it under. Once the ground was ready he hooked up the team and snaked in poles from the hills to build a fence around his garden.

Mary showed no interest in the planting and did not join in the work. She did please Clay, however, by boiling water in her largest containers and using it to wash their clothes. But when he suggested that they scrub out the cabins Mary shrugged her shoulders.

The cow herd had increased that spring by three calves. To Clay's vexation only one of the new calves was a heifer. He castrated the little bulls, flipped out their horn buds with the same blade, and then branded them all with a homemade running iron. The brand he used was a reversed B K connected. The Baker-Kelly brand.

One morning when he went out to milk, Clay found Little Dick Pierce sitting by the corral. "Howdy!" said Dick.

"Howdy yourself! Where did you drop from?"

"Oooh. Come in the night. I learnt night-travelin' a long time back. Ya need to get ya a dog. He'd let ya know when the Injuns start showin' up. I could fetch one in from the fort."

"You goin' to Eagle Rock?" Clay asked.

"Yep, the signs are right. I figgered you'd let me have some horses to take my fur out."

"I don't want the dog yet, but I'd like you to take my fur out, too."

"I'll do her. But how do ya know I won't blow all your money on women and red whiskey?"

"You give my fur to Marv Feltch. He'll take out what I owe him and hold the rest for me."

"Done," said Dick. "I want to move quick now afore the river gits any higher. She started runnin' mud the other day."

At breakfast Mary and Dick engaged in an animated conversation in Shoshone. Clay was pleased and surprised that this time he understood some of it. Mary was boasting of how many horses they had now that Jack and Dutch were dead.

Dick turned to Clay, speaking English, "I knowed ya finally rubbed out them two bed bugs up the Little Gros Ventre. It was good work."

The compliment made Clay uncomfortable. "No, not me. Two deputy marshals came in after the last big storm. They did the shooting. They almost got me, too."

"Wouldn'ta mattered to 'em neither," said Dick. "Man's gotta look out fer hisself when he's treatin' with the law. Most of 'ems as crooked as the fellers they're after."

Clay was noncommittal. He preferred that the old trapper didn't know the details of his involvement at the cabin on the Little Gros Ventre. To change the subject, he began talking about their furs.

Clay learned to his surprise that Little Dick had carried his furs to a cache near the ranch. The old man had made several trips back and forth from the hills to bring down his excellent catch of furs.

These were packed into the ranch that afternoon and stored in the empty room in Clay's cabin. In the evening they sewed Clay's furs into waterproof mantas of canvas and elk skin. Dick said, "We got a river ta cross. Don't want them pretty martens a yourn ta get wet and go moldy."

The horses that were to make up the pack string were brought in and corraled that night. Clay fed them the last spears of hay from the stackyard. Long before daylight the next morning Mary and the two men were outside, packing the horses. The plan was to cross the river early when the flow would be at its lowest. Then, depending upon how Little Dick appraised the "signs," Clay might ride part way to Eagle Rock with him. With some reluctance Mary agreed to stay home and perhaps milk the cow.

The Snake River was running hard when they reached the ford. Dick appeared undaunted. He rode up and down the bank twice, studying the river. "We'll start here an' head fer that leanin' cottonwood yonder." So saying, the trapper forced his horse into the swift water. Clay followed cautiously.

When his lead pack animal temporarily balked, Clay jerked the lead rope savagely. The horse came on obediently, and the crossing under Dick's guidance was made swiftly and without further incident.

"Git your feet wet?" Dick asked when the pair were on the far shore.

"No. Just my pants. This river scares the hell out of me."

"Keep it that way," said Dick, "an' it'll never git ya."

Dick took the lead, examining the trail ahead for tracks. He said, "We may be the first ones over the pass this year. Could be plenty snow higher up. You better ride along, Clay."

It was well that Clay stayed with the older man. Because higher up they ran into several huge snow drifts and had to fight their horses across them. Dick might not have been able to manage alone.

By early afternoon the worst was behind them and they had crossed the divide. At sundown they were camped in a secluded glade well off the main trail. The horses were picketed and avidly clipping the fresh, new grass.

The men sat by a small fire eating a dinner of elk jerky and dried trout. "I know places like this here all through this country," said Dick. "I'd be a tol'able guide if I felt less puny."

Clay said, "Johnny told me that sports from back East needed guides in this country. There were some in huntin' last fall."

"Yep," said Dick. "There's easy money to be made there. I've heered five dollars a day fer a guide an' four bits for saddle horses. Just thinka that! An' takin' them sissies around is easy. Why you could even go up to that blamed park they made outa the Yellerstone an' guide sissies all summer. Make ya a bar'la money."

Clay fell asleep pondering a summer of "sissy" guiding. The next day he continued on with Dick because the danger of being waylaid and robbed was on the old man's mind. Well before noon Dick called a halt. "I'll hide up in the quakers an' go the resta the way after dark. Should be in Marv Feltch's yard afore daylight. You kin go home now."

It gave Clay a pang to wheel around and go back to Jackson's Hole when he was just a few miles short of civilization. But he knew he had no alternative.

He found the Snake higher than it had been thirty-six hours earlier. Its color was a uniform gray-brown that obscured the bottom a few feet from shore. He wondered what Little Dick's signs said now. And because he had no idea, Clay took the old man's line at the ford and made the crossing without difficulty.

Not far from the river he shot a young buck antelope. It was one of the earlier migrants returning to the valley from the sage plains beyond the mountains to the southeast. He tied the carcass behind the cantle of his saddle and reached the ranch that night. While Clay attended to his weary horse, Mary skinned the buck and quartered the carcass.

Clay would have been glad to do the butchering if it had encouraged Mary to spend more of her time keeping house. But it did not. In good weather Mary preferred to cook outdoors.

The neat vegetable garden didn't interest her, either. Clay noted with impatience that a ground squirrel had been busy there in his absence. He shot the little rodent within an hour after first noticing his burrowing. Also, the cow had not been milked and Mary's irresponsibility had cost them a third of an already limited milk supply. Clay guessed that Mary had spent most of the time while he was away watching the horse herd.

But he realized that it would do no good to reveal his dissatisfaction to Mary. She sang "Buffalo Gals" and the "Alphabet Song" again and again while cooking their evening meal. Clay tried to ignore it. But finally, to make her stop, he sought her opinion of a guiding venture in the Yellowstone that summer.

Any lengthy conversation with Mary was a halting and often exasperating one. But, before he gave it up, Clay had put his idea across. Mary was interested in going, but she rejected Clay's idea that she stay home and tend the ranch. Just packing up and going was ingrained in Mary's nomadic soul. She could not conceive of going on a long trip in search of a job.

Such differences made Mary's relationship with Clay as difficult as his was with her. For her part Mary found this young man not as preoccupied with horses, hunting, and lusting as other men. She couldn't understand why he spent so much time with the cattle. He took far better care of them than he did the horses. Even now there were horses in the herd that should be trained and ridden. But Clay neglected them to build a fence or chop weeds in the garden.

Now he was talking about leaving but not to hunt or seek out his enemies. He wanted to ride north and help white people he did not even know. This made no sense to Mary. But, because her nature and training were to accept a man's decisions she would do as he wanted—so long as he took her with him. She was tired of this cold valley. It was never meant to live here all year. There was a restlessness in her. Johnny's spirit was here, but it would follow her if she left.

All of Clay's plans were abruptly changed when he got up the next morning and saw Indians and their ponies in the meadow. Outside he found four blanket-wrapped bucks squatting in the dooryard.

Trying not to appear uneasy Clay returned to his room and picked up his rifle and hunting knife. With the knife in his belt and the Winchester over his shoulder he approached the squatting bucks. "How," he said. The men looked sulkily at him and grunted. Two of them wore low-crowned, wide-brimmed gray hats with black bands. As was typical, their hat brims were unshaped and the crowns were as smooth as mushroom tops. One of the bare-headed men had long, unkempt hair that hung to his shoulders. The other wore his hair in braids and had on a necklace of bleached bird bones and hawk talons intermingled with bits of brass, fur, and red cloth. The rusty barrels of two old guns spiked up from under the blankets of two of the braves.

The Indians watched Clay with silent intensity as he passed by them and knocked on Mary's door. She opened it. Her hair was unkempt but her face was placid. And not until Clay was inside did he realize that someone else was there with her.

Sitting on the bed was an Indian man, perhaps forty years old. He had piercing black eyes and a brass ring in his right ear lobe. The Indian wore a soiled cotton shirt under a tight-fitting, blue vest. He had on blue Army pants with the ubiquitous blanket folded Indian-style around his hips. The man did not move when Clay entered but his eyes flashed with savage interest.

"Mornin'," said Clay, leaning his rifle against the cabin wall.

"I speak Hinglish," said the Indian.

"Good," said Clay. "What can we do for you?" He saw that the rum bottle given them by the marshal was on the bed beside him, empty.

"I Crow Dog," said the Indian.

"I'm Clay Baker," and when he was sure the Indian wasn't going to move, Clay went over to the bunk and shook hands with him.

Clay next got himself a cup of coffee from the pot on the stove. He extended the pot to Crow Dog who nodded, yes. Clay poured the man a cup and placed it on the table, waiting until the Indian came and sat down.

"We camp here! Maybe go Lemhi," said Crow Dog.

"Fine," said Clay, hoping he sounded more enthusiastic than he felt.

"This my people. Our land," said Crow Dog, sweeping his arm over the table. "We hunt here long time." Then he began speaking to Mary in Shoshone.

"He want race, trade horses," said Mary.

Clay made a wry face, "Maybe trade, maybe race. Horses are not mine. They belong to the U.S.A."

The Indian made a face of his own and spat on the floor, "Damn, son-a'-bitch U.S.A.! Steal! All time steal!"

Clay looked at Mary for support. But she sat placidly on her bench by the stove and said nothing. To change the subject Clay asked her if she was going to fix something to eat.

Crow Dog said, "Warriors heap Goddamn hungry."

"So that's it," Clay muttered. He spoke loudly to Mary, "Cook up a lot of pancakes. Put plenty of molasses on 'em. They'll like that."

In minutes Mary had sourdough hot cakes sizzling in two frying pans. When they were brown, Clay slid them out of the pans and into a large, graniteware basin. He poured molasses over them, then took the cakes out to the still-squatting Indians. The men wolfed down the hot cakes, eating as if they were starved, then licked their filthy hands and wrists to capture the molasses before it ran down their arms.

Mary served hot cakes until the Indians began lying back on the ground belching and groaning and waving her away. Then she placed a platter of the cakes on the table between Clay and Crow Dog. Clay pretended not to notice that the Indian ignored the fork Mary had placed beside his plate and ate with his fingers.

"Crow Dog," said Clay filling his own plate with pancakes, "I have fed you. You are welcome in this house. Your people are welcome to camp in the fields. But you must not steal."

"White man steal," said Crow Dog. "Shoshone not steal. We heap friends." With that the Indian held out a sticky hand and Clay gripped it. "Shake!" said the Indian.

"Shake!" said Clay.

After breakfast Clay went outside and saw that four tipis had been pitched in the meadow. The women were in the willow patches gathering dry wood and cow chips for their fires. Beside the stream some of the men were shooting at trout with a smoke-belching muzzle-loader. They did not get many fish, but their enjoyment obviously made up for that lack.

Clay returned to Mary's cabin and drank tea with Crow Dog until the Indian left. Half the morning was gone and Clay asked Mary how long she thought the Indians would stay. She did not know. Perhaps, as Crow Dog suggested, they would only stay a few days. But they might stay all summer. Indian people, she told him with an amused expression, did not plan their trips as far ahead as white people.

There was nothing Clay could do about his new neighbors. The Shoshones might be his guests, but he was their prisoner.

Chapter Eleven

There were seven men in Crow Dog's band along with eleven women and perhaps twenty children. Clay remembered later, with some amusement, that "The little buggers popped in and out of the tipis so fast and hid in the willow bushes until even a bookkeeper couldn't keep track of 'em."

He did get close enough to some of the Indian boys to engage them to hunt ground squirrels in his garden with their bows and arrows. Clay paid the boys a nail for every ten ground squirrel tails they brought him. The animals themselves ended up in the Shoshone cooking pots.

When the Shoshone men were not horse racing or playing some gambling game they hunted. Antelope were abundant, but the pronghorns were by no means their sole quarry. Nesting geese, ducks and their eggs, sandhill cranes, swans, and sage grouse also went into the Indians' omniverous bag. One afternoon they killed a huge, old buffalo near some warm springs above the Little Gros Ventre. It was a tough, strong-tasting old bull, but his capture set off two days of feasting and celebration.

Clay did not begrudge the Indians the game. He believed it kept them from butchering his beef. But the Indians' large horse herd did concern him. The herd numbered sixty animals and they were stripping the meadows used by his animals. He had also planned to cut hay there. To save some of the grass Clay began to build a fence.

His project was well along until the morning Clay went out to work and found the meadow empty of all the horses, both his and the Indians'. He soon discovered the reason for as he walked through the meadow clouds of mosquitoes swarmed up to attack him. For a while Clay tried to work. But, at last with bites covering his face and hands, Clay threw down the pole he was holding and sprinted to the cabin.

The horses and cattle had moved onto the adjacent butte to avoid the mosquitoes. In the meadow the Indian women were dropping their tipis. They too had been driven off by the mosquitoes.

"I guess the damned mosquitoes are good for something," Clay said as he watched the Indians' preparations to depart. Mary had built a smoky fire in front of her cabin and Clay sat with her in its protective pall watching the Indians.

The squaws went about their tasks with a kind of disorganized order. Kids and dogs dashed helter-skelter. Horses, maddened by the stinging insects, were breaking loose and running through the camp. But, in spite of it all, the squaws were getting packed.

Before they left, Crow Dog and another man came to see Clay. Crow Dog was leading two of the Kellys' horses while the other Shoshone led two Indian ponies.

"We trade," said Crow Dog.

One of the Indian ponies was lame and the other had kidney sores as large as a man's hand. Clay shook his head, no. The horses Crow Dog wanted were two of the best in the Kellys' herd.

Crow Dog trotted his pony around in a tight circle, jerking on the ropes tied around the horses' necks. "We trade!" He swept his arm out from his chest in a manner that indicated the bargain was already made.

Clay again shook his head and walked over to the two Indian ponies. The man holding them wore a sullen expression. Clay ignored him and placed his hand on the sore-backed animal. Its flesh shuddered involuntarily. "No good," said Clay. Then he moved to the other horse and raised a hoof that was badly broken. "No good," he said again.

Crow Dog threw down the ropes of the horses he was leading. He then rode over and seized the lead ropes of his horses and threw them down.

Clay shrugged and went to his two horses. He ran his hand down their backs and rubbed them between the ears. He would, he said, trade either horse for the two Indian ponies plus the two horses the Indians were riding and Crow Dog's saddle.

Crow Dog swung his fist down hard against his thigh. "No!"

But as the bartering continued Clay saw him weakening. Eventually a bargain was struck; Crow Dog would give up the four Indian horses for one Kelly horse and six plugs of Johnny's chewing tobacco. Once the exchange was complete Crow Dog waved to his companion to climb up behind him on his new horse and together they trotted away, obviously pleased with themselves.

Clay ran the four new horses into the corral to keep them from following the Indian band as it left the valley. Then, to be sure that none of his other stock accompanied the Indians, Clay followed along with them until they reached the ford on Snake River.

Turning back he wished that something now would turn up to drive the mosquitoes away. But nothing daunts a Jackson's Hole mosquito although a sticky dope that Mary made did help. Once Clay had smeared on enough to make himself feel varnished Mary's preparation was effective. By using the dope and working during the hours when the insects were not so active he dammed the creek and irrigated about ten acres of wild hay.

The results were nearly magical. The dark, green grass grew so rapidly Clay thought he could see it rising. On the Fourth of July Clay got out a scythe and began mowing the hay. During those hot days he could not keep up with the grasses' growth.

While Clay worked in the fields, Mary mounted her pony and herded the horses and cattle so that they would not be tempted to eat the hay before it could be stacked in the corrals. She moved the stock well to the west so they wouldn't move back into the hay fields at night. It was a task that required a lot of riding, but Mary loved it.

Mowing was not enjoyable. The scythe blade had to be kept razor sharp. Also, the scythes' two handles had to be adjusted until Clay found the blade angle that was both reasonably comfortable to swing and efficient for mowing. But nothing kept the sweat from running into and burning his eyes. Nothing eased the ache caused by steadily rotating his hips or relieved the cramp in his right forearm. The mosquitoes rose incessantly from their shaded hiding places in the grass to attack him. Clay recalled the long days when he had sat on a mowing machine and bounced along behind a team of horses. And that, he thought ruefully, had seemed like work!

Nevertheless the tall grass fell and cured rapidly in the hot sunshine. Clay used a homemade, wooden rake to gather the hay into windrows. Later he pitchforked the windrowed hay into conical piles called "shocks." Shocking the hay not only protected it while it was still in the field but facilitated loading it on the flat, wooden slip. The slip was a raftlike affair made of light poles fastened together and pulled along on the ground by the horses. It was used to move the hay to the corrals where it was stacked.

When Clay was hauling hay Mary left her herding job to climb up on the stacks and both spread the hay evenly and tramp it down as Clay pitched it up to her. Mary hated this work and did it half-heartedly. And Clay, his humor much reduced by hard work and insects, inwardly fumed about her laziness and pitched the hay up to her in huge fork loads. After an hour of this work they hated each other.

Such was Clay's preoccupation with his work that he took only brief notice of a significant event. Settlers moved into the valley. These were not horse-wrangling ex-trappers with squaws instead of wives, but white men with white women.

Actually it was just one woman. There were two sunburned young brothers named Lars and Iver Andvik. With these husky Swedes was Iver's wife, Helga. She had two children, a towheaded boy of six and another son who was barely two and still nursed his mother.

The Andvik brothers came to meet Clay, and he shook their hands warmly. He introduced them to Mary saying, "Her husband, Johnny Kelly, died last winter. I'm helpin' her out till I know what she's gonna do with the place." Clay was then quick to add that he and the Kellys claimed all the meadow land to the south and east of the creek and marsh. And when the Andviks said they planned to trap that winter Clay showed them the ridges in the eastern mountains where he and Little Dick had trap lines.

"There's plenty of room for us all," Clay said, "but we ought to understand one another right off. It will save us trouble later on."

The Andviks agreed readily to this. They did not want neighbor trouble. It was one of the reasons they had come to this lonely valley where they could work by themselves. Because the season was advancing these competent-appearing Scandinavians explained that they were primarily interested in building a cabin and cutting enough hay to winter their stock. In addition to their pack string of horses and mules, they had driven eight Durham cows over the pass. The brothers had chosen to build their cabin a couple of miles north of the Kelly ranch. It was a good site, both for a ranch and for not being too close to the determined young man named Clay Baker.

Clay was happy to have neighbors, so Mary's reaction to the Andviks was disappointing. Her dark face took on an expression that he had not seen since Johnny died.

"What's the matter?" he asked. "Don't you want neighbors?"

"No," said Mary. "No white woman, no good."

"I see. But these are good men. We can help each other. We'll work in each others' hay, an' you won't have to do it anymore."

Mary said nothing.

"You'll see," said Clay. "Mrs. Andvik will need your help. She'll be coming to see you any day, I'll bet on it."

Clay would have lost. Mrs. Helga Andvik, a good, Christian woman of boundless energy and courage would never call on Mary Kelly.

But Clay scarcely noticed. The summer was too short and the work too abundant for him to worry about Mary. No sooner had he finished the haying in early August than it was time to cut wood and bring in more poles for fences and corrals.

It was while Clay was cutting poles and dragging them into the ranch that the two men came. He found them sitting on the bench beside Mary's cabin. Tied to the corral were two jaded-looking horses. Their riders looked equally tired and dirty with unkempt hair and beards. Their clothing hung in tatters while they wore boots that were split and broken open at the toes.

"Howdy men," said Clay. "I'll unhook my team and be with you."

"Hidy, Mr. Baker," said the smaller of the pair, rising to shake hands. "I'm Joe McGraw. My partner here is Herman. But he's a Dutchy an' don't speak much English."

Clay shook hands with both men. "What can I do for you?"

"We been prospectin'," said McGraw. "There's another feller up at our diggin's. We thought we had a placer mine, but after the first show we ain't made much more'n our wages. Our horses, all but these two, got away. We're about outa grub and just down on our luck."

Clay sat on a block of wood and faced the men. "This is a bad country to be down on your luck in."

"We run onto that Andvik feller this mornin'," said McGraw. "He thought you might fix us up with some horses an' grub enough to git out to Eagle Rock."

"We're a little low on grub ourselves. My winter's supplies aren't here yet. We could get you some antelope, you could jerk it. Do you know yamp root? I can show you what it looks like."

"We're not begging, Mr. Baker," said McGraw. "I can pay you in gold or yellowbacks."

"Well, money talks all right. But out here there's no place to spend it, so it only whispers. Some of the horses are just boardin'; I couldn't let you have them. I'm short on saddles and bridles, too."

"We've all got saddles plus a half-dozen pack outfits," said the miner. "Maybe we'd throw them and our horses an' camp stuff in on a trade."

"Maybe," said Clay. "I'd have to see it. But why don't you pull the saddles off your ponies? Give 'em a rest while we have some dinner."

Watching the two miners unsaddle proved to Clay that neither was much of a horseman. Clay called Mary from the cabin, explaining, "Mrs. Kelly is the horse expert. I'd like her to look over your horses."

"Sure."

Mary came out and examined each horse, looking in their eyes and speaking softly to be sure they heard. She ran her hands over their backs and down each front leg, feeling there for such faults as ringbone. Both horses were young, she said, four and five years old. Their main fault appeared to have resulted from a lack of food. The miners had probably kept them tied too much after their other horses ran off.

As she finished her examination Mary made a querulous mouth. "Maybe good—next spring," she said.

"Well, gents," said Clay, "that's what the expert says. Come in now and have some dinner. Maybe we can work something out."

The miners ate hungrily, almost gorging themselves on antelope steaks, watercress from the spring, and boiled yampa root. When their intake began to slow Clay said, "I've got three horses you could have. They're not fancy, but they'll take you to Eagle Rock and a lot farther if you want to go. You could sell 'em there for seventy-five or a hundred apiece."

"How much?"

"Two hundred apiece, your horses plus your camp and outfits—except for what you need to get over the pass."

"Damn! That's a sight of money for three plugs."

"They're not plugs. You'll need a good horse under you to get across Snake River. I've had trouble there myself, so I wouldn't set a man out to drown himself. Tell you what, we'll throw in a ten-pound sack of flour."

"Done," said McGraw, opening his ragged shirt and pulling a sweat-darkened, leather money belt from around his waist.

Clay took the money, four hundred dollars in gold coins and two hundred dollars in yellowback currency. "I'll put this in my belt, then go get your horses." But Clay didn't own a money belt. He wanted no one, not even Mary, to know about the cache he had made in the floor of his cabin. It was where he hid the money J. J. Parker had paid him.

Two of the horses he drove in were the best of the four Indian ponies he had traded for with Crow Dog. The third was a slab-hipped bay; a good walker but hard riding.

It was late afternoon before Clay had an outfit ready to go with the miners to their camp in the Gros Ventre mountains east of Jackson's Hole. In addition to the saddle horses Clay led four pack horses that he would need to carry in the miners' outfit.

The miners led Clay up the trail that follows the Gros Ventre River. Much larger than the creek of similar name, the Gros Ventre is a lovely mountain stream. Clay saw many riffles and knee-deep runs where trout and whitefish were rising. As the light began to fail the men stopped and made camp beside the river. They had chosen a grassy swale that was also being used by dozens of sage grouse. Before the light failed Clay shot the heads from three of the birds to supplement the food Mary had sent with them.

After supper they made simple beds with their saddle blankets and used their saddles for pillows. As they lay before the dying campfire Clay asked, "How do you look for a mine, anyway?"

"Lots of ways. Sometimes you find a little color in a creek an' foller it up, hopin' you'll hit the lode somewhere along it. That's what we did here," said McGraw. "We built a washing operation an' washed gravel for two months. The gold was there but it was flour gold, so damn fine it just washed on over the rifflers in the trough. We didn't get a tenth of what we washed out."

Clay said, "I think I know how you must feel. They ought to call this 'Almost Valley.' It's where everything almost happens."

McGraw chuckled and Clay stopped talking, remembering now that it was not "Almost Valley" for Dutch, Jack, and Johnny Kelly.

The men set out again early in the morning. They soon left the river trail to follow a small creek to the diggings. The man who had been left behind verged on hysteria at the sight of his companions. "Hi boys!" he cried, gripping their hands. "I wondered if ye'd left me! The damn wolves howl an' there was a she bear came by with two cubs. I spent one night up that tree!"

"Why didn't you plug her?" Clay asked.

"I was ascared to."

Clay couldn't help smiling. It was a wonder that the miners' ineptness hadn't killed them all weeks ago. But, apparently, they knew mining and had moved a lot of dirt and gravel. The creek bank was pocked with holes and the creek itself ran sluggishly through the newly made mud and gravel bars left from their ore washing.

"Looks like you've done a lot of hard work," said Clay.

"It paid pretty good for a while," said McGraw, "but we never struck the lode. And havin' our horse run off pretty much ruint the proposition."

Clay found the miners' camp gear run down from hard use and neglect. There were some useful tools and a half-dozen good pack outfits. While he loaded these things on his pack horses, the miners were making up small packs of camp gear and food to tie behind their saddles.

Joseph McGraw came to where Clay was working. "We're ready. You made us a hard bargain, but I guess you were fair, considerin'. So thanks and good-by."

Clay said, "You came in over the Gros Ventre trail. Don't you want me to show you the Snake River ford?"

"Naw, the river's low. We want to get outa here. You said the trail goes past your place and right to the river—then on west across the pass?"

"That's right," said Clay. "When you get to the ford take a line on the big leanin' cottonwood on the far bank. Put the bay in the river first. He's crossed lots of times. The other horses will follow him."

"Thanks to you then," said the miner, reaching out to shake hands. "Maybe I'll see you again next summer. We're thinkin' of puttin' in a placer mine on Snake River."

"Good," said Clay. "Maybe we can trade horses again."

McGraw gave a derisive laugh. "Only if we hit the mother lode." In ten minutes the three miners had ridden out of sight down the creek.

Clay did not reach home until midnight. Mary had waited up for him and came out to help when she heard him. After the horses were unsaddled and turned loose Clay carried the packs into the cabin where Mary tore into them like a ten-year-old opening Christmas packages. It amused him to see how gleeful she became upon discovering some commonplace and often dirty utensil.

Mary's childish delight in opening box after box of surprises amused Clay. Tired as he was, he stayed up and watched her until the last pannier had been emptied. That summer Mary had virtually given up housekeeping and this was the first time in weeks that Clay had seen her interested in anything except the horses. He hoped her present attitude lasted until she had cleaned and put away some of her own things.

Mary was still looking at the miners' things when Clay went to bed. When Mary shook him, he awakened angry. He thought she wanted to show him something from the miners.

"Clay! You come, Clay!"

"Huh? What's the matter?" Clay squinted in the morning light. Mary was too excited to wait while he dressed. She pulled him to the door. "Looky," she said, "horse come home!"

"Oh, oh, look out. I gotta get my boots on."

The bay horse he had sold the miners was back with the other horses in the pasture. It was still wearing the saddle. But the saddle had turned and was hanging under its belly, much the worse for some kicking. The bay still wore its bridle, too, but the dragging reins had been stepped on and broken off short.

A saddle horse was always kept in the corral at night for just this kind of need. In ten minutes Clay had caught and saddled it, then caught the bay. He removed the battered saddle. The leather was soaked. "They got as far as the river," he told Mary. "I hope this old horse just got away from them. They were poor hands."

Clay reset the saddle on the bay's back and fastened a halter and lead rope on the animal. He told Mary, "I'll look for 'em. If they come back here, tell 'em to wait."

He wasn't sure Mary had understood his instructions. But this time he didn't care because he was almost certain that the miners would never be back; at least not Joe McGraw, who had been riding the bay.

The miners' trail was easy to follow. The men had ridden straight to the river. Clay reconstructed what had happened then. The miners had struck the river a hundred yards below the ford. Instead of reconnoitering, they had ridden directly into the river well downstream from the fording place. And although they may have headed for the leaning cottonwood tree, their route took them straight into the deep channel where Clay had nearly drowned the previous fall. McGraw had probably failed to check his cinch and the saddle turned, spilling him into the river. His heavy work boot may have hung up in the stirrup, making such a fall even more dangerous.

Tying the bay to a tree Clay rode his own horse across the river. There he found the tracks of two horses. They had come from downriver and then turned up the trail that led over the pass to Idaho. Clay backtracked them until he came upon a rock cairn. Jutting out of the cairn was a piece of driftwood. And scratched on the wood Clay read, "J. MCGRAW LOST HERE 8/11/85."

Clay returned to the ford and crossed over. Then, leading the bay horse again, he went down river, carefully examining every bar and eddy. He rode for an hour before he saw a mixed flock of ravens and magpies sitting with some seagulls on a half-submerged object at the end of a gravel bar.

The birds had been pecking at the miner's sodden clothing, but their major efforts had been concentrated on the unprotected flesh. Little now remained of Joseph McGraw's face.

"Ufff!" Clay spun away, then stood for a moment, swallowing hard and taking deep breaths. A few feet up the bar he found a piece of driftwood and used it to scrape out a shallow depression in the gravel. When he had finished he returned to the corpse. Keeping his back to the ruined face, Clay stepped astraddle the body. In the coat he found some ore samples, two cartridges, and a clasp knife. An inner pocket yielded a sodden leather billfold that contained a picture of a woman that disintegrated in Clay's hands and his own receipt for the horse payment. He tossed this aside, then pulled open the man's shirt at the waist and stripped off the money belt he found there. In it were fifty dollars in coins, a wad of currency too wet to be separated, and a long, tubelike leather sack half-filled with fine gold dust. Clay weighed the sack in his palm; about a pound he guessed, three hundred dollars.

He fastened the money belt around his own waist, then

grabbed the corpse at the back of its coat collar. Trying not to look at the face, Clay dragged the body to the depression he had dug and rolled it in. He covered McGraw with gravel and some larger stones he picked up along the bar. Back on shore Clay cut an "X" in a big spruce and below that he carved the initials, "J.M."

That night he tossed McGraw's possessions on the table in front of Mary. She looked at them, "Him dead?"

"Colder'n a wedge. There's about four hundred dollars there. I'll hold the money in case his partners come back. Maybe Marv Feltch will hear something. McGraw had a picture of a woman, maybe a relative."

In bed that night the image of the miner's wrecked face seemed to hang white and shiny-wet in the blackness above Clay's head. He wanted to despise the pecking birds, but he could not. His own image of himself bending over the corpse and stripping away the valuables was almost as unpleasant. But what was he to do? Leave them there? No. He decided that he had acted as naturally as the birds had.

Clay went to the Andviks' the next day to tell them about the accident and stayed to help them shingle their cabin roof. As the men worked they questioned Clay about some of the valley's other residents.

"Mary says there's a man livin' down on the river, below where the Hoback comes in. He's got a placer mine and doesn't like company. Guess he's a little touched. Then there's Dick Pierce. He's a real old-time mountain man. More Injun than some Injuns an' kind of sickly. But Dick's all right—if he likes you. Just don't try readin' him your Bible.

"Until this spring there were two other fellas here. But they were rustlers, and the law came in an' shot 'em both. Anyway, that leaves the two of us, the five of you, plus Dick. That makes nine with the placer miner. But Mary says there'll be a lot more when the Injuns come in to make their winter's meat."

The Andvik brothers stopped work at the mention of Indians. "You tink day giff us troubles?" asked Lars.

Clay replied, "They've left us alone, but that may be because Mary's one of 'em. I have a hunch they stole those miners' horses last June." Clay warned the brothers not to let their stock wander or leave things lying around. "If your missis goes out with the kids pickin' chokecherries one of you better go with her."

An hour before sunset the men finished shingling the roof. "Py golly, Clay Baker, you done a goot day's vork! Come now and haf some supper," said Iver.

Clay declined, explaining that he had to go home and milk. Later, as he rode through the evening twilight, he was struck by the stark ruggedness of the Teton peaks. The deep strength of these great mountains was emphasized by the last rays of sunlight streaming against their backs from the west. He was conscious, too, of a chill in the air. It was mid-August but already there was a hint of fall. It reminded him of all the work still to do before winter.

The late summer coolness combined with the drying of the meadows to end the plague of mosquitoes. Clay took advantage of that to finish building his fence. It was, not counting the garden fence, the first fence in Jackson's Hole and enclosed about ten acres. Clay was just finishing it when Little Dick rode into the yard leading a pack string.

"Hi! Dick!" Clay called, putting down his tools and swinging aboard the saddle horse he used to ride to and from the meadow.

Little Dick Pierce was standing in the dooryard and jabbering in Shoshone with Mary. While they talked they were untying the hitches on the pack stock.

The trapper and Clay shook hands warmly, "Dick, you look good, new clothes and all. That red whiskey and high livin' must have been good for you."

Dick shrugged, "Naw. I din't take on mucha that. I seen onea your white doctors. Prob'ly a quack, but damned if I don't feel better. Might make a few more winters yet. By the way, I had to borry a couple more pack outfits to bring in ever'thin' ya ordered plus what Marv figgered ya really needed."

Of the eight pack animals, three carried Dick's winter supplies and the other five bore over a half-ton of supplies for Mary and Clay. There was flour, new clothes, boots, overshoes, bolts of cloth, nails, stovepipe, and wire, a coffee grinder, coffee, and tea plus castor oil, candles, a new oil lamp, and five gallons of kerosene; only a part of which had leaked from the can. There was salt, whiskey, traps, horseshoes, and horseshoe nails, gun powder, lead, primers, baking soda, molasses, a box of salt pork, some cans of fruit and vegetables, two sacks of oats, and three books: The Holy Bible, *The Complete Works of Wm. Shakespeare,* and *Dr. Foster's Encyclopedia of Home Cures and Remedies.* Packed in the same pannier with the books were garden seeds and two big cans of hard candy. Mary snatched one of the candy tins as soon as it was unpacked.

"Hey," Clay said, "give us some." And Mary, her mouth too full to reply, came forward, holding out the can.

"Not for me," said Dick. "Doc said I had to lay off sech stuff on accounta my liver. I ain't ever 'sposed to drink, but I ain't goin' that far."

Later Clay showed Mary how to grind coffee beans in the new grinder. Dick said, "It beats whackin' 'em with a rock, though I ain't convinced it makes as good a coffee."

"Say," said Dick, "I damn near forgot. I brung ya some mail." He took five crumpled envelopes from inside his shirt and handed them to Clay. "You're awful important. I ain't got five letters in my hull life. Carried one aroun' fer a year afore I found someone who could read it ta me."

Clay's fingers moved eagerly through the envelopes. His parents had sent two of the letters, another was from Ab Duckett in Montana. The fourth letter was from Marv Feltch, while the fifth and last was from a bank in Iowa.

He read Duckett's letter first. It was brief and full of misspellings. Duckett said that the ranchers whose cattle were in the Kellys' herd had relinquished all claims to the animals in appreciation of Clay's helping the deputies. Also, Duckett wrote, the owners of missing horses could only claim five from the list Clay had made. Therefore, he could either sell the horses and send on the money after deducting his board bill or he could buy the lot for five dollars a head.

"Well," said Clay with a grin, "we doubled our horse herd for twenty-five dollars. Not bad." But Mary did not understand why they had to pay anything for horses that already belonged to them. Dick tried, unsuccessfully, to explain it to her.

Marv Feltch's letter stated that Clay's furs had been sold for $490. The 488 pairs of elk teeth had earned $1.25 a pair. The combined value of the fur and elk teeth had been $1,100. From this amount Feltch had subtracted $675 to pay for Clay's first outfit plus the supplies brought in by Little Dick. Clay's balance was $375. He caught his breath as he read that; Feltch owed him $425 not $375. But as Clay read further his frown became a smile.

Clay's parents had written to Feltch, worried because they had not heard from their son in several months. Feltch had answered, explaining that Clay was fine and prospering in a new district. He had also sent Clay's parents fifty dollars in their son's name. Clay was pleased and told Dick.

"Marv told me he done that," said Dick.

"He's a good man. One of the best I ever knew."

"He be that," said Dick, "an' he's a hell of a rich 'un, too. All us ol' brush rats do business with him. Even the Injuns trusts Marv."

In his next paragraph Feltch wrote that a banker in Iowa had written him about Clay. Feltch had replied that Clay Baker was developing a potentially rich property in an isolated part of Wyoming Territory.

Marvin Feltch, Clay thought, had a positive genius for putting a genuine gilt edge on any description of the dreariest of western endeavors. But if the banker was curious, Clay was more so. He didn't know a soul in Iowa.

Chapter Twelve

Clay put the other letters in his pocket. These were the last he might receive for a year and he wanted to read them slowly and in privacy.

"That was pretty good news," he said, patting the letters. "I was wonderin', Dick, did you hear about a miner named McGraw gettin' drowned in the Snake?"

"Oh sure. It was the big news fer a couple days. Two fellers come in all excited, ridin' Injun ponies. Marv told me. The fellers said they bought three horses from ya. Man name of McGraw had trouble with his at the ford. He got throwed or his saddle turned. Anyhow, he done what they allus do, pulled his horse's head under the water. The last they seen of McGraw he was fightin' his horse. They couldn't do nothin'. Did you find 'im, Clay?"

"I did. He washed onto a bar about five miles below the ford. I buried him on the bar and marked a big spruce with his initials, 'J.M.'"

Clay then described the gold mine the men had in the Gros Ventre range and also told about the Andviks coming in to settle. Dick's reaction was immediate.

"Settlers? Damn 'em! I seen 'em before, allus sneakin' in some'ers. They'll kill off all the game, ruin the trappin', fence off the water, and drop kids like blow flies layin' eggs. Settlers is the worst varmints ever turned loose on a country!"

Clay tried to defend the Andviks, but Little Dick would hear none of it, saying, "Just gimme a drinka that new whiskey. I decided not to keep my damned ol' liver goin' after all. Settlers!"

That night Clay and Little Dick bunked together in Clay's cabin. "Don't fret yerself," said Dick. "I got rida them body rabbits whilst I was out."

"I'm not worried about that," said Clay. "What does worry me is not being sure of my ground here."

"Damn me! If you ain't got the mind of a settler, too. Nobody ought to own this valley," said Dick. "But Marv says a guv'mint survey is comin'. Once the ground is all marked off so's the settlers knows which little square is thern, they'll be hoppin' all over us like magpies on a gut pile."

"It has to come. You know that, Dick. But we're here first, an' we're damn fools if we don't look out for ourselves."

"There's a heapa difference in a man takin' care of hisself and ever' man for hisself. Which is what it'll be when the settlers comes." Dick rolled over in his blankets thus terminating the conversation.

Clay did not go to bed. By the light of one of his new candles he read the letters from his parents. They were written by his younger brother, Max, but dictated by his parents. These letters reminded him how enormously different their lives had become. His family all attended church every Sunday while Clay never thought about it. His father said the President, Grover "the Good" Cleveland, was going to end the financial panics and put the strikers back to work. Until then Clay had not known, or cared, who the President was. Cleveland ought to send some of those strikers out here, Clay thought. One winter in Jackson's Hole and they'd be damn glad to go back to any job.

He read then reread his parents' letters, both enjoying them and becoming angry because his folks didn't seem to think for themselves and let everyone walk on them. Clay thought, "That's just what old Grover and the rest of the big shots on Wall Street want people to do. Swallow it. It's God's Will if your crops fail and the bank takes your farm. It's God's Will if your team founders or the cows get hit by a train." Clay knew his parents were not satisfied with their pinched lives. Yet they were dead set against trying to change anything for fear that it might be for the worse. They were like the young deer that stood on the ridge deciding which way to run until the hunter put a bullet in his lungs and made the decision unnecessary.

Clay opened the last letter. He had never heard of the banker who wrote it or the town, Aldora, Iowa, from where it came. Still, Clay had guessed what was in the letter before he read it. It began:

"Dear Mr. Baker,
  A valued customer has asked me to write you in the belief that she can perform a service to you both by investing in your current Western enterprise. I have therefore been instructed . . ."

Clay paused before reading on; "she" was Alma Warburton. He knew it. Although the letter never mentioned her name and only that once referred to "she," Clay knew it had to be she. And she was offering to help him! He sat holding the letter but staring beyond it. His mind was on what five or even ten thousand dollars could do in this valley.

Clay read the banker's name again, "M. Theodore Blount." He sounded substantial, and dull. Alma Warburton would have chosen him very carefully. Clay lay awake for hours that night thinking out the reply he would make to Mr. Blount of the Farmers' and Merchants' Bank of Aldora.

In the morning Clay was out early. He looked with fresh perspective at the primitive farmstead and its handmade fixtures. How little there was to show for all the months of privation and endless toil. He realized that skill and enterprise didn't amount to much without money. It was the one tool he had to have if he were not going to end up like Little Dick, railing at progress and cursing the inevitable.

As soon as Dick had packed and gone into the hills Clay thought he could make a fast trip to Eagle Rock and mail his answer to Mr. Blount. But it was not to be. Because, a few minutes later, Dick asked him, "Whyn't ya ride up with me to my main camp? I could use some help, an' that way ya could bring out the horses fer me."

"Sure. It'd do Mary good to get out of here for a day or two."

"Fine," said Dick. "While you're gettin' in the stock I'll ast her."

Clay had the pack stock in the corral when Dick came to

help him. "Mary won't go, Clay. What's a' matter of her? All I seen her do since I got here is set by the stove and eat candy."

Clay jerked angrily on a latigo strap, drawing an ominous look from the mule he was saddling. "Damned if I know. She took Johnny's dyin' hard. But I thought I got her over that. Now all she'll do is ride out an' watch the horses or sit in the cabin." Clay paused, thinking for a moment before saying, "She's been a real friend to me, a big help. I hate to get mad at her, but sometimes I can't help it."

"I lived with Injuns all my life," said Dick. "I think an' smell like one, an' I believe in a lotta the same things they do. But I'm damned if I savvy 'em. Course you got to unnerstan' that Mary ain't really an Injun no more. She lived with Johnny too long. But she ain't white, neither. Maybe you just oughta beat her. I seen that do a lotta good fer a lotta squaws."

"No. I couldn't do that. She's like a kid. I don't know what to do. I just wish she wasn't so damned lazy!" Clay jerked so hard on a lash rope that the mule he was packing was pulled off balance.

Talking about his problem with Mary made Clay feel better and without saying more he returned to his packing. The two men were soon ready to leave.

The old man guided and Clay followed, leading the pack string. They rode east, ascending the grassy foothills in lazy serpentines that made the climb easy on the horses. The hills soon became sprinkled with stands of aspen trees and expanses of sagebrush mixed with thick grasses. Clay mentioned that some of the aspen leaves had already turned color.

Dick replied, "Frosts come early here. Them settler friendsa yourn won't raise no corn for their hogs."

Somehow the ride into the wilderness erased Clay's peevishness about Mary. His obsessive thoughts about the banker in Iowa were replaced by his impressions of the country they passed through. Here and there large sections of timber had been burned. But the fireweed, berry bushes, and wild strawberries had moved in abundantly to hide the blackened scars. On many slopes there were huge Douglas firs, each tree long past its centennial and still growing. Fall was most becoming to Jackson's Hole.

As they rode over the lip of a shallow basin Dick stopped abruptly and slipped down from his horse. "See 'em?" he whispered. Clay nodded. Dick said, "Take the horses back in them trees. Tie 'em up real good."

"We gonna kill it?" Clay whispered.

"You bet. I kill ever' onea the varmints I kin."

The grizzly bear was busily digging ground squirrels from their burrows while Clay and Little Dick stalked him. The men were downwind from the bear. And with that disadvantage added to its limited eyesight, the bear never knew the men were there.

"You got the long rifle," Dick whispered, "take him through the shoulders, 'bout a thirda the way down his hump."

Clay had never seen one of these great bears before. And the sight of this one nearly overawed him. The bear weighed a half-ton and its dark pelt was tipped with white. Remembering the fate of Marv Feltch's late partner, Clay vowed to make his first shot perfect.

He eased the Winchester's hammer back to full cock. Then, taking a rest against an aspen tree, he aligned the sights, holding a trifle low because he was shooting downhill. Clay fired, never feeling the recoil, then automatically levered another cartridge into the chamber.

The heavy bullet struck the bear squarely on the shoulder. The surprised creature fell back on its haunches, emitting a terrible roar. Then it pitched forward as Dick's bullet struck almost on top of Clay's. The animal's once powerful forelegs could no longer support its great weight. Its broad muzzle thudded into the dirt as the bear pitched forward, jaws snapping and blood streaming from the mouth and nostrils.

"That done it," said Dick. "We got the dirty bastard. We'll wait though till he quits kickin'. Then we kin go down an' take his claws. Injuns buy 'em to make necklaces."

"I guess the hide's no good," asked Clay.

"Naw. The hair's patchy this timea year. Be some fine bear grease there, but we ain't got time to fool with that. It's just a good bear now."

Standing beside the bear's carcass Clay was again awed by the animal's great size. Its huge forepaws left a track that easily accommodated his cap. "Damn, that's a big thing! Doesn't smell too good, either." He seized a big paw and began cutting out the long, curved claws.

Dick said, "Ya don't know how many calves an' colts ya jus' saved by pluggin' this ol' bugger."

In half an hour from the time when they had first seen the grizzly, Little Dick and Clay Baker were in the saddle again. Beyond the basin where they left the bear their route now was over brushy slopes to the top of a wooded ridge. Below the ridge was a deep canyon whose steep walls were alternately covered by stands of dark pines or impenetrable rock slides. Across the canyon rose a flat-topped mountain with rocky outcroppings that resembled the turrets and block houses of a mythic fortress. Wandering among these silent battlements were numbers of dun-colored, bighorn sheep.

Little Dick pointed out a band. "There's your real mountain meat. Git ya a young sheep an' ya got the best."

No wild sheep came within rifle range, however. And although there were numerous bands of elk in the aspen, the men had no wish to stop and shoot any.

They reached Dick's cabin in midafternoon. It lay sheltered in a rocky cleft at the foot of the flat-topped mountain. The building was partially hidden by trees, but from its dooryard Dick could see anyone approaching for a half-mile. The cabin was only ten by twelve feet with a steeply pitched roof of split poles. One tiny window, paned with oiled, semitranslucent rawhide, was the sole source of sunlight when the door was closed.

"Don't you feel cooped up in here?" Clay asked.

"On'y if she storms bad fer a few days. But I'm out an' doin' most ever' day. My trap-line cabins is littler than this, I kin tell ya."

A crude but sturdy ladder was lying propped against the cabin. Dick explained, "I need that sometimes to get up on the snow. One winter there was ten an' twelve feeta snow in places here."

A pile of bleached logs stood in front of the cabin. Clay noticed them while they were unpacking and said, "If you'll unsaddle and stake the horses, I'll take my saddle horse and drag you in some more wood. That snow sounds plenty deep to me."

Clay dragged in wood until dark when the old man called him for supper. He had shot a pair of blue grouse and roasted them in a Dutch oven in his stone fireplace.

The men got up early the next morning, tending the horses and then breakfasting on salt pork and dough gods. In another hour they had saddled, packed the string, and were on the way to the nearest of Dick's trap-line cabins. Enroute Clay shot a young bighorn ewe that had stood watching them as they passed within seventy-five yards. The carcass was dressed and hung in a tree to be picked up on their return.

Dick's line cabin was as small as he had said and partially buried in a hillside. "I jus' sleep here," Dick said. "I don't need no palace." Indeed it was not. But it provided shelter and could, as Dick said it had many times, be a warm place to stay during long storms. Here, too, Clay snaked in firewood while Dick cached his supplies and made his shelter ready for the winter.

"This is as far as we go," said Dick. "My other places are easier ta git to on webs, after it snows."

They were back at Dick's main cabin by midmorning. Dick had taken the heart and liver from the sheep but refused Clay's offer of more. "That's my fun up here all alone, gettin' in some meat."

"I hate to go off and leave you all by yourself," said Clay.

"Naw! This is where I'm happy. The speerits talk ta me of nights, an' I'm the heap big chief. This is the life, boy. I'm a free trapper! Onea the very last. Couldn't stand it no other way. Besides, we'll run inta each other trappin' this winter."

"I know, you old ghost. I never know when you're behind a tree watchin' to see if I make the right set."

"Oooh! That's right. The ghost of the mountains, that's me. Git on now. Yer supper'll be cold."

Clay shook hands with the old man. Then, calling to his pack string, "Hey! Wake up!" he rode back the way they had come.

It was after dark when Clay rode into the ranch yard. He was unsaddling when Mary came.

"How, Clay."

"Hi. Everything here OK? We got a nice sheep."

"I fix," said Mary. While Clay put away his pack outfits Mary skinned back part of the hide on the ewe's hindquarter and cut off several steaks.

Mary's cabin was chilly and Clay noticed that she had to kindle a fire in the stove. "Were you sleeping?" he asked.

"Sleep outside now. Better." She patted her thick chest and inhaled.

For as long as Johnny lived Clay had appreciated the pains Mary took with their food. But now she seemed not to care. She fried the sheep steaks in a dirty pan and put them on the table unseasoned and alone. She did not even brew tea. Clay got a cup of water from the bucket outside the door. It had the thinnest skim of ice on it.

He returned to the table. "Not the middle of September an' it's already freezin'."

Mary said, "Bad place. Too cold. Maybe leave."

The steaks were good but too fresh to be tender. Clay had to chew before he could answer. "You're right. But we got a good start here. You an' Johnny did a lot of work. The worst is over now. Look at all the new stuff we got in. Next summer I'm plannin' on a mowing machine. I'll be able to put up hay for a lot more stock. What do you think of that?"

"Hay, muskeeta," said Mary, leaving the table and taking her accustomed seat by the stove.

Clay said nothing. He had lit the lamp and now, by its light, he saw how dirty the cabin had become. Mouse droppings were on the table. The floor had not been swept in days and every corner had its cobwebs. Dirty dishes and pans were piled on the floor.

Clay felt his anger rising. "Well, blow out the lamp when you're through, Mary. Save all the coal oil we can. I'm gonna hit the hay."

In the morning when Clay came to Mary's cabin he found the lamp still burning and a black streak of smoke rising from its sooted chimney.

"Damn it!" He blew out the lamp and noticed that its reservoir of precious fuel, enough for a week, was nearly empty. He felt an impulse to smash the lamp on the dirty floor. Instead, he

built a fire in the stove and began heating water in the big copper boiler Dick had brought them. With the water heating and
a newly cleaned coffee pot sitting beside it, Clay went out to
find Mary.

She was rolled in a blanket in a makeshift tipi near the
spring. She had hung canvas pack covers from the tipi poles to
provide some shelter. Also hanging from the poles were Indian
charms and fetishes that Clay hadn't seen since Johnny's death.
"I'm sure you're gettin' enough air out here."

Mary turned in her blankets, she had been awake. "How,
Clay." She regarded him for a moment then got up; she was
fully dressed. Mary shuffled a few steps from the tipi. Then, before Clay could even turn his back, Mary squatted. Clay pretended to ignore it but he knew what Mary had made was a
sign of contempt. He walked back to the cabin.

Not until they were seated at the cabin table and eating
breakfast did Clay say anything. "Mary, this is your place. You
and Johnny started the ranch. It's amounting to something.
But you have to take care of it or you'll lose it, savvy?"

Mary gave him a blank look. "You take care."

For an instant Clay thought he might hit her. Then he
shook his head in resignation. He remembered hearing how the
great Shoshone chief, Washakie, stabled his horse in the nice
house Uncle Sam had built for him while he, the chief, slept
outside in a tipi. "I guess I will have to take care of it," he
said.

He put his dishes in the pan and began to wash them and
the others that had been lying on the floor. Mary watched for a
while, then went out. Clay saw her go to the corral and catch
her pony. "That's right," he said, "go out and count your
horses again. Make sure the worthless bastards are in the best
feed!"

Clay finished the dishes and began to clean the cabin. It was
while he was on his hands and knees scrubbing the floor that
he heard horses in the dooryard. Curious, he got up to see a
string of four packed horses standing tied to the hitching rail.
They appeared ready to travel. Mary had ridden to the cabin
and was dismounting.

"What's this?" Clay asked her. "You goin' somewhere?"

"Mary heap tired. This place no good no more. You take. Mary go." She stooped and picked up some dust and wood chips from the ground. Mary placed these in Clay's hand, "You keep. Me give, Johnny give."

Clay had a feeling of elation that was immediately followed by one of regret. He could not feel good about this, but neither could he feel very bad. Perhaps he was disturbed most by the unexpectedness of Mary's decision.

"You sure?" he asked. "Don't go yet. There's money comin' to you. I'll get it."

"You give Mary three hunner' dollars." She held up three weathered fingers.

"Wait here." Clay pointed to the ground before hurrying to unearth his cache of money. He took three hundred dollars from it and reburied the can. Next he peeled the label from a can of tomatoes and scribbled out a bill of sale on the back of it.

Finished, Clay took the paper outside. "This is a bill of sale for this place; horses, cows, everything you've left," Clay said. "If you want me to have everything, sign this paper."

He showed Mary where to mark an "X" on the bill of sale. Below that he appended, "Mary Kelly, Her Mark."

Mary took the money Clay had counted into her hand and carelessly stuffed it into the canvas sack hanging from her saddle horn. Then she climbed heavily into the saddle.

"We shake," she said. "Goo-by."

Mary allowed Clay to grasp her fine-boned hand for just an instant before she pulled it away. It was over.

With the stylish ease that Clay had long admired, Mary wheeled her pony and trotted it to the tethered pack string. Without dismounting she leaned down and untied her lead horse's rope, "Gee-up!"

Mary rode northeast and Clay, hands jammed in his hip pockets, stood in the dooryard watching her. He watched her until she disappeared beyond the screen of cottonwoods along the Little Gros Ventre. He supposed that she would turn east on the main Gros Ventre trail, then ride over the range to the Reservation at Fort Washakie.

Clay returned to the cabin and finished scrubbing the floor.

Next he made an inventory. Mary had taken most of the things that she and Johnny had had plus some flour, salt, and tea. She had also taken all the candy. All of her packing must have been done, Clay decided, while he was in the mountains with Little Dick.

That afternoon Clay moved into the new cabin and put fresh hay in the tick. He worked furiously all afternoon. He dug the root crops from his garden and packed them away to remain cool in boxes of soil and sawdust. He dug a pit around the spring and lined it with stones to form a large basin.

At twilight he saddled his horse and rode out to move his cattle and horses nearer the ranch buildings. Both Mary and Little Dick had said that the Indians would be in the valley soon for the fall hunt. He didn't want them to practice on his livestock.

The cabin was dark when he returned. He had to feel his way to the lamp. While he was locating it and finding a match Clay was bemused by a strange, rhythmic sound. He stopped to listen. But the sound stopped, too, then resumed. "Hell," he said. It was his own breathing.

How loud it had seemed in the new stillness. There was no human sound now unless he made it. The scratching of a nesting mouse under the floor had gained new volume. Coyotes howling far down in the meadow seemed, tonight, to be crouched under his window.

Clay cooked and ate his supper. After washing his dishes he sat down again and looked over at the bench beside the stove where Mary so often sat in the evening. Some nights she had made or mended clothes. She also wove baskets and beaded shirts or moccasins. If she had candy she was likely to just sit there and do nothing but dreamily suck on one piece after another. But, no matter what she had done, she had been there, a living, responsive human being.

Now there was no one. And Clay, for the first time since he had lain hurt and abandoned in the back room of the Riggs post office, remembered again how vast are the boundaries of loneliness.

He went to the shelf and took down a book. It was the Holy Bible. He looked at it for a moment, then replaced it and took down another volume, *The Complete Works of Wm. Shakespeare.* Clay sat down at the table, opened the book, and began turning the pages. He discovered that many of them were fastened together at their outer margins. He tried tearing a doubled page at the fold to separate the leaves. But this made a ragged job and inspired Clay to take out his pocket knife and carefully slit open the pages. For twenty minutes he worked, turning the leaves and sliding the knife between each one. He came to an illustration and stopped to look at it.

It was a picture of Julius Caesar wearing a muscled breastplate and a short armored skirt. Clay studied the picture, then turned the page to see if there was any explanation for such a costume. There was none. He resumed cutting open the pages. When he had finished he was disappointed. The book had made him oddly uncomfortable. Its text was difficult to read and he had found nothing in it that would be of any use to him.

Clay turned in his chair, surveying the empty room. The fresh bed tick was fragrant with its smell of new hay. Clay blew out the lamp, undressed, and crawled between his rough blankets. He lay on his back staring into the blackness. He wondered how Mary was getting along.

Chapter Thirteen

Mary was comfortable. She had pitched her tipi on the edge of an alpine meadow. A small stream burbled through the meadow. All around were tall pines, black now in the darkness. Mary sat in her tipi watching the embers of a dying fire. Her horses were picketed and standing quietly in the meadow. It was colder here than it had been at the ranch. She had wrapped herself in a blanket leaving only her head exposed. In her lap was a bag of candy. Periodically her hand sped from inside the blanket to rummage in the candy bag. Once a piece had been chosen she popped it into her mouth.

The next morning Clay arose to see white frost covering the meadow and the tops of the corral poles. A steamy haze rose from the spring. After breakfast Clay went to look around and threw the horse standing there a fork full of hay. When he had washed the dishes and swept the floor Clay got a bucket of water from the spring and set it on the stand beside the door. It was still early. He took his rifle from the corner and cleaned and oiled it until the weapon gleamed. He sharpened his knife, testing its edge on the hairs along his forearm. He sat for a few minutes, doing nothing.

"Damn!" He jumped up. "You can't do this!" Clay got his saddle horse and rode northeast, following Mary's tracks. Mary had always liked to travel at a fast walk and Clay noticed how her horses' hooves had cut sharply into the dry soil, indicating speed.

He would have been surprised, therefore, to know that Mary had not ridden far and was now camped in a lonely canyon a couple of miles off the main Gros Ventre trail.

For a moment Clay considered following her, to see if she had got out of the valley safely. But when he reached the point where he would either have to follow Mary or turn off to the Andviks', he turned off.

In the cottonwoods beside the Little Gros Ventre he found two canvas tipis with smoke-blackened tops. Three dejected-looking ponies stood nearby, tied to trees. A pole drying rack sagged under the weight of the darkened strips of meat hanging from it. Some children came to peek out at him from the dark entrance of one of the tipis. Standing in front of the other was a dour squaw wrapped in a gray blanket. Clay waved to her, calling, "How!" The squaw made no response.

The Andvik brothers were working in their hay meadow as Clay rode up. Their hay had been cut and shocked for some time, but the brothers had been too busy to bring it all into the stack.

"How about a job?" Clay said as he reached the two grinning brothers.

"Oh ja. Dot vould be fine. Ve be grateful to you, Clay."

As they worked Clay said, "I see you got some new neighbors over on the creek."

"Ja," said Lars. "Dey come two days ago. Dey be more camps up de country." He pointed to the north.

"They friendly?" Clay asked.

"No. But dey not mean edder. Ve do our vork and dey do deirs," said Iver.

"You didn't see my Injun with 'em did you? I lost her yesterday."

The Swedes stopped work and leaned on their pitchforks. "No!" said Lars.

"Yep," said Clay. "She sold me the place, lock and stock, then took five horses and outfits and rode off northeast. I guess she's headin' for the Reservation."

"Vell, Clay," Lars said, "maybe it be for da best. You know."

"Maybe," said Clay, beginning to rake again. He worked all day for the Andviks and was happy to have supper with them. Helga Andvik was a good housekeeper. The children were clean. And her floor was freshly scrubbed. She was clean herself in a fresh, if mended dress. One of their cows had calved and Helga was milking her, using some of the milk for custard and puddings and making butter from the cream. That night she put a dollop of cottage cheese on each man's plate.

"Gosh!" Clay exclaimed, "I haven't had pot cheese for a year."

Helga smiled and her husband beamed proudly. "Maybe you get you a *Svenska flicka* now, Clay. A reg'lar vife?"

Clay bridled, then he remembered what Marv Feltch had said about the difficulties of adjusting to the rapidly changing times. "Mary Kelly was a fine woman," he said, "but, you know, most Injuns aren't cut out for housekeepin'." He turned to Helga. "Are there any more at home like you?"

"Oh ja! Many fine Svedish girls. But, oh," Helga paused, her smile fading, "dey are so far avay, so far."

Iver said, "Helga, she get lonely sometime. Maybe you get vife, Clay. Keep Helga comp'n'y."

"Maybe, you know what they say, though—this country's hell on horses and women. I might have trouble findin' one that'd live here."

He didn't mention the woman who had found him, the one he believed was Alma Warburton. But it was mostly on Mrs. Warburton's account that he had come to see the Andviks. Clay said, "It's goin' on a year since I was outside the valley. I figured on trappin' this winter and goin' out next spring. But now, with Mary gone, I'd like to go sooner—if I could get someone to take care of my outfit."

Speaking almost in unison Lars and Iver said, "Ve take care uf you!"

And so, over a buttered, sourdough biscuit with chokecherry syrup poured over it, Clay and the Andviks made a deal. He would help them until early October. Then, before the snows closed them in, Clay would leave for Eagle Rock. He would go on from there to see his parents in Wisconsin. He did not mention that he would also stop in Iowa to see the mysterious banker, Mr. Blount.

The late September days were winey in the morning and warm in the afternoon. But around her camp Mary noticed that the leaves on the willows had all turned a vivid yellow. The meadow grass was buff-colored, and here and there a golden aspen leaf drifted down from the tree branches. Mary puttered around her camp, braiding her hair and fastening medicine bundles to the tipi poles. She cut some willows, then peeled the bark to make a backrest.

One night it snowed and she awoke to a camp that was newly white and winter silent. By afternoon all the snow had melted. Nevertheless, it prompted Mary to gather a great pile of dry wood and place it beside her tipi, within easy reach.

She may have worked too hard for that night she was sick and vomited. She was dizzy, too, and had to crawl on her hands and knees after wood to replenish the fire. When the flames were bright and rising again she lay back on her blankets. A wrenching pain twisted her back causing her to instinctively draw up her legs. When the pain had passed Mary realized the time had come, she was going to have her baby.

She had had babies before. Brown-skinned boys and girls drawn squawling and slick from her by the Indian midwives. But that had been long ago. Johnny Kelly would never give her a baby and she had been ashamed. Later, she forgot her shame. They had both grown too old to want a child.

Before her contractions became too severe and frequent, Mary was able to draw a heavy log onto her fire. Sweat drenched her when she had done it, but she knew she must have yet another or the fire might go out. It was midnight before she was able to get the second heavy log to her fire. And when she had placed it, Mary fell back on her blankets, sick and exhausted.

No sooner had she lain down again than another contraction seized her. It was the worst one so far and she cried out. The child was coming. She wanted to guide it, to help it into the world with her. But she was racked by still another contraction and fell back. Her head thumped on the ground but she scarcely felt it.

Mary caught her breath only to be tortured again and again by almost unbearable pains. During a lull in her agony Mary reached down and felt herself. And what she felt was more horrifying to her than the pain. Her baby was being born backwards.

Mary clenched her hands into fists, breathing deeply and straining. The pains, coming faster than ever, seemed to be ripping her apart. But she would not give into them. With each agonizing contraction she took a deep breath and strained, pushing down with all the strength in her body. It happened over and over again and the pain was endless.

Then, with one final, convulsive shudder, Mary's body heaved and she delivered the child. She lifted it up. In the firelight she could see the cord, twisted tightly around her little boy's neck. He was dead, strangled in what had until so recently been the protective shelter of his mother's body.

Mary lowered the baby and fell back on her blankets. Tears flooded her eyes and ran down her lined cheeks. In a few minutes she was able to reach out for the soft blanket she had made for her baby. She wrapped the still body in the brightly embroidered and beaded blanket, then held it tightly in her arms until morning.

Chapter Fourteen

Sometime in the twilight of early morning, Mary fell asleep. When she awakened it was late afternoon. The sun was shining and her picketed horses were fidgeting on their ropes.

Mary opened her son's blanket one last time to be sure, eternally sure, the child was dead. It was so. The tiny face was shriveled and black. She closed the blanket again; she did not want to see any more.

Using water from a pot beside her, Mary washed. She had a fear that the smell of her blood might attract a coyote or even a scavenging wolf or bear. After she had washed and sat up for an hour Mary felt strong enough to add wood to the still-smoking coals of her fire. Although the afternoon was mild and sunny, the rising flames felt good to her and were company. She ate a piece of jerky and drank a cup of water.

In another hour Mary made herself stand and carry her baby to a pine tree. Using a piece of rawhide rope she tied the little bundle to a branch, then slowly walked away. The words of a death song rose in her mind, but she was too exhausted to bring them to her lips. In her tipi she lay down again and ate a piece of candy. It was almost the last.

What evil spirit, she wondered, had followed her to this place and twisted the cord around her son's neck? Mary looked at the fetishes and medicine bundles hanging from her lodge poles. It would be good to reach Fort Washakie where a shaman of her people would know the right charms to use.

The heat from her fire and also the sun, now high overhead, warmed Mary and made her drowsy. She fell asleep and when she awoke this time it was early morning. She sat up, feeling much stronger. In two or three more days she would resume her journey to the Reservation.

Clay missed Mary and yet, having no inkling of her pregnancy, was also glad she had gone. The work at Andviks, in addition to making his own ranch ready for winter, left him little time for brooding about Mary.

As the settlers built their fences, strengthened their corrals, and banked insulating dirt around the bases of their cabins, they kept a collective eye on the weather. Snow would bring the elk, and they were all eager for the hunt to begin. In early October it snowed six inches in Jackson's Hole. A few elk migrated into the valley and Clay helped the Andviks shoot five fat cows. After the carcasses were dressed and hung on the shady sides of the Andvik cabin, Clay said it was time he left.

In addition to his saddle and pack horses, Clay decided to take eight other horses to sell in Eagle Rock. There was a snake-headed white gelding that he especially wanted to be rid of.

Lars Andvik came on the afternoon of October 9, 1885, and moved into Clay's cabin. The next morning he rode with Clay to the ford and helped him push the loose stock across the river.

Once Clay was safely across, Lars took off his cap and waved a vigorous farewell. Clay raised his arm, "So long, Lars!" Then he turned his horse and crowded the loose string up the trail ahead of him.

It was a chilly, overcast day, a good day for traveling. The bunch took the trail well, and by early afternoon Clay had pushed them across the divide and begun the long descent into Idaho Territory. Before sundown Clay herded his remuda into the small clearing where he and Little Dick had camped that summer.

He tied his pack horse to a tree while he unsaddled and picketed the saddle horse. From the pack he took a small bag of oats. Using the grain for bait, Clay quickly lured in and caught all the loose horses—except the white gelding. He let the white horse roam, knowing it would hang around its picketed companions.

It was a good camp, but something Clay found there made him uneasy. Someone had camped in the meadow since he and

Little Dick had been there. The horse droppings he found were too fresh. Clay slept lightly that night and close to his rifle.

Morning came with a cold wind that set the tree tops swaying. Clay was up and packing at first light. He did not risk building a fire. He tied five of the loose horses behind his pack horse, knotting each animal's lead rope to the tail of the one in front of it. When he rode out he drove the other three horses, including the unruly white gelding, ahead of him. Clay was amused at how easily he handled his horses now when he compared his performance coming into Jackson's Hole a year earlier.

Dense timber bordering the higher sections of the trail helped keep the animals on course. But lower down the thick forest was replaced by more open timber interspersed with patches of aspen. Clay hurried his horses through these open areas, his haste forcing the three animals ahead of him to stay on the trail.

As he rode, Clay maintained a careful watch. But he saw and heard nothing. Even the normally raucous pine squirrels sat quietly on their tree limbs while he passed below them. Clay hoped the menacing weather, not something even more dangerous, had caused the unnatural silence.

The horses Clay was driving began lifting their heads and looking around. The white gelding raised his head and whinnied enthusiastically. Although Clay strained to hear a reply he heard nothing except the thump and clatter of his horses' hooves.

The Indians struck just east of Game Creek. The trail narrowed there along an old stream bed. There were five of them, renegade Sioux. The first to burst from cover and turn his horse sideways in the trail was wearing a round beaver cap with a crucifix on the front. He was quickly followed by two others, all wearing gingham shirts and choker collars made from bone. One carried an old Springfield single-shot carbine. Another brandished a bow and arrows while Fur Cap waved a long-barreled Colt's revolver. The Sioux were grinning.

The other two bucks came in behind Clay, trotting their ponies to catch up. Clay kicked his horse into a trot. The Indian with the Springfield was cocking and aiming it, while Fur Cap continued to brandish his revolver.

"Get out!" Clay's throat was so tight that his voice only croaked. His horses sensed the excitement. The white gelding in front began whinnying and threw up his tail. He was trotting now, head up and almost stylish. Fur Cap was twenty yards ahead. The Sioux behind Clay were gaining; one of them held a knife, apparently planning to cut the lead ropes on Clay's trailing horses.

Realizing he must not stop, Clay banged his heels into his horse's ribs, forcing him to pound over the rocks while the driven horses fled before him. Clay was yelling, incoherent but louder. Without looking back he looped the pack horse's lead rope around his saddle horn and snubbed it there. If the pack horse balked now he could jerk Clay's horse down or rip off the saddle. Clay had gambled to keep the horses close behind him.

Without slowing his pace he jerked his Winchester from the scabbard under his leg. The brave with the Springfield fired but held high to avoid hitting the men behind Clay. Clay raised his own rifle so the Indians would see it and worked the lever.

The wild shot from the Springfield startled the pursuing Indians and made them hang back. Ahead, the bowman was drawing his bow and Fur Cap was holding the Colt's in both hands, aiming. Clay ducked, pressing himself against his horse's neck. He never stopped yelling and in two bounds the driven horses were milling with the Indians' ponies. Without warning the snake-headed white gelding bared his yellow teeth and bit Fur Cap's pony on the cheek.

Instantly, the Indian's pony whirled, trying to kick, and as it did, Fur Cap accidentally fired his revolver. His pony wheeled again, thudding into the bowman's horse. Hooves clattered on rock, the Indians yelled, and jerked savagely on their reins. Horses spun and kicked while their riders fought to control them.

Clay plunged through the gap torn between the blockading horses. As he came abreast of Fur Cap, the Indian was simultaneously turning his pony and cocking the Colt's. Clay reached out and speared him hard in the chest with the muzzle of his Winchester. The blow pitched the Indian out of his saddle and Clay charged ahead; as he went, he flipped the lead rope off his saddle horn. The pack horse veered away, and got the rope tying its tail to the following horse under the tail of an Indian pony. That pony squealed, reared, and threw its rider. Ahead the trail lay open and Clay jammed weight in his stirrups and lashed his horse into a gallop that never slowed in two miles.

Clay glanced back frequently as he fled, but there was no sign of following Sioux. Still, he was afraid to stop until his horse began to lather. Then he slowed the animal gradually, stopping it in a patch of pines. Clay dismounted and led his horse behind some trees where he could watch the back trail. It was there that he found his fingers had cramped around the grip of his rifle. Even more remarkable to Clay was the condition of the rifle itself. The hammer, which had been at full cock when he charged past the Indians, was down. Clay worked the lever and a spent cartridge case sprang from the breech.

He picked up the casing. He did not remember having fired but here was the proof. It had to have happened when he jammed the rifle's muzzle into Fur Cap's chest. And he must have pulled the trigger.

Clay leaned against the tree, resting his forehead on his arm. He felt enormously tired. Inside him there was a new emptiness and he could feel his heart pounding inside it. "I've just killed an Indian," he thought. Later he might want to talk about it, but now he only wanted to get out of there.

He adjusted his saddle, straightening the blankets and tightening the cinch. The horse was breathing easily and cropping the grass at his feet. Clay set out again, riding at a slow lope for a mile, then slowing to a walk for a half mile before lifting the horse into a lope again. When he had gone five miles he stopped and dismounted to walk a half mile. He dared not tire his horse unnecessarily with the strong chance that there were four vengeful Sioux close behind him.

At the first homestead he reached, Clay stopped and told the man there of his skirmish with the Indians.

"I know all about 'em," said the homesteader. "They been aggravatin' the people for a month. They killed onea my heifers an' only took the loins." He added that a detachment of cavalry from Fort Hall was in the district now trying to round up the renegades. The homesteader took Clay's written description of the nine horses he had lost and promised to give it to the soldiers if they passed that way.

Clay said, "The leader was a big buck, about thirty, with a cross on his hat. I think I shot him."

The homesteader, who was a bachelor, said, "Good! I hope ya killed him. All this mollycoddlin' just makes 'em worse." He fed Clay salt pork and beans while Clay's horse worked ravenously at a pile of hay. When they had both eaten, Clay gave the man a dollar and resaddled.

He rode steadily and reached the farm home of Marv Feltch in the early evening. The barking of the merchant's two dogs brought him out.

"Hello! Who's there?"

"Clay Baker from Jackson's Hole!"

"I'll be damned! Didn't expect to see you till next summer."

Clay swung down, knees feeling weak from his long ride. "This ol' horse has had a hard day. Could I bum some grain and give him a feed?"

"You bet. Take him around to the barn. I'll bring a lantern."

While the animal munched noisily on a box full of oats, Clay rubbed and curried it with special care. Feltch was sitting on some sacked grain, watching. "Your horse looks about used up."

"You should have seen him this mornin'." Clay described his brush with the Indians.

When he had finished Feltch said, "I wondered where your pack horse was. I been hearin' 'bout those bucks. Come in here to raise some hell afore they go back to their reserve an' eat on Uncle Sam all winter."

"I guess they'll be wearing my clothes and sleepin' in my blankets now. I hate losin' my horses to 'em."

"You been in a wild country with wild men all right. You sure don't look like the young banker that come here last year."

Clay said, "I've cussed you an' Jackson's Hole a thousand times since I left here. I never knew there were so many ways a man could get killed in a place."

"Now, Clay, you did real well for your first year there."

"Yes, I made about as much money as I'd have made workin' in the bank, maybe more. And I own a ranch now. Mary sold out to me. I was bringing my horses over to sell. But even if I lose 'em all, it still leaves me with over thirty head. About all I can say for my cows, though, is that I pulled 'em through the worst winter I ever saw."

"Come on now and have some supper," said Feltch. "I want to hear about all this."

Mrs. Feltch sat Clay down in her big, lamp-lit kitchen and fed him a huge supper of beef steak, fried potatoes, and corn on the cob. Clay ate four ears, all dripping with butter. Later, he sipped hot coffee and told the Feltches about Jackson's Hole.

"It sounds like a dime novel story," said Clay. He told them about the death of Johnny Kelly and losing his ski in the mountains.

Feltch said, "Little Dick told me about Johnny. I wish Mary had come this way. She could of had a room here and helped my missis for as long as she wanted to stay."

Clay did not mention that before Mary left she had given up cabin living in favor of a tipi. He did say, however, that Mary had apparently become despondent and lost all interest in her ranch. "All she seemed to want to do was ride out with the horses," Clay said.

"Injuns are funny critters," said Feltch, giving his wife an arch look. "I seen others go the same way when they got older. But Mary ought to realize there ain't no life for her over on the reserve. She's not a real Injun no more. They might not take up with her."

"I thought on my way back from the States that I might come through Fort Washakie and see her," said Clay.

"That'd be nice in ya. If ya find her, tell her she's allus got a place here."

It was long after midnight when Feltch finally called a recess, "By hell, boy, you don't know what it's like for me to hear about yer life. I'd give anythin' to be able to git on a horse ag'in an' see the frontier afore she's all gone."

Feltch saw the disbelief in Clay's face and held up a hand. "I know she's hard, and it'll be hard for a while yet. But you'll look back some day, maybe even in the next century, and know ya was a man out there. Not onea these here boosters that comes in here wearin' suits and cowboys' hats. But ya kin tell me more tomorra. It's way past our bedtimes. I'm gonna try ta git them horses back for ya. You'll want ta rest up. I got some mail for ya, too." Feltch took two letters from his desk drawer and handed them to Clay.

One was from his parents in Wisconsin. They had been overjoyed to learn that he was doing well and to receive the fifty dollars. The second letter was from Banker Blount in Aldora, Iowa. But inside the bank's envelope was another addressed to Clay and marked, "PERSONAL." It contained this letter:

"Dear Mr. Baker,

For reasons of my own I wish to remain anonymous for the present. But I also wish to help you financially, or in any other way, with your project out West.

If you will describe your projects and communicate your needs to Mr. Blount at the bank, I will see to it that he helps you. I understand Mr. Feltch will act as an agent in Eagle Rock."

The letter was signed, "A Friend."

Clay went to sleep that night composing a tightly-worded telegram to M. Theodore Blount telling him of his imminent arrival in Aldora.

Feltch was at breakfast when Clay came in the next morning carrying his money belt. In addition to almost five hundred dollars in coins and currency, he had Joseph McGraw's pound of gold dust. "I took the dust off the man that drowned," said Clay placing the belt on the table. "Has there been any word from his family?"

"Nope," said Feltch. "Course that Dutchy with him couldn't talk English and the other feller's backside was on fire to git outa here. I can hold this dust in my safe till you get back. Better yet, I'll cash it for you now. If some McGraws shows up, I'll pay 'em off an' bill ya."

Clay agreed, feeling better to change McGraw's gold for Uncle Sam's currency.

Because Clay Baker was still an outcast in Eagle Rock, Feltch suggested he remain on the farm. "I'll handle your business an' bring ya some travelin' clothes from the store. The train leaves for Ogden ever' mornin' at 8:10. I'll git ya a ticket, then we'll flag it at the crossin' south of town when ya want to go."

On the third day after his arrival Clay was driven by Feltch to the flag stop and put aboard the Ogden train. Clay was amazed at how fast the train flew down the track. And the farther it carried him from Jackson's Hole, the greater became his feeling of exuberant freedom. Without realizing it, Clay was a young man who needed to raise a little hell.

Ogden was a good place to do that. But Clay, pressing his full money belt to be sure it was in place, rented a room in a quiet boardinghouse and put in a call for 5 A.M. He was catching the early train east and did not want to risk missing it. Before going to bed he sat in his room and read the newspapers. How much he had missed in the past year! And how little it really mattered!

Clay was three and a half days on the trains to Cedar Rapids. He rented a hotel room there and took a bath in a great white tub whose water carried with it fine particles of Midwestern grit. They were left on the tub's bottom when he drained it and Clay was embarrassed lest the black porter think it was dirt he'd washed off himself.

That evening was spent reading in his room while a bellboy had his suit out being pressed. Clay rose early the next morning to be shaved in the hotel barber shop and have his hair trimmed.

"Who's been cuttin' your hair, sir?" asked the barber.

"For a while no one cut it; but the wife of a friend of mine trimmed it some before I left Eagle Rock."

"Well, sir, no offense to the lady an' all, but I'd recommend you get a little professional service out there. You've got a fine head of hair, but it don't look like it's been cut right in a year."

"It hasn't."

The barber "tssked," then asked Clay if he was in "the big city to have a little fun?"

"No. I've got to catch a train out to Aldora."

The barber grunted disapprovingly.

In the train Clay sat beside the window looking out. The

trees had been touched by the first frosts and were turning color. They gave the countryside a warm, hospitable look. Every farm house had trees around it. But there were so many farms! Clay thought the land here must be overcrowded and probably expensive. And while he never thought he would, Clay missed the mountains. The Tetons and the Gros Ventre Range to the east of them had once seemed to form prison walls. Now he remembered them as part of home country and something he could depend upon. Iowa, he thought, was just little rises and nobs with more corn and pigs on the other side. So many pigs!

The train made several stops enroute to Aldora. Mail was loaded and unloaded. Clay saw milk cans and crates of eggs standing on depot platforms and once, a stack of crates containing full-grown brown hens. The train's leisurely pace didn't bother him. He could not help being nervous about meeting Blount. And what if "A Friend" weren't Alma Warburton? Would it then be proper to give Blount the fancy box of chocolates he'd bought at the hotel cigar stand? Too bad he couldn't send them out to Mary. Then Clay reminded himself that Aldora wasn't Wall Street and Blount wasn't Mr. Vanderbilt. Blount would have received his telegram and now all that remained was to go to his bank, look him in the eye, and shake hands.

Finally the conductor passed through the car, slapping his hands on the seat backs and announcing, "Aldora, nex' stop. Five minutes."

Clay was waiting in the car's vestibule when the train stopped. The conductor came and put a metal stepstool at the bottom of the car's steps.

"Watch yer step," he said but not to Clay. It was a company regulation. This solid and deeply-tanned young cowboy could obviously watch his step in places far more dangerous than the railway depot in Aldora, Iowa.

As usual, the main street of Aldora was quiet. Two old men were sitting in the sunshine outside the depot. A few buggies and farm wagons stood behind their tethered teams at hitching rails along the street. The Farmers' and Merchants' Bank of Aldora was the two-story brick building up one block and across the street from the depot. Clay took a firmer grip on the handle of his new valise and started toward the bank.

M. Theodore Blount was a middle-aged man with graying hair and a little pot belly that was not quite hidden under his vest. Clay had met a hundred just like him when he was trying to land a job in a bank.

Blount shook hands. "Well, sir. You're Mr. Clay Baker from Wyoming? Always wanted to see your part of the country. Never had the time. I guess you're curious about your new partner—prospective partner, I should say? Yes. Well, the lady I mentioned in my letter is a widow, Mrs. Alma Simpson. She doesn't want to be bothered by promoters and such so she remains anonymous and I manage her affairs."

"Does she live here in town?"

Blount folded his hands on top of his polished desk, "No, the Simpson place is five miles east of here. Mrs. Simpson leases her land, but she lives in the farm house. It's been fixed up considerably since she bought the place."

Clay asked, "She knows I'm coming?"

"Of course. She's sending someone in to pick you up." Blount continued, "That place where you are? Ah . . ."

"Jackson's Hole."

"That's it. It sounds very western and ah, primitive."

"It is," said Clay. "I had to shoot my way out to get here."

Blount gave him a perfunctory smile. "Aha! The Wild West. Seriously, Baker, how much land have you out there?"

"It's never been surveyed. It's all federal land. But I am claiming the Kelly ranch which I bought a few weeks ago plus my own homestead and desert land entry. That's a section. I also claim as my range about a section and a half north and west of the ranch. I may file a timber claim to help hold that. I filed on the other land before I left Eagle Rock. Then, one of my neighbors has promised to sell me his relinquishment on 320 acres. It all adds up to better'n 2,000 acres."

"My word," said Blount. "I never cease to be amazed at the size of western properties."

"Mine's just a little outfit," said Clay. "I plan to have a lot more."

"Is this land fertile?" Blount asked.

"Yes. Course it really helps if you can irrigate it. But you should have seen my vegetable garden last summer; carrots as thick as your wrist, an' lots of spinach and lettuce—till the frost got it. But it's a cattle country. The seasons are short an' the winters last all year."

"How many people live in Jackson's Hole? How close are your markets?"

"Right in the valley there are just the Andviks an' me. That's six. Then, Little Dick Pierce is usually up in the hills, and there's an old miner down the Snake River about twenty-five miles. We're close to a hundred miles from the markets, but I expect the Army up in the new Yellowstone Park to become a market."

Blount was shaking his head, "You're too far from your markets. What do you think an acre of land in Jackson's Hole is worth?"

"The Law say $1.25 an acre, but some of the Wyoming cattlemen are talking a nickel."

"I suspect the cattlemen know more about land values than the government does," said Blount. "How much will it take to bring this valley into production?"

"It'll take a lot. Everything's there, grass, timber, water. But it'll take a lot of work by a lot of people before it amounts to much."

Blount said, "Do you know that in places like yours it's the second and sometimes the third generation that finally makes a profit on such land?"

Clay nodded, "But every generation is gonna need someone to give 'em advice and make their loans. That fella's gonna make money, he can't help it. And I'm gonna be him." Clay hesitated. "Shouldn't I be telling this to Mrs. Simpson?"

"Mrs. Simpson will surely want to ask you a lot more than I have. She wants you to work here in the bank for a few months this winter. She seems to think I can teach you something. But she'll tell you all about that. She's made arrangements for you to live in our boardinghouse. But I see her man out in the street with her rig. You'd better go."

The last doubt about Mrs. Simpson vanished that afternoon when Clay walked into the parlor of her comfortable farm home. Alma Warburton took Clay's hand, "Clay! Come in! That lonely place out in Wyoming must agree with you. You're the picture of health—but you look more like a cowboy than a banker."

"Lately I am more of a cowboy. Iowa seems to favor you, too. You're looking well."

"I've got a lot more gray hair than when you last saw me."

"We've both been through some hard times, Mrs. Simpson."

She took Clay's hand in both of hers, "You can call me Alma. We're going to be partners, aren't we?"

"I hope so."

Alma led Clay into her parlor where they sat down. He asked her, "Do you live out here all by yourself?"

"No. The man who drove you out lives over the stable, and I have a boarder. She teaches in our grade school. She'll be home soon. You'll like her."

They were chatting over coffee when the door opened and a young woman entered, then paused, hesitant.

"Faith! Come in. This is the man, Clay Baker, I've been telling you about."

Clay stood as the young teacher crossed the room. She was not pretty. Faith Ward was large without being fat and nearly as tall as Clay. She had brownish hair done up in a bun at the back of her neck. Faith had broad shoulders and the flounce at the waist of her green dress didn't quite hide the fact that her hips were broad, too. But Faith's smile was warm and revealed her good teeth. They shook hands and Clay liked the strength he found. Some women's hands reminded him of gripping the plucked neck of a dead turkey.

Faith said, "I hope you're going to tell us some of your western adventures. I read all I can find about the West. I loved *The Oregon Trail*, and I've just finished *The Great Divide*."

"I've seen those places," said Clay, "but I haven't had time to read about 'em."

"I've seen them, too," said Alma, "and I don't think most of those places are nearly as romantic as the writers claim. Clay, don't you remember all the dirty, drunken Indians who hung around Eagle Rock begging? They never struck me as 'noble savages.'"

"No, me either. But two of my best friends had Indian wives an' they're both fine women. One of 'em speaks English like a white woman. But they're not like us; neither one can read her own name. The changes out West are hard on the Injuns. A lot of 'em can't understand what's happening."

"You haven't a squaw in a tipi out there in Wyoming, have you, Clay?" Alma asked, just a bit sharply, Clay thought.

"No, nor in my house, either. But I just bought a part of my ranch from an Injun woman. And, for the next few years at least, I'll get along with those people. I have to."

Faith asked him, "Are there truly wild Indians in Jackson's Hole?"

"About as wild as they come. But they don't live there all the time."

"The Indians may be more intelligent than I thought," said Alma.

Faith looked at the watch pinned to her small bosom, "I hope you'll excuse me. There's a choir practice tonight, and I'd like to change before supper. It's nice meeting you, Mr. Baker."

Clay remained standing until the young woman left the room. Alma said, "Sit down, Clay. I hope you like her. Faith is a fine, intelligent person. She'd make you a good wife."

Clay grinned. "Your husband told me he liked seeing his debtors saddled with a husky young wife. Miss Ward's nice, but I came here to see you."

"Clay, you don't really know me. I'm a very practical woman. Too practical I guess or I'd never have married that freckled bag of daily balances named Warburton. Oh, some of our life was all right. He used to discuss the business with me. I like to think I was a good adviser. I'm the one who got him to send for you after I read your employer's letter."

"I never underestimated you. But you still surprise me. How did you get to be Mrs. Simpson?"

"There never was a 'Mr. Simpson'. It seemed wisest after I left Idaho to start fresh, with a new name. When you have some money, Clay, you can be anyone you want to be. So I am Mrs. Simpson."

Alma got up, smiling. "But what are your interests? I have some Kentucky whiskey that's supposed to be very good."

Clay drank the whiskey slowly, with a little water. "The only thing that could possibly improve this is a little of my spring water."

"If you really like that whiskey," said Alma, "I'll have some casks sent out to you."

"Oh, that'd be too expensive. And I'm not much of a drinker."

Alma took a deep breath; she still had a good figure. "Clay, I'm frugal. I'm not sending you back out there like some English lord with a lot of French champagne and a grand piano. But I know a man needs a drink sometimes, and it ought to be a good one. The Lord knows, you haven't many luxuries."

Faith came in at that moment wearing a dark serge dress, and the three of them went into the kitchen to eat. Alma said, "I didn't think you'd mind eating in the kitchen, Clay. It's cozy and we don't have to run back and forth with things for the dining room."

"It's fine. I'm not used to dining rooms."

"Will you be staying long, Mr. Baker?" Faith asked.

"I'm here at Mrs. Simpson's pleasure. We have some business to discuss. When we're finished I'm going on to Wisconsin and visit my folks. I haven't seen them in four years. Then I'll come back here and work in Mr. Blount's bank till the weather breaks and I can get back to Wyoming."

Supper was a huge sirloin roast, savory in its own juices. Alma had baked carrots and big, mild onions with it. There was corn and pickled beets and apple sauce along with tray after tray of hot, crusty rolls.

"We don't eat like this in Wyoming," said Clay, taking his third helping of meat and potatoes.

It pleased Alma to feed such an appreciative guest, "There are lots of things here you won't find in Jackson's Hole. I have ice cream and chocolate cake for dessert."

Clay looked wounded. "I forgot there were such things. I'm pretty full."

"Tell you what, then," said Alma. "You walk Faith down to the church, it's only a mile, and when you come back I'll have my kitchen cleaned up and we'll have our dessert together." Clay agreed.

There was a chill in the air but it was a clear night with a moon so bright that Clay and Faith didn't need the lantern Alma made them carry.

"Fall is certainly here," said Faith.

Clay chuckled. "This is like Dixie for me. I've already seen the first snow at home. I'm enjoying your weather."

"Have you known Mrs. Simpson long?" asked Faith.

"I knew her out West. But I was surprised to hear from her again."

"She's told me about you, and we have been looking forward to your visit since Mr. Blount said you were coming."

"You've both gone to a lot of trouble for me," said Clay. "Everything here seems special. When you're livin' alone you can really get tied up in a little knot. That country out there's so big you wouldn't think so, but it's true."

Faith said, "I hope you have a good visit and enjoy yourself."

Leaving her at the church steps, Clay tipped his hat, then returned to Alma's.

"How was your walk?" Alma asked when she opened her front door for him.

"It was fine. She's a nice woman, and I needed to walk off some of that supper." Clay and Alma were sitting across from each other at the kitchen table. He ate two helpings of cake and ice cream. "I haven't had anything like that since you used to feed me back in Eagle Rock."

A few minutes later Alma's hired man came around with the rig and drove Clay back into town.

Chapter Fifteen

The next morning Clay returned to Alma's farm to talk business. "OK, where do you want to start?"

"I used to love it back in Eagle Rock when you told me all your plans. You had wonderful dreams. It reminded me of the summer days when I was a girl and used to lie on our lawn at home. I'd look up at the clouds and imagine I could see all sorts of things; knights and castles, sailing ships, and sandy beaches with palm trees and buried treasure."

"Was I that silly?"

"No, just ambitious. It was one of the things that made me interested in you."

"After the last year," said Clay, "things don't shine as bright as they used to. I was thinking this morning that I ought to settle down on a place like this. Then I wouldn't have to worry about Injuns, wolves, or forty-below weather any more."

"You can do that," Alma said, "but would you be happy?"

Clay tossed his arms, "I'd be happy for about a month. I know you'd think Jackson's Hole is a hell of a place. And there have been a lot of times when I thought it was worse than that. You'd never guess that such a pretty country has so many ways of killin' you."

"Then why stay? You never have to go back. Do something else."

"I haven't given up on the banking business. But it'll be years before I could get another bank job out West. Someday there'll be a bank in Jackson's Hole, an' I'll own it. That valley has so much potential that I'll be damned if I'll let it beat me. Besides, I own some of it. It's the first land I'ever owned in my life. I never knew how much difference there is in working on your own place an' somebody else's."

"Sometimes you make it sound as if that valley is your enemy. Not that I blame you. I think the West is a terrible place," Alma said.

Clay grinned. "Hasn't there got to be a place for all the terrible people to go? You wouldn't want us all here in Iowa."

"People are people, Clay; they don't change much. But in the banking business we found they're a little nicer when life isn't so hard. Not that things should be too easy for people. But in the West they're often much too hard. The West destroys people."

"Life's gonna be hard in Jackson's Hole. I know that. But somebody's gonna make a go out there, and it might as well be me."

Alma asked, "What would you call 'success,' Clay?"

He thought for a moment then replied, "Being able to wake up in the morning and not worry about money."

"Is that what you do now?"

"Pretty much. I never realized it till Marv Feltch mentioned it. I always wake up thinking or worrying about money."

"Do you like rich people?"

"I like you," said Clay.

Alma laughed. "I'm not rich, my dear. I guess I am what you'd call 'comfortable.' I got our cash out of Eagle Rock, but all the investments were impounded. By the time the attorneys finish milking them, there won't be any investments. I had some money from my father's estate. But most of that is invested. What I am saying is that I'm not rich. I wouldn't want to be rich. The rich are such a dreary, grasping lot."

"So are the poor," said Clay.

Alma said, "My father used to say 'The only thing worse than not having enough money is having too much.' Now, come on. Let me show you my farm."

It was a charming place. They picked themselves an apple, then gathered the eggs and tossed wheat to the clucking chickens. In the pasture Clay admired Alma's sleek driving horses. "They're sure beauties."

"I love them. Let's take them for a drive. We could go past the school this afternoon and bring Faith home." Alma smiled. "Remember, I picked her out for you."

Clay felt embarrassed and Alma smiled at his discomfort. He was more at home discussing the development of Jackson's Hole. And Alma was impressed by the care and concentration of thought Clay had given the project.

When the day came that he was to leave, she saw him off at the station. "Thanks a lot, Alma. I've had the best time I've ever had in my life."

"I'm glad, Clay. Please come back and see me again."

He would have been ashamed to admit it, but Clay's visit to his parents was an anti-climax. His parents seemed to have aged so much in four short years. They were preoccupied with their farm and their church. Nothing else mattered much to them. So, after a week of increasing restlessness Clay made ready to leave. He shook hands with his father, who cried, kissed his mother, who blessed him, and hugged his brothers and sisters to him. Then he climbed onto a wagon seat beside his brother and was driven to the railroad station.

Although he had written Alma of his arrival, there was no buggy waiting at the station to meet him. Clay rented a hack at the town's livery barn and drove to the Simpson farm. He tied his horse to her hitching post, then vigorously spun the bell handle on her front door. There was no answer. He rang again. And from somewhere in the back of the house he heard footsteps. Looking in through the glass in the door he saw a woman coming. But it wasn't Alma, it was Faith Ward.

"Clay, come in!" She was smiling. Faith extended her hand; it was the same firm grip he'd liked before.

"Has Alma gone somewhere? I wrote last week."

"Alma left the day after you did, Clay. She's going to Italy for the winter. She left you this letter," Faith took an envelope from the marble-topped hall table.

Clay read the letter:

"Dear Clay,

I have decided to go to Europe. I have made arrangements with Ted Blount at the bank. You will have an ample line of credit to get your Jackson's Hole project underway. Use the money wisely, but not too frugally.

Ted has a job for you and will teach you all he can before
you go back to Wyoming.

I expect two things of you, Clay. The first is that you be
successful but not rich. The second is that you and Faith
be married and living in that dreadful wilderness by the
time I return to Iowa.

I have thought that by helping you I may be helping
some people out there who have not thought kindly of me
recently."

The letter was signed, "Love, Alma."

Clay said to Faith, "Do you know what is in the letter?"

"I have a general idea. Alma talked to me a lot about you before she left."

"Alma said we were supposed to get married."

Faith dropped her eyes. "I know. Sometimes Alma gets a little too helpful. Have you eaten? I'll fix you a sandwich."

Clay sat in the kitchen while Faith sliced ham. He asked,
"Do you still read all those books?"

"Oh, yes. I've just finished one called, *The Beef Bonanza* or
How to Get Rich on the Plains.

"That's one book I have read. Fella that wrote it was a general."

Faith asked, "What did you think of it?"

"What he says is true enough. But what he left out is even
more true."

"What's left out?" asked Faith.

"For one thing it leaves out the winters. With the buffalo
gone an' the Injuns more or less under control there is a lot of
grass. But, in Jackson's Hole an' a lot of other places, cows
can't get through a winter on their own. You have to have
some damned big haystacks." Clay described the winter he'd
spent in Jackson's Hole and how difficult it had been to save
the cattle. He told about the lop-eared calf and the wolves that
had killed it. Before he realized it, it was seven o'clock, "My
golly, I got wound up. That old horse will think I've deserted
him."

At the door Faith said, "I think Mr. Blount is going to keep
you very busy at his bank this winter. But if you'd like to come

out Saturday afternoon, we could go for a drive, and I'll cook you a good supper after." Clay accepted.

In the morning he presented himself to M. Theodore Blount at the bank for what were to be many agonizing weeks. He soon confirmed his fears: Banker Blount was a martinet. Unlike Mr. Warburton, this banker had no imagination and was excruciatingly precise. But, Clay had to admit, Blount knew his business. It was probably why Alma had chosen him. And, unpleasant as his lessons often were, Mr. Blount taught Clay more about finance in a few months than he had learned in years in Colorado and Idaho banks.

Blount's frequent critiques of Clay's work, held in the embarrassed presence of the other bank employees, were merciless. The slightest error was seized upon and treated as a capital crime.

One Saturday afternoon when Clay drove out to take Faith for a ride he was seething. Blount had closed the business week with a scathing criticism of his work.

Faith greeted Clay with her good smile and obvious happiness at the day's prospects. But his black mood subdued her. After they had ridden for a quiet half hour Faith asked, "Have you had trouble with Mr. Blount again?"

"It's always that bastard. In Jackson's Hole I could plug him an' it'd be a service like killin' a wolf or grizzly."

"Then I'm glad this isn't Jackson's Hole," said Faith.

"I apologize. I guess it's his way of improvin' the breed. But he makes me so damn mad I could wring his neck. He's so careful. He wouldn't take a hundred-to-one bet that tomorrow's Sunday."

"I wonder what he'd think of that book *How to Get Rich on the Plains?*"

"It would give him apoplexy. Remind me to buy him a copy for Christmas." Clay chuckled and hugged Faith to him.

"Now, Clay," she said, "don't take advantage of an old maid schoolmarm." She looked him in the eye with that special way of hers, and he grinned in spite of himself. Before he knew it, it was time for him to start back to town.

At the door Faith asked him, "See you next Saturday?"

"How about tomorrow? I could drive out in the mornin' and take you to church."

After the services Faith asked Clay if he had enjoyed the sermon.

"Your preacher seems to be against most of the things folks enjoy."

"After all," said Faith, "what does he know?"

Churchgoers driving home stared at the gay young couple and were curious to know what they thought was so funny.

Later Faith cooked a big dinner while Clay changed into overalls and attended to the team. When he'd taken care of them he washed the buggy and oiled the harness, lingering to polish the brass studs and buckles until they gleamed.

Finished, he washed and put his suit on again and went into the house. In the kitchen Faith's plain features were rosy from the heat of the stove where she was roasting a leg of lamb. "I hope you like lamb."

"Sure do. Won't be any of that where I'm goin' unless it comes from a wild one."

"Have you eaten mountain sheep?"

"Just the one Dick Pierce and I got last fall. The sheep stick close to the mountains. Elk, deer, and antelope are all easier to get."

"I'd love to see all those animals. Not to shoot them, just to see them."

"You better hurry. They won't last much longer. The game's been pushed back as far as it can go. The Injuns killed an ol' buffalo above the place an' they acted like it was the Second Coming. A few years ago they wouldn't have wasted their time on a bull."

Faith was excited when he told her about all the trout swarming to spawn in the Little Gros Ventre. "Wouldn't it be fun to fish in a stream like that!"

"I never thought about hook-an'-line fishin'. Mary Kelly had the business for fishin' that creek. The most excitement I ever had was shootin' my first elk and that big grizzly bear I told you about."

After dinner Faith and Clay took their coffee into the parlor and sat down on the couch together. For a while they talked about the West, and then Clay put his arm around Faith and kissed her. "You like that?"

"Yes, Clay. I like it very much." Then she pushed him away.

"What's the matter?"

"Oh, Clay, I'm sorry. I can't help it. Let's go for a walk." As they walked Faith held Clay's hand tightly. "Alma told me that if a woman really loves a man she mustn't hold back anything. But, oh, Clay! I just don't feel that free."

"Don't apologize. Maybe it would be easier for both of us if we did something else Alma said to do."

"Do you mean get married?"

"Yes, if you'd like to." The words, when he said them, burst in his brain like bullets striking a tree trunk.

Faith smiled her good, honest smile at him and it made her plain face pretty. "You had better be sure, Mr. Baker. I might take you up on it."

"If you smile at me like that, I'll ask you every hour on the hour."

The next Saturday Faith and Clay took the afternoon train to the little town that was nearest her parents' farm. She had already written them of her engagement, and Mr. and Mrs. Ward, a simple and rosy-cheeked couple, beamed on Clay. Mr. Ward blurted, "Aye gollies, Mum 'n' I was thinkin' we'd have an ol' maid on our hands."

"Oh, Dad!" Faith said.

They were married on a Sunday morning in early May. After a one-night honeymoon in Cedar Rapids the young couple caught a west-bound train.

Chapter Sixteen

In a Wyoming springtime the hills and rolling plains are swathed in vivid greens. Faith was entranced and even Clay enjoyed the view. They saw antelope near the trackside. And Shoshone Indians wrapped in blankets sat on their ponies and watched the train pass by.

At Rawlins they saw a siding where sheds had been built for crews who were shearing thousands of sheep. Faith asked, "Will we raise sheep?"

"No. I don't hate sheep like a lot of cattlemen do. There's good money in them. But, in Jackson's Hole, there are too many hungry varmints. And there's no place to winter a big band unless you took 'em clear to the Idaho desert."

Their train rattled down from the Wasatch Mountains to arrive in Ogden City in late afternoon. Although the community was less than forty years old, the industrious Mormons had planted hundreds of trees that were now full grown and well-watered by an extensive irrigation system.

Faith found it a pleasant town and Clay told her, "This'll be your last look at real civilization for a while. I'll buy you the best dinner in town—if there is such a thing."

He had planned a stopover in Ogden both to give Faith a rest and, almost as important to him, to find a mowing machine. He wanted one that could be disassembled, crated, and carried into Jackson's Hole on pack mules. He planned to make the rounds of the implement dealers in the morning.

But the night was going to be theirs. He bought Faith a roast elk dinner which she thought delicious. Although Clay said, "Wait till fall. I'll get some dry cows that'll be lots better than this." After dinner they went to a variety theater whose noisy acts bored Clay, although he tried not to reveal his boredom.

Clay awoke early the next morning. Faith awakened later to find her groom staring at the ceiling. "Penny for your thoughts."

"It's all those sheep we saw at Rawlins. Unless we get back on our range and hold it, the gypsy sheep outfits might come through and take all our feed."

If Faith had hoped for a more romantic thought she didn't admit it. "Do you think that will happen?"

"They're bound to try, sooner or later." Clay couldn't stay in bed any longer. There was too much on his mind and too much to do. The couple were in the stores, shopping, as soon as they opened. Faith pleased Clay by being his match at hard bargaining. Her smile could charm the crustiest old merchant. And she helped Clay get a better price on a mowing machine than he believed possible. She bought other supplies at rock-bottom prices and got them shipped prepaid to Eagle Rock.

The young couple followed their goods on the morning train. Marv Feltch met them in Eagle Rock and took them out to his house. Faith loved Marv and she was thrilled to meet his Indian wife. She insisted on helping in the kitchen while the two men visited in Feltch's home office. As the men talked they could hear the two women chattering in the kitchen like old chums.

"That's a fine girl ya got there," said Feltch.

"I think so."

"I been wonderin' if ya saw Mary Kelly on your way out?" Feltch asked.

"Never had a chance," said Clay. "I had to get back as quick as I could. Do you hear anything of her?"

Feltch said that some Shoshones had told him Mary was living on the Reservation near Fort Washakie.

"I hope she likes it better over there than she did in Jackson's Hole," said Clay.

"With her man dead, Mary ain't gonna like any place too much. How do ya think Faith'll take to Jackson's Hole?" Feltch asked.

"I think she'll like it. She's interested in everything. She likes to read, an' I got her to bring a lot of her books out. Maybe they'll help keep her from gettin' too lonesome."

"You might have to work on that some yourse'f. She ain't used to bein' all alone. I think, though, that you'll be havin' some new neighbors. Some stampeders has already gone through here."

"Damn!" said Clay. "I've been worryin' all the way out about holdin' my range." He had made arrangements to file his land claims before leaving Eagle Rock in October.

Feltch said, "Boomers and jumpers. I seen 'em all. But you got roots an' backin'. Most of 'em will jus' be poor honyockers lookin' fer somep'n' easy."

"How should I handle 'em?"

"Treat 'em white. You kin buy 'em out or wait 'em out. File on all the water ya kin. But the main thing is to be smarter. That girl a yourn will have 'em eatin' outa her hand if ya turn her loose."

In the morning Faith rode into Eagle Rock with her host. Clay stayed at the farm, still wary of the reception he might find in town. Also, he had the pack string to bring in, horses to shoe, and equipment to get ready. The Army had recovered six of the horses Clay had lost in his skirmish with the Sioux.

The first time Clay really missed Mary Kelly occurred when he and Faith headed out of Idaho toward the Teton Pass with sixteen pack animals. Faith's riding experience was limited to having ridden her father's work horses while he drove them in from his fields. She hadn't the least notion of how a horse was packed, let alone know how to handle one of the snorty, wild-eyed nags. To her credit, however, Faith did everything she could to help her husband. In the process her hands were scratched and her nails torn.

That day on the trail was a series of major and minor catastrophes. The horses were winter-soft and peevish. Their first ten miles were punctuated by numerous stops to straighten or adjust packs.

That evening, once Clay had unpacked and picketed or hobbled all the horses, he collapsed beside the campfire Faith had built. "I know this has been a hell of a day for you, honey. If it makes you feel any better I'm tired, too. I'll unroll our beds if you'll cook somethin' to eat."

"Don't expect too much. I've never cooked over an open

fire." But, despite aching in every joint and muscle, Faith cooked a respectable meal.

The sun was well up the next morning before Clay finished packing and got back on the trail. The animals helped by becoming resigned to their burdens, and Faith began to enjoy the trip. When they had crossed the last divide and she at last saw spread before her the panorama of Jackson's Hole, Faith wept.

"Oh, Clay! I never dreamed it would be so beautiful. You never told me. Those mountains, the Tetons! How could anyone ever call this paradise a 'Hole'?"

"It's easy when you're stuck down in it for a winter. But I said it was pretty. What I like about it is it's so big. Way over by the far end of the last butte is home. What do you think?"

"I think every day here must be a treasure!"

Clay laughed and turned his horse down the trail toward the Snake River. He was satisfied with the way the river looked at the ford but the spring runoff was on. He decided to camp in a meadow west of the river and cross early in the morning when the water was lower.

As they lay in their soogans that night Clay asked, "Remember that narrow place with all the rocks—I said it was Game Creek."

"Very faintly." Faith's voice was heavy with weariness.

"I had trouble with five Injuns there last fall. I killed one of 'em."

"Killed one!" Faith was sitting up. "What happened?"

"I just found out from Marv the other day. My rifle went off when I jabbed that buck with it. I was too scared and busy to notice it till later."

Clay repeated what Feltch had told him and how the Army had recovered six of his horses. The Indian wearing the fur cap was a wanted troublemaker. The brave who had been thrown from his pony had fallen on a rock and broken his arm. He eventually came in for treatment and told the story.

When Clay had finished talking Faith cuddled closer to him. "I didn't expect to marry an Indian fighter or find life here quite so exciting."

"I told you so you'd be damn careful. Don't trust this country 'cause it's pretty. It can eat you up."

Faith helped with the packing the next morning and the river was forded without incident. With all the animals across and on the trail Clay said, "I don't know how good a housekeeper Lars Andvik is. You might find a boar's nest in the cabin."

"A lot of pioneering wives never had a house to move into. I only hope Mr. Andvik hasn't let it burn down. I'll take care of the house. You'll have all you can do worrying about the stock and the land."

The stock was foremost in Clay's mind as they rode toward the meadows between the low buttes where his cattle should be. At the opposite end of the butte from his cabin Clay saw three horses. He rode toward them and found that they were hobbled and not his. They belonged to a gaunt, black-bearded man who they found working on a dugout cabin in the side of the butte.

"Howdy," said Clay.

The man was leaning on a length of pole. "Who're you?"

"I'm Clay Baker and this is my wife, Faith. That's our place at the far end of the butte."

"Oh. My name's Cullie McWilliams. I'm outa Missouri. Your stock has been in here trompin' down my feed an' my garden spot ever since I got here. I liken to taken a gun to 'em."

Clay said, "Glad you didn't. I've been claimin' some of this ground and always let the stock graze this way. So it's my fault more'n theirs. If you'll get some poles, though, I'll help you fence off your garden."

"Your claim! I didn't see no markers here. This here's all open ground, ain't it?" McWilliams was tense.

"I set out markers last summer. Maybe the elk wallered 'em down this winter. But don't get excited, Mr. McWilliams. There's plenty of good land here for us all."

McWilliams softened at this conciliatory approach. And he smiled and pulled off his hat when Faith invited him to supper in a couple of days.

"That was what ol' Cullie needed," Clay said later. "Just a kind word from you, an' he rolled over on his back like a good dog."

"Are you going to let him have your claim?" There was a hint of indignation in Faith's tone.

"Nope. But McWilliams is already up against it. He's goin' to need help gettin' through the summer, let alone the winter. We'll put him to work an' help him move out when the pinch comes."

Clay was pleased to find his cabin neat and clean. But his stock had had a bad winter. There was only one calf to show for the year's production, and two horses had disappeared. Lars Andvik said, "Py golly, she vas a hard vinter! I na'er seen nutting like it." He was eager to receive his pay and the supplies Clay had brought him and move back to his own place.

Clay had nodded sympathetically, but after Lars left he told Faith, "Lars didn't have it any harder than I did my first winter. From the looks of what's left of my woodpile he spent most of the winter tending stove. We may be buying him out sooner than I figured."

That spring and summer Faith did her best to match every ounce of her husband's sweat with one of her own. There was plowing, seeding, and fencing to be done. Clay irrigated twenty acres of wild hay, then mowed it with his new machine. With help from Cullie McWilliams and the Andvik brothers he built a barn and dug a root cellar.

For relaxation Faith planted flower seeds she had brought from Iowa all around the cabin. Clay hauled manure from the corrals and the fertilizer induced the plants to almost explode from the ground. Perhaps the plants grew too eagerly because when Faith went to look at them one morning she found their succulent growth blackened by frost. She could not help crying.

Clay heard and came to put an arm around her. "Don't let this bother you. They may come back. I planted peas here my first year. They came up and podded out as well as anything back in Iowa. Then a frost hit and ruined 'em all."

"It's silly to cry," said Faith, wiping her eyes and pushing Clay away, "but we always loved our flower gardens at home. And I wanted something alive here to remind me."

"But this is home. It's not Iowa, but it's home. You wait, I'll take you with me when I go to cut poles. You'll see all kinds of wild flowers."

"May I bring some home and plant them?"

"Sure. Just don't get upset if these don't make it. You'll get flowers to grow if you don't give up on 'em."

During the summer two more families arrived in the valley. One of them was typical of nineteenth-century American nomads who took up land, built a shack, and then, when their enthusiasm waned, moved on. Clay gave the second family an outside chance of sticking. He had, however, visited them both, taking each an antelope freshly killed and neatly dressed. He also gave the men suggestions about building their cabins and where to find material. Later, when he had time, he returned to help them for a morning or afternoon. But that was not a gift. Labor was accounted for and repaid as scrupulously as if the hours had been dollars.

He found Faith unflagging; throwing herself out of bed and dressing in the dark while Clay lit the lamp and built a fire in the stove. She learned to swing an ax and split wood as well as many men. She would sit on the head of a horse or cow and hold it down while Clay performed whatever operation was necessary. These things and a hundred more made Clay proud of his strong young wife. And in that first year her deeply suntanned face lent exotic beauty to her plain features.

It was not in Clay to deeply enjoy most things. It was enough for him to be satisfied. In their first years together Faith often sought his opinion by asking, "Aren't the mountains beautiful today?" or "Don't you think the little sage hen chicks are darling?"

Clay would always answer, "I guess so." He "guessed so" often enough that Faith eventually stopped asking for his aesthetic opinions. And Clay was relieved; he concealed his emotions and often said, "I've got a lot more important things to think about."

One of the things that he and his new neighbors found more important were the Indians who came to the valley each fall to hunt. Cullie McWilliams advocated calling for federal troops to control the Indians if not to drive them out entirely. McWilliams had made his only money that year by guiding and packing for a party of eastern hunters. He claimed that the Indians killed more game than they could use and that they shot the largest of the bull elk and took only the tusks, hides, and, occasionally, the antlers. This was especially resented because it was these same bulls that the paying sportsmen wanted to shoot.

Clay met with his neighbors and counseled patience, reminding them, "There's a lot more of them than there are of us. Even if troops do come in, they couldn't stay. But the Injuns would be back an' they'd be mad. Let's all agree to get along with the Injuns; at least till there's enough of us to keep 'em in line ourselves." The men realized that Clay was right and all agreed to go out of their way to avoid trouble with the Indians.

A week after this agreement was made, Cullie McWilliams shot an Indian boy. The boy, he claimed later, had been sneaking around McWilliams' dugout. After the shooting McWilliams came looking for Clay; partly to brag and partly to unload some of his guilt and fears of Indian retaliation.

On hearing this news Clay was furious. "Damn you, Cullie! Do you want a massacre? How would you like tryin' to sneak by the villages up north to find federal troops?"

McWilliams, now thoroughly alarmed, tried to excuse himself. "What could I of done? He was up to somep'n. Besides, you've killed an Injun your own self."

"I didn't kill a kid. An' I didn't kill to get a scalp to put on the wall. Now you get on your horse and ride like hell to every homestead. Tell 'em what you did. They might all want to move into one place, even dig some rifle pits. I'll go get the kid and take him back to the villages." Leaving Faith with strict orders to stay indoors with a loaded rifle handy, Clay saddled his bay horse and put a pack saddle on a second animal.

He found the bloated body of a fifteen-year-old boy a hundred yards from McWilliams' dugout. The bullet had passed completely through his chest. Judging from the size and shape of the hole, the boy had been shot in the back. But more disturbing than this was the peculiar appearance of the boy's skin. Clay decided not to handle the corpse but instead to lead the Indians to it.

The weather that afternoon was fine. Crisp air and a clear sky. The jagged Teton peaks gleamed under a light coating of fresh snow. Down by the river the cottonwoods were shedding their leaves in golden showers. Clay would much rather have been hunting elk than an Indian village.

It was late afternoon before he reached the first Indian camp. The tipis were pitched in an open stand of cottonwoods near the river. Clay recognized some of the lodges from the symbols painted on them. The occupants were members of Crow Dog's band. The camp dogs rushed out at him barking fiercely with hackles raised. Wisps of gray smoke rose from the blackened tops of some of the tipis. Everything appeared normal about the camp except for one thing—there were no people.

Clay paused on the fringes of the camp and yelled, "Hullo!" No answer. Riding farther into the camp Clay heard low chanting accompanied by drum beats.

The first corpse he saw was lying on its back behind a tipi and was half-hidden by a pile of pack saddles. Clay rode over and looked down at it. Crow Dog's face was a mass of pustulated sores. Clay shuddered. It was smallpox.

Although he and Faith had both been vaccinated, Clay's first impulse was to dig his heels into his horse's flanks and run. Instead he controlled his urge and reined his horse around, stepping him quickly away from the corpse.

A thin, high-pitched voice startled him. "Ho! Clay?" Turning in his saddle Clay saw an old man in buckskins leaning against a hide stretcher. The man's gaunt face and the whites of his eyes were a sickly yellow.

"Dick! I hardly knew you!" Clay rode up to the old trapper.

"Oooh, it's Little Dick, all right. While I last. Yeller as egg yolks."

"You got the pox?"

"No. I'm 'bout the on'y one in camp that ain't." Dick sagged down until he was sitting on a cottonwood log. His hands trembled badly, although he tried to hold them still by clasping them around one knee.

"Why don't you get on my pack horse and come with me?" Clay asked.

"Oooh, I couldn't leave these folks. Some of 'ems gonna make it. 'Bout all I kin do is keep a pot a meat a stewin'. I crawl aroun' feedin' them 'at kin eat."

"You got plenty of meat? Need flour or anything?"

"If'n ya could kill me three, four antelope it'd be a he'p."

Clay nodded. "I'll get 'em. What else?"

"What we need is a doc," said Little Dick. "I do what I kin, but my charms an' sech ain't right for this pox. It's a hell of a thing the way it takes these Injuns. Poor li'l kids, sores all over 'em—eyes, in the'r mouths. One papoose died yestiddy whilst I was tryin' ta feed it."

"I don't know where we'd find you a doctor," said Clay.

"Course not. Even if they was one, he wouldn't come fer Injuns."

Clay said, "We had some other trouble. An Injun boy got shot. Man claims the kid was sneakin' around in the brush by his cabin, scared him an' he shot."

"Mebbe he was a'ter stealin' somep'n. Likely though he was tryin' ta hide from the pox. Some of 'em believes the pox won't find 'em if they crawl off an' hide in a thick patcha brush."

Clay said nothing. He had found the boy near a patch of sagebrush that was almost head tall.

Dick continued, "This pox is carried by the air. What we need is a good storm to blow this bad air outa here."

Clay replied, "The weather looks good for a while. If you won't come with me now, I'll go hunt you some meat. No sense in me comin' into the camp any more'n necessary. I got a wife at home to look out for now. The meat'll be hangin' in the trees just outside the camp."

"Be fine, Clay. We'll 'preciate it." Dick was still sitting on the log when Clay rode away.

Less than twenty minutes out Clay saw a doe antelope and her fawn. It was an easy stalk, the doe's curiosity overrode her caution, and Clay dropped her with his first shot. The second shot took the fawn as it looked at Clay. After dressing both animals Clay threw their carcasses on his pack horse and took them to the Indian camp. They were still warm when he hung the antelope in a tree and skinned them. While he quartered the carcasses the Indian dogs fought savagely over the scraps and discarded hides. The afternoon light was fading as Clay hung the last quarter in a tree and left the camp.

It was dark when he reached the Andvik homestead. He called and Helga Andvik came out.

"Hello, Helga," Clay called. "I need to talk to Lars and Iver."

"Clay, come on in," Lars was calling to him from the lighted doorway.

"No! I can't. Did McWilliams come here?"

"Not today. Ve not see him for a veek."

"It doesn't matter now," Clay replied. "There's smallpox in the Injun camp. I came to tell you, tell the others . . ." Before he had finished speaking the Andviks' door was slammed in his face. It was an act he never forgot or forgave.

Although Faith had been vaccinated, Clay was afraid to go near her. For the next three weeks, they lived apart. She in the new cabin and Clay batching in the old one. They communicated by yelling across the dooryard to one another.

When Clay first told her of the pestilence Faith called, "Those poor people! What can I do?"

"Nothin' to do. Keep away from 'em so we won't spread it. I hate to see old Dick in there. I'll take 'em a load of meat every couple of days."

"Shouldn't you go for a doctor?"

"Honey, they're *Injuns*. Any doctor that'd come way out here for Injuns wouldn't be worth havin'. It'll just have to burn itself out."

Early the next morning Clay rode to Cullie McWilliams' haphazard claim. He despised the man even more now because he had not alerted the settlers to what he thought were the dangers of an Indian attack. McWilliams was out in front of his dugout jerking the meat of a deer and hanging the strips on a pole to dry. Clay did not ride in or dismount. "Ho, Cullie!"

"Hi! Did ya find them Injuns? They never showed up so I drug that dead 'un off in the brush. It was startin' to stink."

Clay interrupted. "He had the smallpox. Their whole camp's down with it."

McWilliams dropped the knife and a bloody piece of venison. His mouth fell open and even from twenty yards Clay could see his eyes bulging.

"No offense, Cullie, you understand. But don't come near my place for three weeks. Hope ya had a vaccination."

"I never," McWilliams was gasping, trying to get his breath.

Clay called, "Better get out to a doc in Eagle Rock. They'll be able to help ya over there. Nothin' we could do here if ya got sick. So long, Cullie."

McWilliams was frantically saddling his horse as Clay rode away. Clay Baker felt no remorse for whatever McWilliams' fate might be. Clay would come back in a few weeks and burn his cabin.

Part way through the smallpox siege there was a severe snowstorm and the antelope migrated from the valley. But it was not a severe enough storm to force many elk down into the valley. Following a morning of fruitless hunting, Clay rode back to his ranch and butchered a steer. Then, without waiting for the meat to cool, he loaded it on a couple of pack horses.

"Ho, Dick!" he called when he reached the village. At his shout all the camp curs came running. They were getting fat, and Clay knew it was because they were feeding on corpses.

Dick finally appeared, walking slowly and leaning on a staff. A stooped, old squaw shuffled along beside him, one steadying the other.

As the pair approached him Clay said, "Looks like you pulled one of 'em through."

"Had ta save this 'un," said Dick.

The squaw looked up at Clay from beneath the hood of her ragged blanket. One eye was dead and her dark face was covered with partially healed pink scars.

"How, Clay."

"Mary! I didn't know you were here!"

Mary Kelly smiled, the same honest smile Clay had seen when they first started for Jackson's Hole together. Clay gripped his saddle horn not knowing what to say and shocked at Mary's disfigurement.

Finally Dick said, "If the weather holds off, we'll be ready to travel in a week. No more's gettin' sick an' them that ain't kicked off are gettin' better. The worst is over."

"Can I do anything? Maybe gather up your ponies?"

"That'd be a big he'p," said Dick. "Nex' time ya come by push what ponies ya kin find inta camp. Holler an' we'll catch 'em."

Some of the Indian horses had strayed as far as Clay's meadows. He gathered these first and drove them back to the camp. Faith wanted to ride with him but he refused.

Light snow was falling as he rode into the Indian camp. After he called he saw the ghostly shapes of Indians moving through the grayish trees catching their horses.

Clay unloaded a big elk carcass and rode away again. He made several circles that day and succeeded in rounding up most of the Indian ponies. He knew he had driven in far more animals than the depleted band could use, but in their weakened condition the Indians would only be able to catch the gentlest animals.

The snow stopped falling that evening. By morning the clouds had lifted but they did not clear away. The dampness left hanging in the air made the day feel colder than it actually was. It was a cruel day for moving.

But the surviving Indians packed up what they could and left the rest. Clay rode over and watched them lining out across the snowy hillsides, somber tracings against the cold, white background. They were moving east, toward the Reservation.

Clay was relieved to see them go. Winter was drawing down upon the valley. He had to bring in his cattle and horses. They needed more wood for the stove. The root cellar now filled with potatoes, carrots, and turnips had to be sealed against the frost. There was the winter's meat to be made and traps to be readied for the fur season.

One evening Faith said, "I've never felt right about those Indians. We didn't do very much for them."

"Hell! I did all I could. Besides, I couldn't take a chance on you gettin' it. I fed 'em. Gave 'em one of my best steers. Butchered out all their meat and rounded up their ponies for 'em. I'm not worried about those Injuns, I'll tell you."

"What do you worry about, Clay?"

"I worry about money."

Epilogue

Little Dick Pierce died from his jaundice before the party of Indians crossed the divide that separates the Gros Ventre from the Wind River country. He was buried in a tree.

Indian Service officials at Fort Washakie have no record of a Shoshone woman called Mary Kelly. In those years before the turn of the century many of the Indians were nomads, and it was impossible to keep track of 'them all.

Marvin Feltch was one of the best-liked and trusted men in the Idaho Territory. At statehood, legislators tried unsuccessfully to name a county in his honor. In 1887 he and Clay Baker had a falling out and ended their business relationship. Rumors said their trouble grew out of the shooting of two horse thieves on the Little Gros Ventre in the spring of 1885. There were other stories that the men had quarreled over the way Baker acquired some of his property in Jackson's Hole. None of these rumors were ever confirmed. Marvin Feltch died in 1904.

After Wyoming gained statehood Clay Baker was elected a state senator. At one time he sought the Republican nomination for governor. He did not receive the nomination, partially because of stories that linked him to a banking scandal in the 1880s.

Clay and Faith Baker had no children. Clay was bitter about this. And people who knew the Bakers well said that they grew apart because Clay blamed Faith for not giving him a son.

Clay Baker died in his sleep on the first day of winter, 1934. He and Mrs. Baker were at a resort hotel near San Diego where it had become their habit to spend the winters. Mr. Baker's death had been expected. After her husband's death Faith Baker never returned to Wyoming. She died in a nursing home in 1940. Her estate was left to an Iowa teacher's college.

At the time of Clay Baker's death, newspapers throughout Wyoming and southeast Idaho printed long obituaries filled with high praise for this self-made pioneer. It was said that no man had done more to develop a huge region that encompassed parts of two states, Idaho and Wyoming. A peak in the Teton range was named for him.

What none of the obituary writers knew, however, was the true basis of the Bakers' wealth. The money came from a bequest made by a mysterious widow, Alma W. Simpson of Aldora, Iowa. Mrs. Simpson had been injured in a tram accident in Rome and died there of tetanus in April of 1886. Her connection with Clay Baker was never publicized. But it was her money that enabled the Bakers to build a financial empire in the Wyoming land and cattle business.

DATE DUE

DISC-RD

c. 1

Calkins, Frank
The tan-faced children
X58407

BURLINGTON PUBLIC LIBRARY
Burlington. Wisconsin 53105

FINE 5¢ A DA'